Fran Dorricott is an author based in Derby, where she lives with her family, two cats, and three dogs (one of whom weighs more than she does). She holds a degree in American Literature with Creative Writing from the University of East Anglia and an MA with distinction in Creative Writing from City University London.

Fran is also a bookseller working in the Derby branch of Waterstones, which is secretly just a way for her to fuel her ridiculous book-buying addiction.

# THE
# LIGHT
# HOUSE

## FRAN DORRICOTT

avon.

Published by AVON
A division of HarperCollins*Publishers* Ltd
1 London Bridge Street
London SE1 9GF

www.harpercollins.co.uk

HarperCollins*Publishers*
1st Floor, Watermarque Building, Ringsend Road
Dublin 4, Ireland

A Paperback Original 2022

1

First published in Great Britain by HarperCollins*Publishers* 2022

Copyright © HarperCollins*Publishers* 2022

A catalogue copy of this book is
available from the British Library.

ISBN: 978-0-00-844933-9

Typeset in Sabon LT Std by Palimpsest Book Production Limited,
Falkirk, Stirlingshire

Printed and Bound in the UK using 100% Renewable Electricity at
CPI Group (UK) Ltd

MIX
Paper from
responsible sources
FSC™ C007454

This book is produced from independently certified FSC™ paper
to ensure responsible forest management.

For more information visit: www.harpercollins.co.uk/green

For my family, who all feigned surprise when I said
'I'm going to write a creepy island book'

# FRIDAY

# 1

## *Kira*

I see Ora lighthouse before any of the others. The five of them have been busy bickering since we got on the boat, as they always do when we're all together. Lucas is currently telling a work story I heard him boast about a million times when we were still dating, so I've zoned out. James, Moira and Jess have been ribbing him for exaggerating, like always, but that only encourages him. The only difference today is Lucas's new girlfriend, Genevieve, who's listening to his story like she actually believes it.

'Look!' I say, cutting through the punchline. Only Genevieve is listening now anyway because the others have finally seen it properly too.

We all rush to the side of the boat, which is bobbing hard through sharp, dark waves. Up ahead the lighthouse stands tall, no longer obscured by the curve of the island or the mist, which sits, grey and still, on top of the water. When we set off the lighthouse wasn't even a smudge in the distance, but now we're close I can see that the island, which before was only a dark hump in the water, is amber and green, speckled with craggy grey rocks and outcrops of scrubby trees. It's wild to think that only this morning I was in London, all brick and glass and exhaust, and now we're here, alone on the water, mist swallowing us whole.

I feel myself relax a little. The lighthouse looks exactly how I expected, tall and blindingly white on its grassy outcrop. The island is growing larger by the second, isolated and wild. The mainland has long vanished into the mist behind us, and there's a feeling of being stopped in time.

This is the perfect location for our big ten-year reunion weekend. Lots of space to switch off, to reconnect – with nature and with each other. It's been too long since we all got together.

'It's so big!' Moira exclaims, her brown eyes wide. She squeezes her wife's hand excitedly and Jess smiles, a little less enthusiastically. Jess can come across as tightly wound, but she's been especially snippy today. We're all tired, though. Most of us have been up since five this morning, and aside from Lucas snatching a short nap on the plane to Inverness – twenty minutes of blissful quiet for the rest of us – we've hardly stopped talking since we left London. As though if we let ourselves be silent we might not get the same energy back.

'Is that where we're actually staying?' James asks before Lucas can make one of his trademark *That's what she said* jokes. They always fall into the same behaviour when they're together. 'In the lighthouse?'

James rubs his hands together to ward off the cold. It would have been better if we'd been able to do this in the summer, but September is better than nothing.

'The cottages next door,' Jess says. 'Right? That's what you said. I don't think I fancy staying *in* the lighthouse.'

'Gen's been telling her scary stories,' Moira explains when she sees my face. I must have looked hurt, and I try to rein it in. I planned this trip, but I refuse to take responsibility for it like I always would have when we were at uni.

'I didn't mean them to be *scary* stories,' Genevieve says. She scoops her short blonde hair behind one ear, managing to look both apologetic and effortlessly pretty, despite the wind that whips her hair back to wildness after less than a second.

'What scary stories?' Lucas asks, slipping his arms around Genevieve's waist. I have to look away. They're like a pair of lovesick teenagers.

'You know, tales about the sailors who died on the rocks, or the lighthouse keepers who killed themselves when they got too lonely. Or the ones who didn't want to leave when their time was up.' Moira shakes her head but she's smiling. 'Jess always takes that stuff so seriously.'

Jess shrugs. 'I don't like horror movies. What would make you think I'd spend a weekend in a haunted lighthouse?'

'It's *not* haunted,' I say. I don't know why I'm determined to take this so personally. 'It's all shiny and renovated. Nobody's even stayed here yet.'

The guide who met us on the mainland pulls the boat expertly towards the dock. The motor cuts and suddenly I can hear better. It's a different kind of silence here. Your brain says it should be quiet: no traffic, no chatter, and now no motor; but it's not. The silence – if that's what you call it – is loaded. The waves, the wind, the bristle of trees against each other. Like one big reset button.

'It looks amazing, Kira,' James says reassuringly. 'Honest. We are going to have the best weekend.'

'And get very, very drunk,' Lucas is quick to add.

A collective groan eases the tension as we all set about disembarking. The guide is a grizzled-looking man who might be anywhere between thirty and fifty, his hair hidden by a dark beanie. He's got a soft Scottish accent and a deep frown, and I can tell he's not thrilled to bring us to the island. It must be off his usual route.

He helps us to carry our luggage onto a path that leads up a long grassy slope towards the lighthouse. He doesn't struggle with it like we did; his body betrays a lifetime of hard work in the easy way he drops the bags one by one, without a blink.

We've got a lot of stuff between us: suitcases and a wheeled trolley we packed in Inverness full of booze and food supplies to last us the weekend. I think Jess is planning a feast.

'There's a boat once a day when the lighthouse is occupied – except Sundays,' the guide reminds us, 'so I'll be here with the tide in case you have questions or need anything semi-urgently.'

'Thank you, Ben.' Genevieve beams and the man's gruff exterior seems to melt a bit. She seems to have that effect on everybody but me. But then, I didn't even bother to learn the guide's name.

James catches me watching her so I turn away, clutching my camera case to my chest and pretending to examine the lighthouse again. It looks amazing coming out of the mist like that. Actually, this will be a perfect shot for the magazine, all atmospheric and moody. The photos are the main reason we're here, after all. It's one of the perks of my job: paid-for accommodation in unusual locations, which just about makes up for the lack of pay the rest of the time.

It's not often I get sent somewhere with enough beds for a whole group of us to travel, though, so I'm glad it worked out for our reunion.

I focus so hard on the shot that I begin to relax again, letting the others pick up the conversational slack.

'Just be careful on the rocks,' the guide adds. 'The light up top still works – it's automated – but it's still easy to misstep in the dark or the fog. If you think this is bad, wait till it rains. The cliffs aren't as high as they look but they're steep and the sunroom runs close to the edge. We ask people not to go off on their own at night, just to be on the safe side. Getting in touch with nature doesn't mean a midnight tumble into the sea.'

He starts to laugh as though he's said something incredibly funny. Lucas cracks up and James smiles, but Jess doesn't look impressed. Moira nudges her arm.

'Don't worry,' she says loudly. 'We are planning on spending a lot of time inside, and most of the night *sleeping.*'

This makes James raise an eyebrow suggestively and Lucas laughs again. The guide gives us a few more tips, suggests we keep our eyes peeled for a sight of the northern lights when it gets dark if the mist clears up, and then takes the boat out onto the open water with a roar that swallows up the air around us.

I put my camera down and take a deep breath. It's amazing how quickly the sound of the motor is swallowed by the mist, until there's just us and the island. Freedom. The air smells different here. Cleaner, like pine and salt. I know my cheeks are already chapped from the wind on the boat but I don't care. It's so good to be here, to be together.

'A whole weekend with all of us,' I say.

Jess gives the first genuine smile I've seen for hours. 'I know. When was the last time we did this?'

'Nearly three years, I think?' James has started to walk and we all follow him up the chalky path. 'I think the last time we all made it was . . . New Year? In Brighton?'

'Oh yeah, I'd forgotten about that.' I can always tell when Lucas is lying, and he's lying now. He can't have forgotten Brighton, because that's the last holiday we had before we broke up. We fought the whole week and pissed off Jess and Moira, who were pregnant and didn't want the drama.

'It's not like you haven't seen each other since, though. And that's amazing. I never see the people I went to uni with,' Genevieve says. It always feels like she's trying super hard to be nicer than everybody around her. Or maybe she just *is* nice, and I'm a cynic. It's probably the latter. 'I can't believe you've all been friends for ten years.'

'More than ten for most of us,' Lucas says. 'Thirteen actually.' It's not meant to be a dig, but I can't help the little surge of envy I get, same as always. James, Lucas, Jess and Moira all met in first year at uni and have been friends ever since. I only joined their group when I started dating Lucas at the start of our third year, and I've never stopped feeling bad about that.

Still, Genevieve is the *new* newest addition. And this is silly. I'm so tired that if I'm not careful I'll ruin it. The lighthouse awaits, and I know first impressions are every-thing. Besides, I don't want to admit that the mention of Genevieve's scary stories has unsettled me a bit. I'm not normally bothered by that stuff but it's too easy to imagine a brutal death on those rocks at the base of the cliffs: a

8

fall from the lantern room, just a trip, or a careless foot in a rabbit hole in the dark and a short roll down the hill into the ocean. We'll have to be careful.

'Come on,' I say. 'Anybody else desperate for a cuppa?'

# 2

## *Genevieve*

This place is stunning. I've travelled to a lot of places over the years, but already I can tell that Scotland – especially Ora island – is going to be one of my favourites. The wind is fresh and crisp, the scenery rugged and barren, and yet somehow so *alive*, and the lighthouse is so full of energy up close that I get chills.

We've managed to drag the luggage up the hill from the dock and I know I'm not the only one that feels it. Everybody has stopped, even Lucas who doesn't normally feel anything spiritual at all. Old places always have energy like this, but the lighthouse is something else. It is powerful. It must be, to have weathered so many storms.

'Wow,' Moira breathes. 'Just *wow*.'

Kira looks pleased, but I can tell that she's impressed, too. I can't imagine any one of us has ever seen a lighthouse up close before. Lucas points right to the top, where the faint sun reflects the white of the mist off the glass, and we all take it in. Its sleek height; the way the dark windows cut right the way down and seem to drink the light. At the

11

bottom there is a wraparound porch, running to the left in shining glass to form a sunroom where the building gazes out over the ocean.

To the right there is a blocky structure, whitewashed like the lighthouse. It's as short and squat as the lighthouse is tall, but it's charming too.

'Those are the cottages,' Kira says. 'Well, it's just one cottage now, I guess. I think the lighthouse keepers used to live there before the light was automated. Cool, right?'

'Look at that,' Jess murmurs. She's been quiet for most of the journey from London, and I don't know her well enough yet to guess why, but even she seems to have been won over now. 'It's like we're staring at some fantasy land,' she adds. 'Like an island in the clouds.'

She's right. With our backs to the cottage there is only the lighthouse and then the ocean, stretching dark and turbulent until it vanishes into grey. It's like standing on the edge of the world.

'Come on, let's go dump our stuff.'

Kira leads the way to the cottage, and as we follow, James falls in step beside me.

'Is it true?' he asks.

'Is what true?'

'All that stuff about people dying, sailors and lighthouse keepers and everybody.'

I examine his expression. For a second I think I've ruined it; I didn't mean to upset anybody. I've always loved ghost stories, because they often show us what's important about life. The thought that I've unsettled any of Lucas's friends sits heavy in my stomach.

'Well, I don't know about this island specifically,' I say hesitantly, 'but it's quite common. I mean, boats used to

12

crash on places like this all the time. Look at all that mist. That's why we have the lighthouses. There are a lot of folk tales – stories about hauntings and guardians of the sea.'

James is silent for a second. He peers back over his shoulder, taking in the view again. When he turns around he's got a smirk on his face that makes me think of Lucas – cocky and fun – and I smile back, relieved.

'Guess we'd better not get too drunk and fall in then,' he says. 'Wouldn't want to be stuck here as a ghost forever.'

Kira gathers the key from a collection box with a code and we let ourselves into the cottage, which is surprisingly spacious. There are four bedrooms, one large family bathroom and a small kitchen with just enough room for a table and chairs at one end. Everything inside is new, totally unused. Fresh beds and linens that have never been slept in, a coffee maker in the kitchen that Moira whoops over in excitement. The decor is a mixture of kitschy and modern, a blend that sums up the cottage and the lighthouse entirely.

It's gorgeous. I wonder, briefly, who lived here once. How they'd feel about us staying in their home. But the current owners have done a grand job, and by the time we've all run from room to room inspecting the place Kira is grinning from ear to ear.

'Nice,' James intones. 'Really nice. Well done, Kira.'

'Thank you.' She gives a mock bow. 'But you haven't seen the best bit yet.'

'The lighthouse?' Moira asks.

'None other. Come on—'

Lucas and James are already gone, pushing and shoving

13

like teenagers in their rush to get back outside. Jess shakes her head, laughing. 'Such children.'

We hurry after them, still in our jackets and hats. It's getting late in the afternoon now, the weak sunlight dripping away. The lighthouse towers above, its long shadow stretching across the cottage and leaving us all in the cold shade.

'This way!' Kira has caught up with James, and she points at the base of the lighthouse, where the porch is enclosed at the back. There is a door leading inside, which she unlocks with another key from the same set as before, labelled with a green tag.

Up close like this the energy is even stronger. It's like the tug of the wind, pulling me inside. I'm the last one through the door – always the last one in this group, but I don't mind. These are Lucas's friends and I'm honestly just grateful to be included. And so I'm the last one to see it, and I breathe out in awe.

'Holy shit.' This comes from Lucas, and for once I don't laugh. I always laugh at him. I've laughed since the first day we met: when I started at AdZec, when I was his boss and I shouldn't have laughed like that at anything *anybody* said; but he's always surprised the sound out of me anyway.

But this is different. I'm not laughing now, because he's right.

'This is amazing.'

'Jesus, Kira,' James says. 'You've outdone yourself.'

'I know.'

We've entered what can only be described as an entertaining space. It's large and bright, spanning the entire ground floor of the lighthouse and the bulk of the porch extension too. There's a huge circular space in the middle, inside the original lighthouse walls, and within it are homey armchairs, lamps, a coffee table and a bookcase filled with board games and a variety of charity-shop-worn books. To the right, in the enclosed half of the new extension, is what looks like another kitchen, bigger than the one in the cottage. And to the left . . .

We move together, vying to see it: the glass sunroom portion of the porch, terracotta tiles beneath chaise longue-style chairs angled out towards the ocean, and a dining table laid for eight. The view feels endless, just the glass and then the rocks and the waves and the mist for miles, like a wall of white at the edge of the world.

'I think we might be spending a lot of time in here,' Moira says. She turns to her wife and wraps her arm around her waist. 'Whether it's haunted or not.'

'It's not haunted,' Kira repeats, but she's not really paying attention. None of them are. We are, all of us, staring at that view.

But it only takes a minute for the same energy to creep back in, that sensation I got outside. It's stronger in here. I allow myself to wander, picking my way around Lucas and James to get back to the lounge: the lighthouse proper.

There's a spiral staircase, I realise, beginning by the front door. It's mostly enclosed, but the bricks that hide it from view from the lounge are made from some kind of frosted sea glass. I creep towards it, eager to explore.

'Are you going to check out the top?' Moira rushes to join me excitedly. 'Are we allowed up there, Kira?'

'That's the whole point!' Lucas exclaims. 'C'mon!'

Before Kira can answer, Lucas has rushed ahead, Moira not far behind him. Soon we're all hurrying, breathless with

15

excitement and with the climb. There are six floors, the staircase enclosed all the way up, the only light coming from the windows cut into the side of the building. I hang back a little way, feeling the building echo around me. It seems like this place has been empty for too long.

There's a wooden door on every floor; a small landing as the staircase curves. I reach out absently and turn the handle of the first door, wondering if there might be more bedrooms up here. Kira had said, when she booked the holiday, that this place could sleep eight; or was it ten? But the handle won't budge. It's locked.

The other doors are open and they lead into small, strangely shaped rooms. Most are somewhat bare: an old nursing rocking chair and upholstered footstool in one; bookshelves filled with creased paperbacks and a long, beautifully painted wooden coffee table and matching armchairs in another. I find James in the mini library gazing at the shelves, his eyes alight with excitement.

'This is amazing. I haven't read anything in years. I am going to read so many books,' he says earnestly, turning towards me with an Agatha Christie novel in his hands.

'It's only a weekend,' I say. 'How many can you read in two days?'

James laughs. 'Okay,' he corrects himself, 'I am going to read at least one whole book.'

I can tell when the others reach the top because Lucas lets out another 'Holy shit!' and Jess and Moira both burst into laughter. I pause for a second, listening to the sound crashing inside the staircase, before I carry on upstairs.

And the others are right. It's worth every step up. It's like a giant glass doughnut, a concrete walkway around

16

the lamp at the centre. Every inch of it is bathed in white light. It's like being swallowed whole.

'And that,' says Kira, 'is the best bit.'

'I wonder if we'll get to see the whole view while we're here. Can you imagine what this would be like in the middle of summer?' James says.

'Warmer.' Lucas laughs at his own joke, even though his new job was part of the reason we couldn't all make it until now. June or July would have maybe been better, but I've always loved taking a holiday in September.

'Do your keys open all of the doors?' I ask Kira.

She glances down at the keyring she's still holding and then back at me, as if she's surprised I'm talking to her and not Lucas.

'Oh, uh, I guess. Why?'

'There's a locked door downstairs, on the first floor. I just wondered if that's where the other bedroom is.'

'There are no bedrooms in here. Just the entertaining space downstairs. Something about health and safety or means of escape or something—'

'A locked door? Ooooh.' James nudges Jess playfully. 'Spooky.'

'Cut it out.' She waves him away.

'Probably just storage or something,' Moira says. 'Vacuum cleaners, bleach. Boring stuff. Anyway, we've got enough bedrooms already.'

Lucas has appeared behind me. The lamp is sitting in the middle of its own special glass sphere, so there's not much space. His strong arms loop around me and I lean back into him. He's been like this recently: hot one minute and cold the next. Hands all over me, and then he doesn't speak for half an hour, which isn't like him at all.

17

'I know, I just . . .' I stop myself. I just what? 'Never mind. I can't wait to do yoga out there in the morning.'

Lucas moves away and pulls a face. *Girl stuff.* He's always making fun of the yoga, even though I know he'd like it if he tried it. The others laugh too, though, and once again I'm on the outside of some private joke ten years in the making.

'Nice,' James says eventually, taking pity on me. 'I haven't done yoga since the dark ages. I might join you.'

Kira and Moira exchange a glance which I can't read.

'As if you will,' Lucas says. 'You're never up that early. Especially when you're hungover.'

'All right,' Jess says. 'I'm going to go and unpack. I need to try checking in with my parents to see how Emma's doing.' Moira starts to say something but Jess already has her back to us. 'I just hope there's some better signal somewhere on this island, Mo, because otherwise I'm gonna be *pissed* you wouldn't let me call them from Inverness.'

Moira waits until Jess is gone and then shoots us a mocking look at her wife's frustration, but it's not mean so much as tired. An old joke worn thin. Everybody laughs but me.

As we make our way down the stairs Lucas catches up with me again.

'You're quiet today,' he says. 'Everything okay?'

'Oh, yeah. I'm okay. It's just so weird, isn't it? Having all that modern space downstairs and then . . . this. Doesn't it make you feel a bit odd? All these lives, deaths, whatever, just kinda *there* while we're having dinner? All that history?'

'Not really,' Lucas disagrees. 'It's a renovated lighthouse. It's old, and they've made it better. That limbo feeling sort of comes with the territory, right?'

He seems defensive. I think of earlier, how I really hadn't meant to upset Jess. I don't want to annoy him, too, if he thinks I'm getting at Kira. I'm not.

Still, I try to shake off the feeling that something bad must have happened here once, for a place this beautiful to have been empty for so long.

# 3

## *Moira*

Jess spends forty minutes trying to get enough signal to phone her parents while I unpack our bags into the sleek wooden units in our bedroom. I try not to get dragged into another rehash of the same conversation – about how worried she is, how annoyed that I wouldn't let her call earlier. She's still trying when I finish unpacking, so I slip out into the small cottage kitchen with James for a peaceful cup of tea and a shared packet of Hobnobs.

'Where are the others?' I ask. It's been ages since I spent time with just James. We hung out all the time after uni, when he lived close to us and needed the attention, but he moved out of the city a couple of years ago to start a new job so our socialising has largely been via WhatsApp lately.

'Lucas and Kira are still unpacking, and I think Gen's nipped outside to have another look at the view. Looks like the mist is lifting a bit.' He leans back in his chair and sips at his scalding tea, making the kind of slurping noise that Jess could kill me for. He pauses for barely a second before stuffing two Hobnobs into his face and grinning.

'Don't get too carried away,' I say through laughter. 'Jess'll be fuming if you're too full for dinner.'

James rolls his eyes, still crunching. 'I know. Was bad enough when she was dragging us round Marks and Sparks for the bloody prawns. It'll be worse if she caters for the ghosts too.'

We tease Jess a lot, but I still cringe at this. She's been planning the meal for literally *weeks* at this point. It will be a shame if people don't appreciate it. James will probably be all right – it's more Lucas that I'm worried about, since he's the one who usually puts his foot in it.

'I'm just kidding,' James adds quickly. 'I know she's put a lot of effort in. It'll be awesome. I guess it'll give you two a bit of time together, too, which is always a bonus. Speaking of which . . .'

He gestures out of the window behind me, and I see Jess stalking out across the space between the cottage and the lighthouse, her fists balled at her sides. For a second I wonder if she heard us, heard James's comment about the 'bloody prawns', but she can't have. And anyway, we didn't say anything we wouldn't have said to her face.

'I'd better go check on her,' I say. 'Don't want to leave her alone with the ghosts.'

James snorts.

I leave my tea, barely drunk, on the kitchen table – I'll probably need something a little stronger before long – and head out into the late afternoon air, wrapping my cardigan tighter around my waist.

When I get into the bigger, modern lighthouse kitchen Jess has already unpacked all of the food and the booze and bits we bought from Marks before getting on the ferry, and organised it on the counters. She's surveying it with a proud look on her face, which withers when she sees me.

'Hello to you too,' I snipe. An old joke, which fortunately still makes her laugh.

'Sorry. I know I've been a bit . . . Just – you know. Leaving Emma for the whole weekend. I still haven't managed to get through, though I did finally get a text to send. The signal is hideous. I just wish I knew that everything was okay—'

'They will be *fine*.' I step closer and pull Jess into my arms. She rests her head on my shoulder and lets me hold her for a minute. 'Emma's got to learn that we won't be there every second, and it's not like we've left her with a random babysitter. We need to get used to this. What about when she starts nursery in April? It's good for her, too. This is just one weekend. Your mum and dad have done this before. They raised you, didn't they?'

'Yes, but—'

'No, no buts. I know this is uncomfortable. It's weird for me, too, because we've not done it before. But it's healthy for all of us. It's *progress*. And really it's no different to leaving her for an hour or two. She's just as safe. We'll try to call again later. They're not going anywhere. Now come on. Haven't we got a feast to prepare?'

At that Jess pulls back and her expression has shifted again. She's laid the food for tonight in a different pile than the other snacks and bottles of beer that she couldn't fit in the fridge. There's salad and prawns, fancy shop-bought dressing that normally she won't let us eat because *home-cooked is better for you*, and she's even got scallops and cream for Coquilles St Jacques. But she doesn't look content like she normally does when she's cooking. Maybe she's nervous. We've never cooked for Genevieve before.

'What?' I ask.

23

'Nothing. I just . . . You don't think there's anything to what Genevieve was saying earlier, do you? The spooky stories? Ghosts and energies and things?'

I scoff audibly. 'Don't be daft.'

'But I heard you talking to James.'

'We were just joking,' I say firmly, cursing us both for teasing. 'Honestly.'

'Right,' she says, but her expression is still terse. 'Right. Okay. It's just – I could have sworn I bought a different wine for the St Jacques, and now I can't find it. I was sure I put it over there, on the end away from the other stuff, right near the door.'

'It's not either of those?' I point at the two boxes of Sauvignon Blanc, but Jess shakes her head.

'No, I got a Chardonnay, a big bottle.' She frowns.

'Maybe we only got the Sauv? Or maybe Lucas and Genevieve are necking it right now, straight from the bottle.'

Jess is too annoyed to laugh, but she screws up her nose so I know that I've won; diffused another situation before it can get out of hand. I reach for one of the boxes of wine and give it a shake.

'The heathens won't be able to tell the difference anyway. If we find the Chardonnay we'll serve it with dinner.'

Jess nods, and starts to wash her hands. I let our normal roles take over – me in charge of music and making sure there's plenty of beer and wine while we cook, Jess in front of the fancy AGA – but I'm pushing at the niggle at the back of my brain. Jess is right. I remember the Chardonnay – in the trolley, on the conveyor belt, in the bag that we piled into the ferry. And now it's gone. Lucas doesn't drink wine, and nobody else would touch anything before waiting

24

for Jess to unpack, so it must be Genevieve. But why would she take a whole bottle and not just pour herself a glass?

It doesn't matter. I don't want Jess to start worrying, so I keep my mouth shut.

Dinner goes off without a hitch and we're serving up the main course as the sun sets. The mist has burnt off entirely now and the ocean is tinted in reds and golds which reflect on the glass walls of the enclosed porch. We've lit all the candles in the two polished candelabras and the whole room glows, the night closing in around us and making the long, dark windows morph into mirrors.

Lucas and James have already started their usual drinking contest, apparently aiming to see who can fastest consume enough alcohol to forget whether they've eaten dinner or not, but for once Jess doesn't seem to mind. She's chatting with Genevieve about some video they've both seen on Facebook about a rescue dog who learns to skateboard, and now that the food is on the table she's visibly relaxed.

I allow myself a moment of pride in how good a cook she is – I often let myself forget, since we still usually hardly have the time or the energy to feed ourselves anything other than soggy beans on toast between naps and bedtimes, play dates and work. I'd thought once that things would be easier as Emma got older but, if anything, Jess has become more anxious, not even willing for both of us to leave our daughter with our parents or a babysitter for more than a couple of hours. I'm clinging to the hope that this weekend will help break the spell.

I pour myself a large glass of wine and lean back. It hits different after the beer; smooth and sweet. Kira has ended up sitting next to Lucas, which I can't imagine she's thrilled about, but she's on her best behaviour, laughing at his jokes and letting him talk about his new job as if she cares. When they broke up things were dicey for a couple of years, but she seems okay tonight.

I drink my wine a bit too fast. It's going to my head. But it doesn't matter: Jess is fine and I don't have to worry about Emma and it's really been too long since we've all been together. The Coquilles St Jacques are delicious. James has seconds, his face ruddy with pleasure.

'Isn't it *so good*?' he asks the table. 'I've missed you all.'

Genevieve smiles and the rest of us cheer rowdily, the noise reverberating inside the glass walls like it might echo on forever. I'd forgotten what it feels like to be surrounded by so many people, so many adults. None of the others have kids; they don't know what it's like.

'God, yes,' I say. 'I've missed the company. I'm so happy not to have to talk about Paw Patrol or Peppa for five minutes.' I take another big gulp of wine, feeling its fingers knead the knots in my neck, my shoulders.

Jess catches my eye across the table but she's not smiling right now. Then James is leaning over and reminding me of the time we kept the shells from the first time Jess ever made Coquilles St Jacques – an expensive, dangerous experiment while we were still living in halls in our first year. We drilled holes in the shells and made bras out of them, and then Lucas and James wore them any time Jess cooked for the next month.

'Mate, that was hilarious!' Lucas is laughing so hard he's crying. Kira rolls her eyes, unimpressed – probably because she wasn't there back then. You had to be there.

'It wasn't funny then and it's still not funny now,' Jess

26

complains. 'Don't you remember? Somebody complained that we were making *porn* in the kitchen—'

Jess's expression is a long-suffering one and we all dissolve into fits of laughter again. Even Genevieve is laughing, probably picturing Lucas in nothing but scallop shells.

'I could have done without that image in my head, thanks,' Kira says drily, even though she's heard the story many times before. 'Ugh. What a sight. Although I do wish somebody had taken a photo – would have made great blackmail.'

Between jokes and stories, it's somehow gone eleven before we get around to dessert. Somebody has cleared the plates away, probably James being his ever-helpful self, but I didn't even notice. I'm three, maybe four, glasses of wine deep and I'm not sure how many beers before that. Distantly I know I'll regret it tomorrow – beer and wine are the *worst* combination after all – but right now I'm too busy being wrapped up in how wonderful it feels to relax, how easy it is to be with these guys again. We're all different, all older and – well – some of us are wiser, but it's just like always.

Then I realise that it's gone quiet. Lucas and Genevieve have their heads bent together and they're still murmuring to each other softly, but James and Kira have both stopped and turned to look at Jess, who's now standing at the head of the table with an empty bottle in her hand. She looks angry.

'What's up?' I ask.

Jess shakes the bottle – at me, as though I should know.

'What's—' James shifts in his chair but Jess shakes her head.

27

'It's the bottle of Chardonnay,' she says pointedly. Again, directed at me.

'The one you couldn't find earlier?'

'Yes.'

Her lips are thin with annoyance.

'Where did you find it?'

'Outside on the ground.'

'What were you doing outside?' I ask at the same time as James says, 'How did it get there?'

'It doesn't matter what I was doing,' Jess grumbles. 'Somebody took the wine and dumped the bottle outside. It was for the St Jacques!'

She's had a fair bit to drink, same as me, and she's starting to get upset. James gets up and takes the bottle from her gently, then glances at me.

'Why is everybody looking at me?' I scan the faces of everybody at the table and they're all staring at me now, even Gen and Lucas. 'We looked for it together, Jess. Anyway, it's just wine, Jesus.'

'I know it's just wine. I'm just saying that I found it, and somebody drank it, and I'm not losing it.'

'I never said—'

Jess throws up her hands and then sinks into her seat at the table, taking a huge swig from her glass. 'Sorry,' she mutters. 'I'm so tired. Is anybody else tired? I feel like it's been three hundred years since I slept. Didn't mean to bring the mood down.'

'Don't be sorry,' James swoops in, ever the gentleman, cheering up my wife so I don't have to. Not that I'm bitter about that. 'It's not a big deal. And anyway, if you want to talk about bringing the mood down, we should talk about the time Lucas threw up in the bath over winter break in third year and we all came back to the whole house needing to be fumigated. What a Christmas present. Now *that* brought the mood down.'

'Yeah, yeah,' Lucas drawls, but he's grinning. 'Keep ragging on Lucas. You all know the only reason I did that was because you arseholes left me alone in that shitty student house for *three weeks* and didn't call once . . .'

I zone out and sit back in my chair. James leans over and gives me a gentle nudge, a searching question in his eyes. I shrug and put on my happy face. Jess has been like this lately, but it's nothing I can't handle on my own. She's right: we're both tired, wound up, and we need this break. But I'm not really thinking about Jess. Instead I'm thinking about the wine bottle, empty – outside. The lads have had a lot to drink so I can't imagine it's either of them, taste in booze notwithstanding. Gen's had two glasses of wine with dinner and she seems completely fine, not drunk at all, so she can't have had a whole bottle of Chardonnay as well, can she? My alcohol-addled brain can't make sense of it.

But I don't have time to think about it too much, because then Genevieve lets out an excited shriek. She points towards the sky overhead, and I look up with my vision only slightly swimming to see what she can see. Swirls of green and blue like Van Gogh's *Starry Night* across the black expanse. I can't work out what I'm looking at, until . . .

'Oh my God, northern lights!' Kira jumps up, chair legs scraping across the tiles. 'I gotta get my camera.'

'I've got champagne,' Jess says, her grumpiness swiftly forgotten. 'Quick, let's grab it and go down to the beach. We can take blankets and watch them.'

'Yes!' Lucas pumps a fist in the air – probably more at

the champagne than the lights, since it's the only kind of wine he'll drink – and then locks his arm around Genevieve's shoulders. She giggles and lets him drag her away, gaze still fixed on the glass roof and the endless night and the lights like a whole universe of swirling ghosts above.

Jess has grabbed two bottles of cold champagne from the kitchen. I let her press one of them into my hands and then also take my jacket, which she offers with a small smile. As though she's forgiven me. As though she still thinks I did something wrong. James is watching, so I smile back.

# 4

## *Kira*

I loop my camera strap over my head and jam my feet back into my walking boots. It takes two attempts – the wine has absolutely gone to my head – but I manage it, and then I'm following the others, stumbling out of the warm glow of the lighthouse and into the darkness.

This is probably stupid, dangerous, but we've got plenty of torches, on our phones and the real thing – although only because *I* dug them out of a drawer in the kitchen earlier. Lucas has two picnic blankets slung over his shoulders as though he's about to go swimming and Genevieve is tugging at his muscular arm.

'Come on! I want to enjoy every minute. Let's *go!*'

She's like a child, but for once I don't begrudge her excitement. For once it doesn't feel trite, or forced. I'm excited too; it's a tremble that says *this is exactly what I was hoping for*. The night air has dropped cold but we don't really feel it. I let James lead the way as he picks out the path back down to the dock where we arrived earlier and to the small cove that's right nearby, sand disappearing into the darkness beneath the lighthouse, pressed on one side against steadily rising cliffs.

The wind nudges at our backs until we reach the beach and then drops silent, as if we've entered a cocoon. Silver sand spreads like glitter around the curve of the island, the lighthouse looming on the rise ahead. I'm not sure how far the beach goes, but it looks like a trail leading right into the black ocean.

'Can you *believe* how cool they look in person?' Genevieve says. 'I've always wanted to see them. Never thought it would be here.' She's stopped about ten feet from the edge of the water and is just staring straight up, right at the sky. I follow her gaze and wobble – not from the booze but from the gravity of it.

The lights aren't anything like I thought; not really. They're so much bigger – so much *more*. The whole universe seems alive with them, whorls and waves and great swipes of green and blue, tinged with red like the embers of a dying sun. I wobble again, and this time I don't fight it, just let myself plonk right onto the sand.

A startled laugh explodes from my chest like relief.

'You all right?' James is breathless as he sits down next to me, as if he's just come running along the beach.

'I'm great. I'm perfect. I'm . . .' I fumble for my camera. I've probably had too much wine to get a decent shot but I'm going to try, fingers numbly changing zoom and aperture.

James hooks his arms around his knees, drawing them to his chest. There's a loud pop as somebody yanks the cork from the first bottle of champagne. James jumps and then laughs at himself. I snap a few shots and then lower my camera.

'Scared the ghosts will get you?' I joke. He shakes his head. He doesn't seem as fun as he normally is when he's drunk. Maybe he's had too much. He's thoughtful, watching Lucas. I wonder if they had words earlier, on the way down here.

'Are you okay?'

James stares down the beach until I nudge him.

'Just drunk,' he says.

'Maybe you should slow down,' I caution. He should. I know better than most how he gets when he's had too much.

'Oh damn!' Jess exclaims somewhere behind me. 'We don't have glasses! No offence but I don't wanna have to share the bottle like we're eighteen.'

Moira snorts but Lucas reaches under the picnic blankets he's still wearing – like a toga now – and pulls out some plastic cups. That's forward thinking the likes of which I've never seen from him, but Genevieve is nodding as though it was her idea and I'm not surprised. Perhaps we're not that different. Lucas has always needed somebody to look after him.

'Kira?'

'Huh?' I turn and Moira's handing me a glass filled with sparkling bubbles. 'Oh, thanks.' I take a sip and sigh. It's good stuff. A little sweet, but not too much. I drink more, feeling the fizz and pop on my tongue and turn my eyes back to the sky, my camera forgotten again.

'It's good to be back together, isn't it?' I murmur. 'All of us in one place. A bit like old times.'

'Mm-hmm.' Moira's already filling her glass again. 'Almost.'

I think back to a night like this at the end of third year, when we'd all driven down to Brighton for the day in

James's car, carrying cans of cider and picnic nibbles onto the beach between us like treasured gems. We stayed until it got late and dark, and we lay in the sand and made plans for after graduation. I'd thought then that Lucas might propose; that we'd be together forever like Mo and Jess. I still sometimes wonder what it might have looked like if things had gone the way I'd planned. We clung on for years but things had been going wrong since before we even graduated.

Now Lucas is sprawled on one of the picnic blankets with Genevieve, their hands entwined as they gaze upwards into infinity.

'Yeah. Almost.'

My glass is full again. Moira must have filled it already. I laugh and dump half the champagne into my mouth in one go. Everything's swimming a bit, waves rolling onto the beach. I wonder if the tide will come in and swallow us up, but the water doesn't seem to be getting much closer.

Moira is quiet. I'm not sure where Jess is, or when James left either, but Moira's still perched beside me on the sand, her hands pressed between her knees. She seems uneasy, or annoyed, probably because of Jess having a go earlier. I wonder if they'll have a proper argument later like they used to, or if it'll just bubble under the surface. It's not my job to mediate, but I've always liked how calm Moira is, even when she's angry. Still waters and all that.

'You okay?' I ask. It feels like tonight's mantra, a bit of fraying twine holding us all together.

'I'm fine. Why?' She brushes her hair back off her face and pulls her jacket a bit closer. The temperature has dropped again and my nose is cold but I don't care. There's a fire in my belly from the champagne and I swallow more.

'Just . . .' I gesture.

'Earlier? Not a big deal. She just gets so tired, you know. It's been hard for her since I got this job. I think she thought I'd change my mind about wanting to manage another auction house. She wanted me to keep doing the freelance stuff, work from home like her. She's on her own with Emma a lot now, but I can handle it. I always do.'

The aurora casts Moira's face in sickly relief, dark hollows under her eyes where earlier I couldn't have sworn to their existence. But she's not lying. She's been looking out for Jess for years, and it's no different now – except they have Emma.

'Good,' I say, a bit slurred. 'I mean good you can handle it, not good that Jess is tired. Is it good to be managing again?'

Moira sags. I can't tell if it's guilt or relief when she says, 'Yes.'

We lapse into silence. Jess laughs at something somebody else has said somewhere behind us and Lucas is talking loudly about God knows what. I tune him out and listen instead to the dim, steady roar of the waves, the crunch of sand under my fingertips. It's nice.

'I'm glad you found this place,' Moira says after a while. 'It's really cool. I like it here. Especially tonight, with the lights and everything. It feels more normal now, doesn't it? Like we're more . . . ourselves. Although Jess is still freaked out about the stories. And there was a thing with . . .' She trails off.

'With what?'

'Oh, nothing. Just the thing with the wine. Not a big deal. I think we're just getting ourselves all wound up over nothing. Anyway, I do think it's really cool. I wish we could get in that other door in the lighthouse though, don't you?'

'Not really.' I shrug. 'Bit of mystery is good. And like I said earlier, it's probably just cleaning products.'

'I know, but if we could make sure that there's nothing cool or exciting in there then Jess would probably chill—'

We both start laughing. Jess will never chill out. We both know that. Moira snorts and wipes her sleeve across her face and I realise that she's made herself laugh so hard she's crying.

'Jesus, Mo,' I say. 'Are you sure you're okay?'

'I haven't been properly drunk in six months!' she exclaims. 'Cut me some slack. We hardly ever go out any more – and never together. This is a novelty.'

She drops back onto the sand, staring up at the sky. I swivel a bit, better to see the others who are crowded behind me. It's dark enough that I can hardly see Jess in her black jacket, but Lucas's white shirt collar glows and I can see the shiny blonde of Genevieve's crown pressed against his chest.

'We should have got a bonfire or a barbecue going. That would have been amazing. Could have done marshmallows.' Jess drains another glass of champagne. I don't know how many she's had now, but it's more than me. We're all worse for wear, though. 'I love marshmallows.'

'Ew,' Moira says with a laugh. 'No. Too sweet! And after what you're always saying to Em.'

'I know, I know.' Jess shakes her head. 'It's a weakness.'

'We could, though.'

Genevieve lifts her head off Lucas's chest.

'Could what?' I ask. 'We didn't buy any marshmallows.'

'No, the fire I mean. We could make one.'

'How?'

'It's not that hard. There are matches up there, right?'

'You know how to make a fire?' Lucas pulls a face, surprise and pride mingled together. 'Full of surprises, this one!'

'I did tell you last time we lit the fire pit. It's not that hard, just technique. I can do it without matches but I'll do it with them if we've got them.'

'What about wood?' I ask, almost like I'm determined to prove that she can't do it. I don't know why I'm doing it, but I can't stop myself. 'It's not like you can magic *that* out of thin air.'

'The cottage has a wood stove. There are logs piled in the store outside.' Genevieve seems oblivious to my tone and I'm both relieved and annoyed. How is she so chill all the time? 'I noticed them earlier since it's getting pretty cold already. I didn't want us to be cold in the night so I had a look how to make the stove work. Ideally I'd prefer clean energy but an old-fashioned wood fire is certainly fitting for the environment.' She smiles.

'That *would* be neat.' James sits up and I jump. I hadn't seen where he'd disappeared off to but he's just behind Jess. 'A fire, I mean. Let's do it. It'll be like the Scouts—'

'I didn't know you were a Scout,' Moira says. 'Makes sense though, little angel like you. Of course you were.'

'You were a Scout too,' Jess points out. 'You're always going on about how you were in the first mixed-gender group in the village. A *girl* Scout! Ha. Why can't *you* light a fire? Didn't they teach you that?'

'Hey, they taught me a lot of things thanks. I just don't always brag about it . . .'

James and Lucas are both standing up now, and Genevieve gets up to join them. 'I'll go get the wood. You sort out the matches? There were definitely some in that drawer in the kitchen.'

'Here,' I say thickly, my head still woolly from the wine. 'Take the torch. Somebody take it.' I wave it blindly until somebody takes it.

'For God's sake Lucas, it's fine, let me go. I know where I'm looking.'

'Gen said—'

I've let myself sink down onto the sand, my camera heavy on my chest, so I can't see them now, but Lucas and James are the ones arguing this time. They both sound, from this angle, like they're well and truly sloshed.

'I don't care what Gen said, you don't have to do everything she tells you, do you?'

'Aw c'mon Jay, that's not nice.'

'I'm just saying I'll go, Jesus.'

'Well I need to go off and grab another beer anyway; can't stand this champagne. Too . . . champagney, y'know?'

There's something bubbling under their words that wasn't there earlier, but I'm not really paying attention. I hear both their footsteps as they storm off across the sand, and then it's blissfully quiet again. Jess and Mo are lying together next to me, or at least I think they are, but my eyes are caught up in the lights overhead. Everything is so pretty. It's just like it used to be when the three of us would hang out in uni, back on those hot summer nights when we'd drag blankets out into the garden and sit and smoke for hours while the lads played Xbox.

'Want one?'

Moira props herself up on her elbow and waves a small packet.

'Oh man, I was just thinking about that.'

'What?' Jess sits up and eyeballs the cigarettes. 'Mo, what

the hell? I thought you quit. We both quit. You said you were done!'

'I am!' Moira shakes the box. 'But we're on holiday. They don't count if we're on holiday.'

'Of course they flipping count!'

'Christ, Jess . . .' Moira chucks the packet at me and it hits me square in the chest. I fumble with the cellophane and pull out one of the cigarettes.

Jess hisses at me in disgust but I ignore her. Moira's right. We're on holiday; it doesn't count. It's an embarrassing few seconds before I realise I haven't got any way to light it, though, and nobody's back yet. I put the cigarette in my jacket pocket and throw the packet back to Moira.

Jess snatches them out of the air with surprising reflexes and stuffs them into her own pocket.

'No, Mo,' she says firmly.

'That's my only pack,' Moira grumbles, flopping back onto the sand good-naturedly enough. It's probably not worth the battle.

I close my eyes, listening to the rush and pull of the waves, my face numb with the cold. I hear footsteps as Moira, or Jess, or both of them, get up and leave. Or not. Maybe they're still there, silent together, or whispering quieter than the world. I'm not paying attention to anything but my body, my heart beating loud and slow, the salt and pine scent inside my nostrils. Bliss.

At some point I hear footsteps behind me, and struggle upright again, fully cold now and out of champagne. I see Jess and Moira first.

'I cannot wait to get a fire going,' I mutter at nobody in particular. 'It's freezing.'

Genevieve and Lucas are shadows against the sky as they

appear again moments later. They drop the wood they're both carrying and all of us set about building a circle of stones and piling the wood into a fire-shaped thing. It's not until we're done, all of us pleased with our handiwork in the dim beam of the flashlight, that Genevieve pauses and looks about.

'What's up?' Lucas asks.

Genevieve's eyes scan us each in turn. I wobble a bit and grab Moira's arm for support.

'Huh?' I say, echoing the question.

'The matches. Has anybody seen James?'

# 5

## *Genevieve*

Everybody is silent and staring at me. I didn't realise how much noise we were making until we stopped. Now the *wash-wash* of the waves on the beach seems to fill the air like static.

'What?' Kira asks. She has a vacant expression on her face, but I know she's understood me because she's starting to scramble off her knees. 'Wasn't he . . .' She looks around.

Moira and Jess exchange a glance, searching, but it's obvious now that none of us have seen him in a while. I feel awful. I didn't notice because I was too busy directing Lucas where to put the kindling at the heart of the fire, feeling proud that I could be useful. A small part of me always loves it when I know something he doesn't, as if I'm reclaiming that early assertion I had, before I let myself melt into *Lucas-and-Gen*.

'He was getting the matches,' Lucas says stupidly. 'He . . . Didn't he come back?'

'No.' Kira's shaking her head. 'Nobody's been back here since you all left. You were with him. Did he say anything?'

Lucas looks a bit sheepish. I can see that even in the dark. The northern lights overhead have faded a bit now and we've been using the torches to see what we're doing.

'He . . . I dunno. He went the other way to us. We were getting the wood. I haven't . . .'

'You were bickering,' Moira says pointedly. 'Whatever. I'm sure he's just still in the lighthouse looking for the matches or something. I'll call him.'

She fishes her phone out of her pocket and finds James's name in her contacts. I'm standing just outside the glow of the torches. Something feels off. I can't say exactly what it is, and I know I've not known James for as long as the others, but we've spent some time together, the odd day here and there, Chinese takeaway in the flat Lucas and I share, and this doesn't feel right. He doesn't seem like the sort of guy who'd just wander off and not tell anybody he was going, especially not after what Ben said earlier about being careful in the dark. James has always reminded me of a golden retriever at heart: obedient and a little silly.

Jess's expression is strained as Moira holds her phone to her ear, and I just know she's thinking about those stories I told her earlier. Missing lighthouse keepers and ghosts of sailors. I wish now that I'd kept my mouth shut.

'I'm sure he's fine, but I think I'm going to start walking up to the cottage,' I say. 'Just to see if he needs help finding them.'

'Hang on,' Jess says, 'why don't you wait until—'

'Signal's no good.' Moira looks worried now, too, her golden skin blanched by the sickly green light overhead. 'I wonder if he's – I don't know, on the toilet. He has had a lot to drink. Maybe he's throwing up?'

'Really?' Lucas rolls his eyes. 'If anything, he's probably passed out on the sofa.'

'He wasn't that drunk, was he?' Kira's eyes are wide and she's moving with the grace of a baby horse. 'I mean, I know we're all . . . But the man said – the cliff . . .'

'I'm going to check the cottage,' I say again. This time I don't wait for anybody to agree with me, but the others fall into step as we leave our pile of wood and rocks and picnic blankets scattered on the sand, plastic glasses shining like half a dozen dying stars.

Lucas jogs to catch up with me. 'I'm sure he's fine.'

'I'm sure he is.'

But we don't talk as we all head up to the cottage. The tension is thick in the air. None of us want to talk about how worried we are when it could easily be an overreaction, but it doesn't really make sense. Maybe one of us should have offered to stay on the beach. I'm trying to remember if James even walked up here with us earlier. Lucas was ranting and I wasn't paying attention.

'When did anybody last see him?' Kira asks.

'When we left the beach.'

'Yes, but did he come with you?'

'I don't know, okay?' This comes out harsher than I intend and I'm immediately awash with embarrassment. 'Sorry. I mean – I'm sorry, but I wasn't paying attention.'

'He was,' Lucas says firmly. 'I'm sure he was.'

'You don't think he left the lighthouse by the other door, do you? The one in the kitchen?' Jess asks. We're halfway up the hill and she's breathless, but there's more than just exertion making her voice tremble like it does. She sounds like she's on the verge of tears. 'In the dark . . .'

'Why on earth would he do that?' Moira shuts her down. 'He's not stupid.'

'I know but maybe he thought it would be quicker. He might have . . .'

She doesn't say the word *fallen* but it's what we're all thinking. My limbs are buzzing, slipping out of the remains of the drunkenness I've been chasing all evening. The crunch of the chalky gravel is loud underfoot and Lucas is breathing heavily. It's cold now and getting darker as the night wears on.

The lighthouse looms above, its beam cutting through the darkness like a silver knife before disappearing again. The cottage is still and ghostly white, windows black just as Lucas and I left it when we headed back down to the beach with the wood. How long ago was that? We didn't hurry. Memories of Lucas's face pressed against mine, tongue searching, rough hands in my hair and a wall against my back, a few moments stolen from the others in the darkness . . .

'What do you think?'

Moira is ahead of me now and she stops so quickly I almost walk into her.

'What do I think?'

'We should split up, shouldn't we? Check the lighthouse and the cottage. I'm sure he'll be somewhere around here. Maybe he went up to see what it's like up there at this time of night, with the lights and everything?' She gestures at the lighthouse. Something makes me shiver. Maybe it's just the cold.

'Yeah, I guess that makes sense. Lucas and I can check the cottage, and you guys can take the lighthouse?'

Jess doesn't look thrilled at my suggestion but Moira is

already walking towards the lighthouse with a purposeful stride. Jess follows quickly, stumbling a little and grabbing for her wife's arm. Kira waits for a moment, indecisive. She looks from me to Lucas, her expression unreadable. Then she grips her torch tighter and follows the others, leaving the two of us alone in the dark.

'Come on,' I say. 'Let's hope he's just gone to bed.'

Lucas doesn't speak, but there's something hanging between us. I wonder why James and Lucas were bickering earlier. I didn't catch most of it, just the part where they were going back and forth about the matches, but I know it's not the first time today they've sniped at each other. Things have been that way for a while, though. Come to think of it, I can't remember the last time he came for dinner at ours.

The door to the cottage is unlocked and we let ourselves in. Everything is blanketed in darkness, except for a flickering green light that sits above the alarm. I snap on the light switch, casting the entry in wan yellow light. The lounge is empty, and so is the kitchen. There is a packet of biscuits on the table, two of them spilling out carelessly.

All of the bedrooms are empty too. We search each one in turn, Lucas right behind me as I turn on light after light, lamps illuminating every corner, marking our progress like glowing pins in a map.

'James?' Lucas calls. 'Jay, you in here mate?'

We're greeted only by silence.

'He's not in here,' I say. I don't admit that I suspected all along he wouldn't have come back here. Why would he? But it's getting late now, and there's more reason than ever for him to turn up here.

We head back outside and Lucas tries James's mobile

45

again. I can hear the distant *brr-brr* of the dial tone as Lucas's breath hitches.

'Come on,' I say, more forcefully than normal. 'Let's check a bit further. Maybe he wandered the wrong way.'

'He's drunk, not stupid.'

I pull a face which I hope is light-hearted enough to hide my very real fears: of the cliffs, the darkness, the uneven ground. But Lucas follows me without any more argument and we cut across the yard between the lighthouse and the keeper's cottage, heading away from the path that leads down to the beach.

Lucas still has one of the torches and he clicks it on again now, swiping left to right in a way that leaves me dizzy. I reach over and snatch it from him, pointing it straight ahead. He grunts but keeps quiet, following just behind me as we wander along a path in the grass that spills out ahead. It's thin, more of a trail really, through the lush grass that grows in thick tufts and larger mounds. The new bit of the lighthouse extension follows the general shape of the path, so I know the cliffs must be coming up ahead, but I can't see much of them or the ocean. Everything is dark outside my beam of light.

As we come parallel to the extension a light flickers on and the kitchen windows flare to life. Seconds later I hear the door open and a voice which might be Jess's, but it's hard to tell.

'James!'

'We haven't found him yet,' I call back, wary of them thinking Lucas is James and rushing out here. We're too close to the cliff's edge for that to be safe.

'Not in the cottage?' calls Moira.

'No. He's not been back there since we were there,

46

I don't think. Hard to tell but doesn't look like it anyway. Can you find the matches at least?'

All three of them are heading out of the kitchen door now, one bright torch beam and two pale lights flickering from phones until they meet us. The wind whips my hair across my forehead and I brush it back impatiently. I'm worried that it'll rain, and that will make the visibility even worse. Already I can see dark clouds forming, blocking out the lights overhead: the moon is hidden.

'They're still in the drawer.'

Up close I can really feel the shift in everybody's attitudes. I start to feel a real hum of fear in my bones then. Up until now it's been . . . not *funny*, but there's been room for error. A mistake. Something to laugh about in an hour, with a roaring fire at our feet and the ocean distant at our backs. Now . . . Well, now we're all scared.

'You searched the whole lighthouse?'

'Top to bottom,' Moira says. 'Everywhere but that locked room, yeah. We checked the sofas, the bathroom, the kitchen and the dining area, and right up at the top . . . I'm not sure he's even been in there since we left but I don't know how to tell. We didn't lock the door so he could have been and then gone back down to the beach looking for us.'

We're all sober now. Or definitely not as drunk as we were before. The fear and the cold wind have seen to that. We're gathered in a circle, arm to arm, all of us frozen. But we can't just stand here.

'We were going to walk a bit further along here,' I say. 'Make sure he's not come out this way and got lost. Do you think somebody ought to go back to the beach just in case?'

'I tried calling him again,' Jess says, her voice reedy.

'Still nothing. I've tried texting him too but it won't go through.'

'We tried to call again as well.' Lucas's jaw is tense.

'He can't have gone far,' I say, trying to stay calm. 'I bet he's just wandering about.'

'Why?' Kira has been surprisingly quiet until now, but this one word cuts through the rest of our reassurances. 'Why would he go anywhere at all? He was told not to wander off. He's not stupid. I know he was a bit weird earlier . . .' she trails off as though she just realises what she's said.

'Weird how?' Moira asks.

'Not weird. Just – I don't know. I think we're all a bit excitable today. I don't know how to describe it. A bit quiet, I think. Jumpy. But I'm probably imagining it.'

'He was fine,' Lucas insists. 'Just being a dick.'

'He wasn't—'

'We can't just stand here,' I insist, stopping the argument before it can start. It doesn't matter right now; Lucas and Kira's egos are the last thing on my mind. What matters is that we find him. 'We're on an island. He literally can only have gone so far. We need to check the beach and this path, okay?'

Everybody looks at me. Kira is frowning at the way I cut her off, but she doesn't disagree. Moira nods and Jess grabs her arm, starting to pull her away.

'We'll go and check the beach again then, make sure he's not—'

'I think we should stay up here actually,' Moira says. 'Or I will, anyway. You and Kira go down to the beach, but I want to make sure we have a proper look up here.'

'Because of the rocks.' Jess is starting to panic again. Her chest heaves and she blows out a long stream of clouded air. 'Okay. Okay, yes. He probably came back down and wandered off that way.'

'He did seem fascinated by the beach,' Kira adds, reassuring once more. 'I bet he's down there now trying to light that bloody fire.'

Kira grabs Jess's arm and they walk away without saying anything else. The rest of us wait for a second, until we're sure they're safely back on the path that leads down to the beach, and then we turn inwards again.

'Without matches. Hmph. If he fell . . .' Moira says.

'I know,' I say.

'He won't have,' Lucas snaps. 'He's fine. Let's just check here and then we'll go down the beach.'

'We don't even know where it goes,' Moira says. 'I wish we had some sort of map, or a bigger torch or something.'

'We'll just follow the path,' I say. I feel calmer, now that we have a direction again. Now that Jess and Kira are gone. It feels awful to even admit that to myself, but both of them have trouble staying relaxed. Moira is a different matter. 'Single file.'

We fall into line and I light the path ahead as best I can with the beam of the torch. The ground is uneven, just a dirt track running through the grass, which is short in some places and much longer in others. Twice I stumble, but catch myself before I fall.

I'm not sure how far we've come, only that the lighthouse seems impossibly tall behind us when I turn to look over my shoulder, even as it drops away as the path works its way uphill. The lighthouse beam bounces out across the ocean, highlighting stripes of black water, so far down that it seems like it would be solid if we fell. I can't see how

49

close we are to the cliff, but I can smell the salt on the air, feel the wind grow sharper with every second. If James came out here by himself . . . If he fell . . .

'This is stupid,' Lucas mutters darkly. 'I'm sure he's—'

'Wait.' I stop, pulse thundering in my ears. Lucas slams into my back and Moira lets out a yelp.

'Jesus, Gen!'

'What's . . .?'

'There's something ahead.'

# 6

## *Moira*

I can't see more than a few inches in front of us, even with my phone torch trained on the uneven ground. Lucas's back is strong and dark in front of me, the grass and dirt damp underfoot, and all I can feel is my blood rushing through my frozen limbs. I force the panic down and try to be sensible.

'What is it?' I ask. My voice comes out quiet. Timid. 'I can't see—'

And then Lucas is moving, chasing after Gen. She rushes ahead with the light and all I've got is my phone, fumbling for a better grip as I push my body into action. Gen's almost running, a graceful loping sort of pace that I struggle to match even despite a few half marathons under my belt.

'What . . .' I start to ask again, but then I see it.

It's a building. A small one, I think, made of some kind of wood. It's like a shack or a cottage, but even from here and in the dark I can tell that it's not been used for a long time. The roof slants at an odd angle and I'm surprised that the wind off the sea hasn't dragged it away before now.

'What's that?' I ask, breathless.

We come to a halt just before it. The dirt track leads right up to the threshold before branching off again into the darkness. We're still close to the edge of the cliff, but not as near as I'd feared, and beside the cottage the wind drops right off so I can suddenly hear better. Lucas and Gen are illuminated faintly by the torch as Genevieve shines it against the front of the building.

It's got glass windows but they're so filthy we can't see what's inside. The door that leads onto the path has a small wooden porch out front that sags dangerously under Genevieve's weight as she steps up close. She gives the door a shove, glances back nervously, and then tests the handle.

'Gen, I don't know if—' Lucas starts to protest, but she's already pushing the handle downwards and swinging the door. It resists a little, wood dragging on wood as she forces it open and steps inside.

'I don't . . .'

'Do you think . . .?'

Lucas and I exchange a glance, but it's clear neither of us wants Genevieve wandering in there alone.

'James?' she calls. 'Are you in here?'

We follow her inside, but I'm careful to make sure the door stays wedged open. We come into a large open room. There's a stone fireplace to my right, dusty and caked with layers of old ash. The floorboards under our feet creak loudly but fortunately seem to hold.

'Wow.' Genevieve turns back to us, pointing the torch from wall to wall, scanning the whole room.

It's an open space, filled only with an old dining table that looks to be carved from solid wood, grubby place settings and a candlestick in the middle. There are a couple of chairs, and a ratty old armchair that could easily be infested with mice. Overhead there's a mezzanine but there's no ladder in sight. Beneath the mezzanine there's a door that leads to a bathroom or kitchen, or maybe more than that – but it's hard to tell how far back it goes in the dark. The whole place must be empty, though. It's cold and damp. Silent. Real silence, too, even the ocean dulled to nothing by the rotting wood.

'He can't have climbed up there, can he?' Genevieve asks. Lucas shakes his head emphatically and I agree.

'Not a chance,' he says. 'He's not here. Come on, this place gives me the creeps.'

I know what he means. There's something . . . *untouched* about it. Not just because it's been empty for a long while, but because it seems abandoned. As if whoever used to live here didn't think they'd be coming back. As if they knew that it would fall to ruin without them.

'What do you think this place is?' I ask.

Genevieve swoops the torch across the space again, her face thoughtful.

'Probably the old groundskeeper's cabin or something. I bet they had groundskeepers *and* lighthouse keepers here back in the day. Or maybe it's where the lighthouse keepers lived before they moved in next to the lighthouse.'

'James?' I call out again, just to be sure. But the only sound that comes back is the muffled echo of my own voice and the creaking of the boards under Lucas's feet as he turns back towards the door.

'He's not here. I told you, we should check the beach again.'

'But the path continues from here,' Genevieve points out. 'He might have just kept walking.'

'Why?' Lucas snaps. 'I don't get why he'd come out here.'

'I think Lucas is right,' I say quietly. I don't really want to agree with him when he speaks to people like that, but I *do* think he's got a point. Why would James even walk this way? Three hundred beers couldn't invent a reason. 'I think we should go back to the beach. In case . . .'

'In case he fell?' Genevieve looks stricken, but she nods eventually. 'Okay. You're right. If he did come this way there's nothing we can do in the dark.'

I don't add that the reason I want to leave is that I don't like the idea of being out here any more. Not even with all three of us together. I can't shake Jess's nervousness earlier, the way that bottle of wine disappeared and turned up later. What if James drank it? It isn't like him at all. What if – I don't even want to think it, but what if he *hurt himself*? Would James do that? He isn't always the bright, bubbly guy people think he is. There's always been a darkness there, a magnetism that tugs him towards the melancholy. Sad poetry, old romance movies . . . But this?

Fear worms inside me as we head back out into the wind, rain now stinging our faces as we pull our coats tighter and head back down the path. I don't know what we're heading towards but I'm glad to leave the cabin behind.

We find Kira and Jess on the beach, standing beside what would have been our little campfire. Neither of them looks happy, and Jess's relief at seeing me lasts only a second before they realise that we are alone too.

'You didn't find him,' she says.

'Not yet.'

I draw her into my arms and let her rest her head on my shoulder, relishing in the feeling of her solid warmth against me, suddenly glad in a grasping, primal way for the tightness of her grip, her fingers digging into my hips. It's spitting with rain and the air is frigid now that the booze has worn off. Jess shifts, drawing back. She tucks her hands into mine and I warm her cold fingers as best I can.

'We did find some kind of – I dunno, a shack, I guess,' Lucas says.

'But he wasn't there. I don't think anybody has been in it in forever. Very abandoned vibes,' I add.

'Where the fuck *is* he?' Kira shakes her head, kicking at the stone circle we built around the wood pile. She's still wearing her camera and it swings against her chest.

'He can't have gone far,' I say. Again. As though any of us believes that now. The island isn't big but it's a monster of dark hills, little wooded groves, cliffs and caves and treacherous tumbles into the ocean. 'Really. He can't have.'

'What are we going to do? If he doesn't turn up . . .' Jess looks at me with wide eyes. She's really panicking now. This is exactly what we didn't want to happen on this trip. It was supposed to be easy, fun. Fucking James. Why couldn't he just fetch the matches and come back like he was supposed to?

I realise I'm gripping Jess's hands hard and I try to make myself relax. Getting angry won't solve anything.

'We'll need to call the coastguard,' Genevieve says.

'Are you kidding me?' Kira is doing a worse job of hiding her anger than I am. She's started to pace, and Genevieve looks affronted as she waves her arms around. 'We're in the middle of nowhere. What are they going to do?'

'We'll have to call if he doesn't turn up,' Lucas agrees. 'There's no good snapping at Gen as if it's her fault.'

'Well the fire wasn't *my* idea.'

Jess steps back as though Kira has slapped her. 'I didn't exactly demand one,' she says. 'I just said it would be nice.'

'I wasn't saying you did!' Kira lets out an exasperated grunt.

'Anyway I'm not the one who's been sniping at him all day.' Jess turns on Lucas. 'What did you say to him earlier?'

'Whoa, whoa,' Lucas says, holding his hands up defensively. 'I didn't say anything. James is – you know, he's *James*.'

'Yeah and you take the piss out of him constantly,' Kira agrees. 'You know how sensitive he can be. Did you wind him up? Is that why he's stormed off? What did you argue about?'

'We didn't even bloody argue!' Lucas loses his temper in one cresting wave, kicking out at the sand and sending bits of wood from the destroyed fire flying. 'For God's sake, I was just checking in because he was being weird today. Don't start acting like I've gone and upset him.'

'I told you he was being weird and you acted like I was imagining things,' Kira says.

'No, you said he was jumpy tonight. I'm talking about earlier. He kept getting in all these digs about my job, about us coming here so late in the year, about Gen and you and everything.'

Genevieve is watching this whole argument like we've all got three heads. If we don't get it together soon we'll be in full-blown riot mode. It's starting to feel like we're out of control, hovering around an option nobody wants to admit. That maybe, if he has hurt himself, that it wasn't by accident. That maybe he's done this on purpose. Or worse – somebody else did. The thought chills me, and I can't believe I'm even giving it a second's thought.

I grab Jess's arm and pull her back to my side, and then hold my hands up.

'All right, everybody just shut up a second.'

'I don't—'

'I said shut it, Lucas.' I give him my best stare – one I've not used on him in years, but he's not forgotten. Used to be I had to be the boss of the lot of them, back when we were still kids. 'Look, arguing isn't going to solve anything. Neither is panicking. We've all had a lot to drink, we're all a bit freaked out. I'm sure that there's nothing wrong.'

'But—'

'But nothing. Listen to me. It's . . .' I check my phone again. No missed calls or texts from James – no signal either – but I fight back the concern. If managing the auction house has taught me anything it's that people don't think things through. They never just send a quick, logical text message; they never think how their actions could hold other people up or make them worry. This is no different. James is no different. 'It's nearly three o'clock now. I suggest we do another search down here, check anywhere he might have fallen, that patch of rocks down there at the bottom of the cliff, near where we were earlier – I know, it's dark and we can't see well. But this time we won't split up. We'll stay together and if we see anything worrying or reach a break in the beach we'll stop. Okay? And then, in the morning, if he's still not turned up, we'll call the people we need to call.'

'Oh God.' Jess is crying. She rubs at her cheeks and lets out a long breath. 'His mum is going to freak—'

'No.' I cut her off before she can get herself any more worked up. 'We're not going to think about that yet, because I'm sure he's fine. The island is big enough that there could be a hundred places we haven't looked. For all we know he decided to go for a walk and found a nice spot to have a lie down. Maybe there's another one of those weird huts we found and he's curled up all cosy.' This sounds feeble even to my ears, but I forge on. 'The more we panic, the less likely we are to spot him if he has hurt himself. Okay?'

Four faces stare nervously back at me and I feel my insides twist. Lucas looks like he wants to say something, his dark eyes watching me intently, but he keeps his thoughts to himself and gives me a curt nod instead.

'We already searched the beach though,' Jess says quietly. 'We went as far as we could go before the sea cut us off.'

'Which way?'

Jess points along the shore towards the cliff where the lighthouse stands proud in the darkness, the intermittent beam still slicing through the night. This feels pointless. If James had gone any way other than up the hill, surely it would be the way they've just searched. But I don't say that. I clench my fists and bite the inside of my cheek, ignoring the feeling that's settling over me. That James is in trouble. That we're all in trouble if we don't find him.

'Well, then we try the other way, head left when we get to the dock instead of right. Just in case he got turned around in the dark. Maybe he saw something interesting. Maybe he's trying to find 4G. In any case it's safer together.'

And, I think faintly, if we do it together we can all trust that we've searched properly.

# 7

## *Kira*

'It's no good. We can't go any further along here – the sea's too far in.'

Moira turns back to the rest of us, swinging the torch so it bounces off the cliffs to our backs. This side of the beach is much rockier, with black jagged outcrops and rock pools underfoot. We've managed to get this far by sheer determination and team effort, but she's right. The beach ahead has been totally swallowed by the ocean, just like on the other side of the dock, and even if we waded through it doesn't look safe.

'The tide looks like it's come in all the way now,' Genevieve says. She's got the other torch and she shines it ahead, the light dipping into more dark ocean. 'We're going to have to go back.'

I don't want to say anything, but I'm as relieved as I am worried and angry. It's bloody freezing and we've been on our feet for hours now. I can feel the exhaustion in my bones, my skin and hair gritty with salt that cracks the corners of my lips whenever I wince. I know I'm not the only one who's given up. Jess is behind me and when I turn around she's already marching back along the way we've come, splashing through shallow pools carelessly, not even waiting for her wife.

We head back towards the dock in silence. The night is still dark, speckled with a thousand tiny stars. The lighthouse on the cliff in the distance is barely visible but still there, still watching over us like a sentry. This wasn't the way I'd wanted things to go when I arranged this break. I couldn't have predicted any of this.

The relief has soon worn off as we traipse along. All that is left is a hollow exhaustion. Now that we've turned back it's like we have to admit we've failed. We haven't found James. If he's hurt, it's our fault. I can't believe he'd get himself into such a mess.

'I'm sure he's fine,' Moira whispers to herself. I barely hear her, her words only carried by some trick of the ocean wind, and I refuse to acknowledge it again. If he's fine, if we find him now, he won't be fine for long because at least one of us will firmly kick his arse. I prefer the anger to the fear. At least the anger helps to keep me warm; helps me to put one foot in front of the other.

The trek back up the hill to the cottage feels like it's miles not feet, and by the time we reach the top I'm out of breath. My camera, still strapped around my neck, feels like it weighs half a tonne. Jess falls back until she's walking beside me and for a while we don't say anything.

'Do you . . .' she starts. Then stops.

'Hmm?'

'Nothing.' Her breath hitches. 'I can't stop thinking about those stories,' she says. 'The ones Genevieve was telling today – yesterday – about the sailors who went wild and killed themselves when they were made to leave. Do you . . .'

'Do I what?' I haven't got the patience right now. 'Think he went and threw himself off the cliff?'

Jess freezes and I have to force myself to stop too. I didn't mean to say that. It just came out. Jess looks panicked again though, as if that's exactly what she has been thinking. A bubble of anger rises in my chest but I check it before it can explode.

'No,' I say. 'I'm sorry I said that. I don't think that's what happened.'

'What's what happened?' Moira reaches us and takes one look at Jess's face before turning to me. 'What did you say?'

'I didn't say anything. Jess was asking if – the sailors. If that had anything to do with . . .' I can't even say it now, it sounds so stupid. 'But I said no. James isn't suicidal. He didn't fling himself into – he wouldn't do anything like that. Not now, not here. Not like that.'

Moira glances between Jess and me again and I can't work out the expression on her face, but it looks like fear. Although whether she's more afraid of ghost stories or the idea of James purposefully throwing himself off a cliff, I'm not sure. I feel sick.

'I didn't mean . . .' Jess heaves a sigh that sounds full of unshed tears. 'I'm just really afraid.'

'I know.' Moira draws her wife to her chest and holds her close, resting her lips on Jess's forehead. 'It's okay. We'll figure it out.'

'How, though? We've looked everywhere. If he . . . The ocean . . .?'

Jess begins to pull away, but Moira holds her tight, as

if she needs the hug as much as Jess. I want to say something reassuring, to come up with a believable story that will explain everything that's happened tonight, but I can't even think of a fiction that makes sense. James has just vanished into thin air.

And now I'm thinking about the stupid ghost stories. They're nonsense – obviously they are – but I can't help dwelling on them now. Being out here as the sun is cresting over the water, the air freezing and wild and pine and salt scented, I'm being reminded constantly how raw a place this is. How I chose it. How this is all my fault.

Genevieve catches up with us next, but she has the good sense not to interrupt Jess and Moira. Instead she sidles up next to me and gives me a once-over. I must look terrible, but she doesn't look great either so for once I don't mind the way she runs her gaze over me.

'You can stop looking worried that I'm going to punch you,' I say.

'I wasn't . . .'

'I'm not going to. I'm a bit preoccupied, if you hadn't noticed.'

Genevieve looks stricken at that, as if I have actually slapped her. She opens her mouth and closes it again, words failing her. I haven't got the energy to argue, or even to question why I'm lashing out at her when she clearly hasn't done anything wrong; in fact she's been nothing but helpful the entire time. But if she hadn't agreed to light that fucking fire then we wouldn't be in this mess, and I can't stop thinking about it. If Lucas had just left her at home – or never decided to sleep with his boss in the bloody first place – then this holiday could have been, *would* have been perfect.

Except that's not true, and I know it. Things haven't been perfect for a long time.

I turn back towards the cottage, which feels impossibly quiet. I think of James earlier, sat in the kitchen with Moira. I heard them chatting, heard James stuffing his face with biscuits while I unpacked my weekend stuff into my single room and tried to ignore the sounds of Lucas and Genevieve making out next door, as though nobody could hear them. I can't shake how normal that felt, how easy it was to pretend that everything was fine, and how everything has spiralled out of control so quickly. I don't think I can stomach going back in there; not yet. It's not like we'll be able to pretend now. We can't just go into our separate rooms and go to sleep and act like nothing has happened.

We need to decide what we're going to do.

'I think we should go into the lighthouse and try to work out a plan,' I say quietly. 'We're going to have to call somebody, but with the tides I'm not sure when they'll be able to get here. I . . . I think somebody should also volunteer to have a nap and then go back down to the beach in a few hours when the sun is up. We need to check to see if we can see anything, if he maybe dropped anything like a shoe or a jacket or whatever. If he . . . if he was washed away there might be something that'll be easier to see in the daylight.'

There's a lump in my throat and I swallow hard. Everybody looks at me, the silence weighing on us all, but then Moira nods and so does Genevieve, so together we trudge towards the lighthouse.

The lighthouse doesn't fill me with the same joy as it did only hours ago. Earlier I had this feeling of being part of something much larger, a history so complex it can't be summed up just using words. Now I resent it. It stands there, towering in the darkness, dwarfing us so that I feel like nothing. I don't want to be here any more. I don't want to take photographs for the magazine; I don't want to experience the bracing freedom of nature. I just want all of us to be here, to be okay, and then I want to go home.

I didn't bother to lock it – it's not like there's anybody around to come in and steal stuff – so I push against the door and slip through first into the warmth, which feels like a hot breath on my frozen face. I've got a pounding headache, right across my eyes and down my neck, and everything hurts.

My whole body feels heavy, weighed down by cold and exhaustion and my damp clothes, so I don't notice it right away. Not until Lucas follows me inside, stops dead in his tracks, and says 'What the actual *fuck*?'

I glance up from inspecting my sodden trainers and jeans and see what Lucas has seen. Recognition shoots like electricity through my veins. My heart feels like it's in my throat, like I can hardly breathe, and I let out an involuntary gasp.

'*James?*'

# SATURDAY

# 8

## *Genevieve*

The lights are out except for one, which illuminates a shaft of the lounge, the armchairs and the sofa and the little coffee table in between. I step around Kira and Lucas. And – it's him. It's James.

He's sitting with his head in his hands, elbows on his knees; he looks half asleep and he starts when he hears Lucas's profanity. Jess lets out a screech that might be in anger or excitement and rushes over to him. He seems alarmed, and raises a hand to his head and squints as though the light and the noise hurt.

'What?' he mumbles. 'Why are you all . . .?'

'Where the hell have you been?' Kira is definitely all anger. There's no softness in her now as she marches over to James, who looks alive and perfectly well, if hideously hungover. His eyes are red rimmed and his skin pale. He rubs his hands over his face and has the decency to look sheepish.

Moira glances at me. I widen my eyes. Disbelief has rendered me speechless.

'What . . .?' James says again.

'Where. Have. You. Been?' Kira is right up in his face now. I'm actually genuinely concerned that she's going to hit him or at least shake the living daylights out of him. Yet I'm too shocked to intervene. 'Have you got any fucking idea how worried we were about you? We thought you were *dead*!'

'Wait, what?' James's curly brown hair is sticking on end as though he's been running his fingers through it. He catches himself halfway to another run-through and crosses his arms instead. 'You what?'

'You disappeared! We thought you'd tripped in a ditch or fallen from the cliff or something!' Kira's cheeks flush darker as her anger blossoms.

James looks at each of us one by one, as if asking whether she's telling the truth. What he sees clearly scares him, because his face pales and he lets out a shudder.

'I . . . I didn't mean to,' he says. 'I was – I came up here and then . . . I don't know.'

'Are you still drunk?' Lucas accuses him.

'Aren't you?' James rubs his bleary eyes again. 'I think I drank enough to knock out a horse.'

'Where were you?' Kira demands.

'I was – outside? I don't know. I went for a walk.'

'You're telling me you've been wandering around outside all night, by yourself, for no goddamn reason at all?' Kira looks to Moira for backup, but she remains silent, processing.

'I . . .' James winces, but there's something cartoonish about the way he does it. As though he's hiding something about why he left us on the beach. I glance at Lucas to see if he's noticed it as well, but he's staring straight at the wall working his jaw and trying not to get angry. 'I guess, yeah,' James says. 'I'm really sorry. I didn't mean to worry you.'

Kira growls and throws her hands up in the air, then marches out of the lounge towards the lighthouse kitchen. I hear the splash of water in the kettle and then the rumble as she puts it on to boil.

Jess, who's been hovering by James's side since we walked through the door, seems to have collected herself a bit more now. She pulls a crumpled packet of cigarettes out of her pocket, tossing it unceremoniously onto the coffee table before crossing back to Moira and wrapping her arms around her. Moira stands half-stunned, accepting. I feel a prickle of something at the base of my skull, something that feels like a lie, but I don't know how to examine it. What possible reason would James have not to tell us the truth?

'We genuinely thought . . .' Moira trails off. Stops. 'I'm glad you're okay. I really am. But my God am I going to kill you myself if you ever pull another stunt like that.'

She unpicks herself from Jess's grip and steps back to take in her wife's face. A shadow of concern flits across her expression, but she smiles and it's gone.

'I think,' she says, much more brightly, 'that we need to go and have a lie down.'

Once she and Jess are gone, Lucas comes to stand by my side, his hand searching for mine. He's hardly spoken to me all night, second-guessed almost every idea I've had, and still I find myself melting into him, grateful for his solidness. I'm so tired I feel like I could fall asleep standing up, but I know the minute I try to sleep I won't be able to. My leggings are soaked, my skin prickling with the cold as I slowly begin to thaw. It feels like my knees are on fire.

'I'm . . . I'm going to go and help Kira in the kitchen,'

James says. He gets to his feet unsteadily, grabbing for the arm of the chair so he doesn't stumble, and shuffles off.

I start to say something, to stop him, but what am I going to do? Pin him down and ask him what he's lying about? He can't have just been wandering about, surely. We followed the path, we found the hut and he wasn't in there. Why would he have gone further than that on his own? And his face – his expression when we walked in, before he knew we were here . . .

'You all right?' Lucas asks. I jump and then laugh at myself.

'Sure,' I lie. 'Fine now.'

There is something James isn't telling us, but there's nothing I can do about it now.

Pretty much everybody drifts off to their respective bedrooms after Kira finishes doling out tea as if it's medicine. Even Lucas heads off to lie down and 'rest his eyes' – or more likely take a bunch of painkillers and nap off the boozy hangover headache I'm sure we're all currently feeling.

I want to sleep but I can't make myself sit still, not in the lighthouse where every sound seems to make me jump, and not in the cottage where the pressure of sleep, bodies pressed close behind closed doors, makes me squirm. I lie awake for hours, counting Lucas's breaths until I think I might wake him with my fidgeting. I wait until the morning light tickles the edges of the curtains and then change into a clean pair of leggings and take myself out into the fresh air. The sky is clear but the wind is bitter. I pull up the collar on my sports jacket as I begin to stretch.

I'm about twenty minutes into a yoga flow that's so

familiar I could do it in my sleep when I feel a presence behind me. I ignore it for a minute, finish up my cool-down pose, and then turn around. Kira's perched on the doorstep leading into the cottage holding a steaming mug of tea between both hands and staring out, past the lighthouse towards the seemingly endless ocean. Her camera sits tucked carefully between her feet, as though she'd been planning to take photographs.

'Am I . . . in the way?' I ask.

Kira jumps, as if I've startled her by speaking. As if she didn't see me – which is ridiculous. I feel a burble of hurt in my chest. I've tried so hard to be nice to Kira, to make her realise that I don't see her as a threat. I want us to be friends. I know there's something like bad blood between her and Lucas – I know things didn't end well – but I don't want to be a thorn in her side, and it's not like Lucas and Kira will ever be able to stop being friends if they want to keep everybody else. Besides, Lucas and Kira were over long before I even met him.

'No,' Kira says. Her voice is surprisingly warm. 'Sorry, I was just lost in thought. You go on.'

'I'm done now.'

'Oh.' She sips her tea. A ray of sun peeks past the shadow of the lighthouse and makes her cheekbones flare a deep golden brown; she lifts her hand to shade her eyes. 'I didn't mean to interrupt you.'

'You didn't.'

I feel a bit awkward standing here while she sits and drinks her tea. I consider telling her I'm going to go for a walk, but I'm getting cold now and actually dying to go and sit down somewhere warm. It feels like I've been awake forever – and I guess it has been a good twenty-four hours at this point. I'm not sure I even slept for a minute last night.

'Should you . . . I mean . . .' Kira huffs at herself, her words getting tangled, 'is it good to do yoga outside when it's this cold?'

I shrug. 'I think it's fine as long as you stretch properly. It's not *that* cold, and I'm wearing a jacket.' I try not to take her question as a criticism, since I'm sure that's not how she meant it. This is unusual to say the least. It's like she's making an effort. But something about the tense way she holds her shoulders makes me think she didn't come out here just to make peace or talk about my yoga practices. I know I should ignore it, but the manager in me wants things out in the open. 'Kira, what's on your mind?'

She frowns, refusing to meet my gaze for a second. When she eventually talks, she checks over her shoulder first.

'I couldn't sleep,' she says. 'I just lay there and kept thinking and thinking about last night. About – *James*.' She whispers his name, hunching forward and pressing the mug to her chest. 'I said before that he was . . . I dunno, weird. Right? There were a few times yesterday where he just . . . He was distracted by something. I don't know if it was the ghost stories . . .' She trails off but looks at me expectantly.

'Everybody keeps going on about those stories, but I didn't mean to wind anybody up. I just thought it was interesting. Normally people like that macabre stuff, don't they? I didn't even tell James the stories. Jess was asking about the history of lighthouses and why the place would have only been renovated recently and I was trying to explain that lots of bad things happened on these sorts of islands and it put people off. That's all.'

'No, no, I know,' Kira says quickly. 'I didn't mean it like

74

that. It's just . . .' She stops. The words must weigh heavily on her because she moves her mouth soundlessly for a moment before they come tumbling out. 'It's just . . . it's got me thinking about something from a long time ago. I don't know if I should talk about it; whether it's relevant. It's probably not.'

'You can tell me,' I say. 'If you want. I . . . I guess I'm an outside perspective? Or as close as you'll get.'

Kira purses her lips thoughtfully. She's definitely conflicted.

'If it's something to do with what happened last night maybe somebody should know?' I suggest.

'I don't want James to think I'm betraying his confidence,' Kira says, 'but I'm also worried about him. You know?'

She finally looks at me – properly looks at me, our eyes meeting – and I can see that she really means it. She doesn't want to hurt James, but she's scared. I have to admit I'm nervous too. He must have known we'd be worried about him. He'd had a lot to drink, sure, but that doesn't make it any less scary. In fact, it makes it worse.

'What happened before?' I ask gently. 'I promise I won't judge. I won't say anything if you don't want me to.'

Kira glances down and places her mug, now empty, on the ground out of the way of the door. She picks up her camera and cradles it, thoughtful.

'All right, but not here. Can we walk a little way? I can take some nice shots of the lighthouse extension from the front while we talk, and then I won't feel so hideous. But you have to promise not to tell Lucas. Or any of the others. Nobody else can know.'

# 9

## *Moira*

It's not even ten o'clock by the time we've all finished breakfast. Things have been subdued this morning, but they're slowly edging back towards normality. James seems much brighter, definitely more sober, and although he doesn't talk much over the eggs Jess has lovingly fried up (with my help on toast duty), by the time we're done eating he's joking with none of the sheepishness of earlier.

'Okay, okay,' Kira says over the chatter at the table, her voice echoing off the glass walls of the sunroom. She waves her hands, back to her usual bossy self. 'So, we have a plan for today, if we're not too tired. I was thinking we could go fishing—'

'Oh my God, are you kidding?' Lucas groans. '*Fishing*? What are we, your grandparents?'

'Shut up,' she retorts without missing a beat. 'Apparently there's a spot on the other side of the island that's absolutely amazing for catching fish – and then we can have a proper, fresh seafood lunch. Jess?'

We all look at Jess, who grins. She told me she was

excited about lunch and now I know why. There's nothing my wife loves more than experimental cooking.

Lucas groans again, this time louder. '*Really?*'

'Yes, really.' Jess pouts. 'Come on, we're on an island in the middle of nowhere, what did you think we'd be eating?'

'I dunno, lamb? Beef? Chicken? Anything but more fish.'

Genevieve looks distraught and is about to intervene when I say quickly, 'He's joking. Honest. He's not that much of a dick. Jess knows that.'

'Speak for yourself,' Lucas grins. 'I'm on holiday. I've got to get all of this arseholery out of my system before I'm back to work.'

Genevieve lets out a startled laugh. 'Oh, *arseholery*. So that's what that was. I just thought you were trying to be charming.'

Even James laughs at that. 'This one's never been charming in his life.'

'Says you.'

'Says me! It's the truth.'

'Yeah, well at least I didn't fuck off and almost get myself killed like a real arsehole.'

There's a moment where we all wait, whether for insult or silence or anything at all, but then James lets out a snorting laugh that sounds so natural, so normal, that we all join in. The tension seeps away, leaving us all breathless with relief.

'All right,' Kira says. 'Enough of that. We should head off now before it gets too late, yeah?'

Everybody sets about clearing up the breakfast plates and dumping them in the Belfast sink, and then there's the usual flurry of coats and scarves and boots while Kira roots around in a cupboard for the rods the owners told her about. We all set out together in a gaggle of noise and celebration, drunk on something other than booze for a change. But as we head out into the cold I notice Genevieve hanging back, a glance passing between her and Kira that looks . . . if not *friendly*, then at least *conspiratorial*. But then Jess is grabbing my hand and pulling me outside into the air that's cold enough to make me think twice, her warm lips on my cheek, a rush of good feeling in my belly. It was probably just my imagination; everybody knows how Kira feels about Genevieve.

The walk to the small, sandy fishing cove takes less than twenty minutes but a lot of that is off-road, which explains why we didn't try it last night in the dark. There is a narrow track that begins behind the cottage, away through the tufty, damp grass. There's a copse of trees, lush and green and swaying in the frigid wind, that leads to a gradual slope down to the cove.

The wind is wild here. Jess shoves her hands deep in her pockets and Lucas mutters curse after muffled curse about how he didn't think to bring a hat. Kira looks jubilant, her cheeks scorched pink by the wind. I have to admit I love it. It feels fresh and free and the icy breath on my face blows away the remnants of last night like sticky, ghostly webs of fear blasted to nothing. It makes me think of my dissertation, the time I spent researching Scottish painters, of Francis E. Jamieson's *Ballachulish*, which I still see sometimes when I close my eyes – green, brown, blue. Pine trees and mountains and still, dark waters. The tranquillity. The isolation.

James is being uncharacteristically quiet. I suspect it's because he still feels embarrassed about last night, so I wait until the others are rushing down to the cove, Kira whooping and kicking up sand while Genevieve runs with her arms flung out to the wind, and then I sidle up next to him.

For a minute neither of us says anything. I stand watching the grey waves, which are calmer on this side of the island today, and enjoying the sight of Lucas and Jess trying to figure out how to set up the fishing rods with the bait. Jess grimaces but gets on with it. Lucas, on the other hand . . .

'What a twat,' I say.

'Who?' James looks alarmed. 'Me?'

'No, Lucas.' I pause. 'But maybe you, too. What on earth did you think you were doing last night?'

James takes what looks like an involuntary step away from me, and then stops himself.

'I told you,' he says defensively. 'I went for a walk.'

'I know what you said. I want to know why you thought it was a good idea.'

'For God's sake, you don't need to mother me Mo, I'm thirty years old. I just decided to go for a walk. Is that a crime?'

I rein in my frustration by laughing loudly at Kira as she trips in the sand. She catches her camera easily enough and shoots me a dirty look as she goes back to trying to line up a shot of Lucas and Jess.

'I know, James,' I say as calmly as I can. 'But we were really, really worried about you. Couldn't you have told us? Brought the matches like you said you were going to and *then* gone? Why did you have to disappear without telling anybody?'

'I was drunk, okay? I didn't think.'

I sigh. I don't want this to become a whole big thing, but something about it doesn't sit well with me. I've known James for over ten years and he's never been this kind of impulsive. Last-minute studying; making a fry-up at midnight? Sure. But something serious? Never.

But I guess there's a lot about his life right now that I don't have any input into. He stopped asking me for advice years ago.

'Is something else going on?' I ask. 'Did we say something to upset you? Are you . . .' I think back to that last year of uni; the few dark weeks after we graduated when James didn't really hang out with us, just holed himself up in his room playing on his computer. He drank a lot, too. It wasn't long afterwards that he left for Nepal, although he'd only ever joked about it before. It took all of us by surprise, and I always said to Jess there was more to his decision than he let on. I never asked him about it because I knew he wouldn't talk. I don't want to make the same mistake now. 'Are you okay?' I ask tentatively.

'I'm *fine*.' James turns to me, looking me fully in the face. 'Honest. Just – I don't know. I got a bit spooked, I think. Those stories. They got in my head. I went for a walk. Had this weird dream, and then . . . you guys turned up. Nothing major. Okay?'

'Okay,' I say. 'Okay. Forget about it. Let's go and try to catch some fish, maybe?'

James shrugs and walks towards the ocean with his hands in the pockets of his jeans, projecting an air of casualness that he isn't really mastering. When I turn away, I realise that Kira is watching me. She gives a small smile and waves me over.

'I'm a bit worried about the rain,' she says urgently.

'Is it forecast?'

'No, I checked half an hour ago – but look at those clouds.'

She points towards the horizon and I realise that she's right. Ahead it's clear and bright, but to the right there's a massive gathering of tar-dark clouds. The wind smells like rain, too: heavy and thick with the moisture of it.

'Maybe it'll pass?' Jess says hopefully. She's left Lucas and Genevieve to it now, and James is rooting through the bag we brought with us for the Thermos of hot chocolate. She wipes her hands on her jeans and comes in for a hug.

'Ew, not with bait fingers,' I joke. Jess blinks at me slowly. Great. I've offended her again. I open my arms for her, but she stays where she is and turns back to Kira.

'Or maybe it won't. I don't know. I'm not a weather app.'

Kira frowns and tugs at a rogue curl. 'I hope it doesn't. I love being outside, don't you? It's so refreshing.'

'Honestly, I spent enough time outside last night to last me a lifetime and a half,' Jess mutters, quietly enough so that James can't hear her. 'But I do fancy some fish, so here we are. Guess we'll just have to see if our good fortune holds.'

Kira rolls her eyes and stalks away, leaving just the two of us. The wind swoops over the sand, sending it spraying up the backs of our legs, and Jess winces as it prickles through her leggings.

'Did you call home this morning like I asked you to?' she asks. 'You didn't say.'

'No. Not yet. I'll give them a ring later, before dinner.'

'And what if we can't get through again? You promised you'd try while I was in the shower.' Jess gives me a look that's verging on evil. I fight the urge to lose my temper with her over this, feel my anger bubbling away like a little cauldron over a hearth, but I bite my tongue. Fighting won't help. We have to get to the root of this.

'Emma won't know any better,' I say. 'I mean – of course she misses us, but it's just for a weekend. It's not like the signal would ever be good enough for FaceTime, so she can't even see us. Can't we just . . . chill? Surely we have to be able to get *some* time together, don't we? Parenthood shouldn't eradicate who we are as a couple.'

Even though my tone is even, Jess looks like I've slapped her.

'I didn't mean anything bad by that,' I add quickly. 'It's just that we're still *us*, aren't we? Still Mo and Jess? Jess and Mo? We've come here to have a nice weekend with our friends. I don't want to be panicking every few minutes that something is going to go wrong at home, because I know it won't. Your parents are more than capable of looking after her, and they'd call if there was a problem.'

'What if they can't get in touch with *us*, though?' Jess says. She's staring at her feet, her voice muffled by the collar of her jacket. 'I bet the signal comes and goes with the weather. What if they have a problem and they can't reach us?'

'Well they'll leave a message. They know where we are. We both have our phones. Worst case, I'm sure they'd find a way to get in touch as soon as possible. And besides, we're on an island. There's only so much we'd be able to do if something did go wrong.'

This is, obviously, the wrong thing to say. I realise as soon as the words leave my lips, but Jess is just as quick; she whips her head up so she can stare at me with horror.

'I can't believe you, Mo,' she mutters. 'Really, I can't. At least when James is stupid he has the sense to apologise.'

83

And then she storms off and leaves me. But even as my cheeks burn with Jess's reprimand I'm distracted by James, who is standing away from the others again, Thermos in his hands. He stares back towards the lighthouse, which is hidden behind the trees, a look of concern on his face. His shoulders are hunched, his back rounded against more than the wind.

He looks as though he's seen a ghost.

# 10

## *Kira*

We haven't been set up more than forty minutes when the clouds become so thick and black overhead that I start to think this isn't a good idea after all. We haven't caught a single fish, and rather than being the cheerful morning of fun I had planned, everybody seems miserable. Jess and Moira have been niggling at each other again about their daughter – I didn't mean to overhear but it was hard to ignore them when I was standing downwind – and James is still sullen, cupping his head and popping more painkillers when he thinks nobody is watching.

I'm about to say that we'll give it another half an hour and give up when a great crack of thunder rolls overhead. It's a boom so loud it shakes me, making me drop the box of bait I'm holding into the sand. I curse and glance around, but everybody else is doing the same thing. All eyes are on the sky now, and we collectively marvel at the lightning arcing over the water.

'Jesus, that's close,' Lucas says. 'Never seen it like that before.'

'I have,' James says. 'When I was in Nepal after graduation. Pretty scary.'

'Should we be outside in that?' Jess asks. She looks a bit nervous, and I can't really blame her. As much as this would make a fantastic moody shot of the island, I'm not in any hurry to get myself, or my camera, soaked.

'Not really. We should probably head back. Seems like it might . . .' Freezing droplets of water begin to plummet from the sky. 'Rain.'

Moira laughs, a tight but genuine chuckle. 'Too late.'

Genevieve looks like she's about to argue about leaving – everybody here knows how much she loves nature, and even I've stalked her Instagram once or twice and been impressed at all the shots of her walking in the wilds – but she seems to come around in record time.

'All right,' she says. 'No use getting frazzled, I guess.'

We start to pack up at a casual pace, but within seconds the rain is roaring down around us and we're going faster than ever, grabbing the tackle box and the rods like they're made of spun sugar and might melt at any moment. Moira lets out an excited shriek as a drop of water makes its way down the back of her coat, and Jess laughs darkly.

'Karma,' she says.

We hurry up the slope leading back towards the trees and make a beeline for the shelter they provide. The rain is heavy and the wind is sharp, cutting at our skin.

'Fuck!' Lucas shouts, but he doesn't sound angry or even frustrated. He actually sounds a bit like he's having fun.

I stop at the tree line to catch my breath and the others do the same. James looks like a drowned rat, his curls plastered to his forehead and his nose dripping. Moira's tan cheeks are rosy from the cold and Jess looks like she's run a marathon, sweaty and wet, her blonde ponytail dripping onto the front of her coat. Lucas slaps his free hand onto his thigh and we can all hear the sound of the moisture.

'Good idea, Kira,' Lucas says drily.

I meet his gaze, about to retort, when I notice the mischievous sparkle there. I haven't seen it directed at me in a long while and it warms something deep in my belly, even though it shouldn't. I let out a bark of surprised laughter.

And then Lucas joins in, followed by Genevieve, who manages to look pretty, even with her blonde hair askew and her fancy North Face puffer jacket soaked and somehow smudged with tree sap or muddy sand. And within seconds everybody is laughing, even James. It's the kind of hysterical laughter you can't explain, but which catches you by the belly and doesn't let go until you're exhausted.

We let it run its course, until we're even wetter and even colder than we'd probably have been if we'd stayed on the beach. Gathered like this, huddled against the elements, it's easy to forget what happened last night; easier still to forget the tension between us all this morning. This is how it should be, even though nothing so far this weekend seems to have gone to plan. At least we have this.

'I'm absolutely fr-frozen,' Jess chatters. 'I can't fe-feel my hands.'

Moira takes a tentative step towards her wife, and when Jess doesn't pull away, she offers her palms to warm Jess's fingers. Jess gives her a small smile that looks like a truce, if not an acceptance of a lost battle. I feel another swell of warmth towards them, the way that they can sometimes communicate with each other, no words required. I know they've been having a tough time but they still have that sense of love between them that could conquer all.

But then Jess pulls back and the smile is gone. The wind kicks up and the cold really is painful now. The rain isn't slowing and my camera is getting damp even tucked under my jacket.

'Come on,' I say.

We move off more quietly, still comfortable with each other, but there's a hint again of that tension, that lack of cohesion that we've never had before. Not like this. It's striking; I wonder what it is, what exactly has grown in the cracks that time has carved between us. Is it Genevieve, disrupting the balance we've always had? Is it James, wandering off last night without an explanation, dodging questions today? Is it me, forcing alliances that are no longer strong enough to hold? Or is it the island itself; the light-house; the ghosts that permeate the air even if they're only folklore?

We trudge back to the cottage, making it in again just as another boom of thunder shakes the air around us. James jumps and ducks his head only just in time to avoid smacking it against the low ceiling that leads into his bedroom. Lucas and Genevieve peel off too, and then Jess and Moira, until it's just me, standing alone in the kitchen.

I wander to the sink, popping my camera on the counter. The view out of the kitchen window is of the lighthouse and not much else. It seems so big, so solid, disappearing far above my head. The rain obscures it, and there's fog moving off the water again like yesterday. If it carries on, soon we won't be able to see much at all.

I shuck off my jacket and drape it, still dripping, on the back of one of the wooden chairs. I fill the kettle, and then move back to the sink. The boil of the water is the burbling of my thoughts. I try not to, but I keep circling back to my conversation with Genevieve this morning. I consider the temporary ceasefire that we reached, and how it hasn't helped at all.

Genevieve seemed concerned when I explained why I was so worried about James. It's a secret I haven't shared in the group, ever – I promised I wouldn't – and now I'm eaten alive by the knowledge that somebody else knows. I shouldn't have told her. It wasn't only my secret to share. And if Lucas ever finds out . . . Things will never be the same.

If I could just get Genevieve alone again, maybe I could tell her to forget it – that I was exaggerating. I've seen the funny way she's looked at James since. On the beach she avoided him, although whether that was by accident or design wasn't obvious. I think . . . I think she's unnerved by him now.

'You look deep in thought.'

I jump at the sound of James's voice. The mug, empty in my hands, waiting for tea, drops into the sink with a crash. I wince and fish it out quickly.

'Shit, sorry. Didn't mean to scare you,' he says.

'You didn't. I wasn't paying attention.'

'Is it broken?'

I lift the mug for inspection. 'Just a small chip. Nothing some glue won't fix.' My cheeks burn. My thoughts weren't obvious; couldn't have been; but James is looking at me with an odd expression now. 'Wanker,' I say fondly.

'Hey, that's not fair. It was an accident. I said sorry.'

I shake my head to dispel my concerns. This is James – *our* James. I've known him forever. He's still the same boy who encouraged me to date Lucas, even though he fancied me as well; he's still the boy who would walk me home from clubs after Lucas got so drunk he had to leave early. What happened back then doesn't mean anything. It was an accident.

'It's all right. I take it back. You're just trying to get me to think about ghosts again. I get it. You're trying to give us all nightmares.'

I'm not sure if it's my imagination or if James pales at that, but he lets out a little chuckle and heads to the kettle as it finishes boiling, pulling two fresh mugs from the mug tree and throwing tea bags in.

We don't speak for a while. I can hear Moira and Jess speaking in urgent voices in the hall, their door closed but not enough to silence another tiff.

'Do you think they're okay?' James asks. 'Jess has been—'

'More tightly wound than usual?' I keep my voice down. James nods. 'I know. I tried to talk to Mo about it. She's being her usual self, refusing to really talk about the problem. I think it must be to do with Emma. Mo's back at the auction house so I guess Jess is just . . . frustrated? Tired? Probably feeling the pressure. It must be hard. I know she wanted Mo to be able to work from home so they could both be there for Emma, but I think Mo's right to try to get them out of the house more. Jess is so withdrawn. It's not good for either of them. I don't want to stick my nose in though.'

'Sure,' James says. 'Obviously. I'm not gonna get involved. It just – sucks. Them, and you and Lucas and Gen . . .' He trails off. 'Well, you know.'

'That's not fair,' I say, mimicking his earlier plea without playfulness. 'I'm being civil.'

'Well, yes, but I'm a bit worried that you and her going at it winds Jess up even more. She's already on one about the ghosts and—'

'No, I am being *civil*,' I assert. 'I invited her on *our* trip and I'm including her. Nobody said I had to be a saint, but I am trying. You're one to talk about that anyway, winding Jess up. After last night?'

'I didn't mean to upset you. I know you're trying, and it must be hard for you with the two of them.'

'I'm not upset, James. I'm annoyed. Don't have a go at me for not being all perky rainbows and unicorns when you're the one who's been freaking everybody out. We were so worried about you last night.'

My words hang between us for a second and I see real regret on James's face. But then he recovers and sets his features into a scowl the likes of which I haven't seen since the days when he used to spend all his time yelling at strangers through his Xbox headset.

'Why does everybody keep going on about that?' James puts his tea down calmly, but I can see that it takes real effort. 'I apologised. I was drunk. Why can't we just drop it?'

'I don't think you realise how big a deal it was,' I say. 'We thought you were dead. We were deciding when to call your parents; the coastguard. We literally spent *hours* searching for you. I'm annoyed and I'm tired. We're not kids any more. This was supposed to be a fun, no-pressure weekend where we could all reconnect, and . . .' I sigh. It isn't just about what happened last night, and it's not fair to blame it all on James. 'And we're all just grumbling at each other. I just wish it could be like it used to be.'

There are a hundred thousand moments that stand

between the people we were and the people we are now. I get that. I knew that this trip wouldn't be perfect, but I was hoping for – well, something better than this. At least for once I don't feel as if *I've* ruined it.

James softens. 'I am sorry,' he says again. 'Really I am. I don't know. It was a weird night. But look, it's not even one o'clock yet. We still have the rest of the weekend. Why don't we try to gather everybody together and see if we can't get some of the fun back?'

I gnaw on my lip, watching the steam rise off my tea. I need to change out of my wet clothes. James is right. The weekend isn't over until it's over. We still have time to have some fun.

'Okay, but you have to promise me one thing. I know you'll hate it, but you are the minority in this group.'

James narrows his eyes, but there's a small smile on his face.

'What's that?' he asks.

'You *have* to play Monopoly with us—'

He groans.

'No, listen. You have to play, and you absolutely are *not* allowed to be the banker. You're too good at embezzlement for that. Deal?'

# 11

## *Genevieve*

I'm so cold when we get back to the cottage that I decide to take a shower. I don't rush, enjoying the feeling of hot water over the tension in my shoulders, and by the time I get out I'm feeling much better. It was fun on the beach, but I haven't been able to ignore my conversation with Kira this morning.

I know she wasn't telling me to freak me out, and I know that it's not a big deal – it's ancient history – but I can't quite reconcile Kira's story with the James I've been getting to know. It's only one side of the story, though, and a lapse in judgement. I can't weigh in without knowing all the facts. Still, alongside his behaviour last night, I have to wonder if we should be keeping a closer eye on him.

I heard my phone ping while I was in the shower, and I take a moment to read the three text messages that have come through all bunched together. Two are from Sarah at work, panicking because she forgot to file a piece of paperwork yesterday afternoon, and the third is from my oldest brother Ted asking if he can borrow my iPad while his is in for repair. I spend a couple of minutes tapping out a reply to Sarah but by the time I'm ready to send it the signal has gone again.

'Damn,' I murmur.

There's nobody in the cottage when I emerge from the bathroom. I can tell without checking the bedrooms or the kitchen. There's an eerie quiet to the place, a sense of abandonment, which I haven't really felt since we arrived. Everything has been bustle and panic and casual bickering, but now it's . . . not quite peaceful. It feels more like *waiting*.

I throw on a fresh jumper from my bedroom and I'm just heading to the kitchen to check through the window if the others have all gone across to the lighthouse when I catch a glimpse of something moving down the other end of the corridor, where there's a window that looks out over the windswept grass that leads, eventually, towards more ocean.

Lucas?

It's just the sort of prank he'd pull, waiting there to follow me when I leave the cottage, jump out and scare me. But he still hasn't learned that I'm better at this than he is. I grew up with three older brothers, and I've never liked to lose at these sorts of games.

I hurry down to the end of the corridor as quickly and quietly as I can, careful to keep to the side so hopefully he won't see me coming. It's cold down here – freezing, actually – and I pull my sleeves down over my fingers. There's the dark blur of a shape at the corner of the glass, an outline I can't quite make out, and I try to stifle my glee as I reach for the icy catch on the window. I ease it up, an inch at a time, laughter building like a balloon inside my chest.

The shape at the side of the window shifts but I hardly

notice. It feels like there's something heavy ahead, like a forcefield my body pushes against, but I pay the feeling no attention, flinging open the window with a warrior's cry.

'Aha!'

I pause. Nothing.

No reaction at all. Lucas has been practising. Normally he'd curse at me, maybe slam the window shut. I lean out a short way, wary that he might try to grab me and kiss me roughly, which would be equally his style, but would absolutely signify me losing, and that's not on.

But there's nobody there.

'Lucas?'

I peer to the right, and then to the left where the grass leads back towards the trees, but I can't see far enough. The air out here is strangely warm though. No, not warm, just not as icy as the air at my back, as though there's something there, something behind me generating that cold. Somebody must have left a window open inside. I resist the strange urge to turn and look behind me, leaning further out instead to see how far I can see. But I still can't see Lucas. I bet he's run off, thinking he's scared me. A celebratory kiss would have been nicer than this.

I sigh and swing the window shut. Now he'll be gloating all afternoon about how he *got* me. Sometimes I think that I got more than I bargained for when I let him charm me the way he did; he's nothing but a big kid sometimes and it's given me a taste of what it might be like to have children with him. Hard work.

But fun, too.

I grab my jacket, which is still soaked through, and grimace as I put it on. Then I hurry back to the entry and out into the cold. The lighthouse is warm and welcoming, lights on, and as soon as I make it through the front door I realise that somebody has lit a fire. The whole central lounge glows orange with it, and the warmth trickles right down to my toes.

I follow the general din into the dining area, where everybody is gathered around the table again. It looks like Jess has been busy while I was getting changed, and there's another feast. It's not fresh fish, but there are little triangle sandwiches and mini pork pies, posh cocktail sausages and a quiche that Moira's already digging into with a knife.

'Mmm,' I say. 'Looks amazing.'

'Right?'

I glance sharply to the head of the table, where Lucas is halfway through a scotch egg. He finishes his mouthful and grins.

'How did you get in here so fast?' I say, unable to contain my surprise.

'I . . . walked?' Lucas pulls a face and slopes one shoulder in a nonchalant shrug. 'You were faffing in the bathroom for long enough.'

I think about calling him out, but telling him that *he's* the reason I took so long will probably lead to a few smirks and raised eyebrows from the others. James especially is likely to make a dirty joke and I'm not really feeling that vibe. Instead I scrunch my nose up and then find a seat at the table, selecting grapes and cheese and a handful of prawn cocktail crisps.

'It's like a party,' Kira says. She looks at Jess fondly, clearly glad she didn't have to worry about this part of the weekend. Jess beams and Moira smiles proudly.

'Except with less booze,' Lucas jokes.

'Hey, there's plenty of beer,' Jess says. 'You can have one if you want?'

James shakes his head. He looks a bit ill at the thought. 'No thanks,' he murmurs. 'I'm good.'

'Ruined on the first night.' Lucas shakes his head, mock disappointment on his features. 'I told you not to go so hard.'

'You absolutely did not,' James says. 'If I recall properly you were egging me on!'

'I did nothing of the sort.'

'I think that's a lie,' I say, smirking.

'A blatant one,' Kira adds. She meets my gaze and there's no real hostility there now, which makes a nice change. I wonder if this morning's conversation might have started to mend the awkwardness between us. I wish it didn't have to be like that – that we didn't have to have a secret in order to be friends – but I do understand.

'Damn. Well, I didn't exactly put the beer into his hands, did I?' Lucas asks.

'Erm . . .' Jess squints. 'I distinctly remember you coming into the kitchen at seven o'clock and demanding I give you two beers – and I quote – "one is for James".'

'Maybe I was lying. Maybe they were both for me.'

'While I wouldn't put that past you, I saw you give it to him,' Moira points out.

'Okay, okay. I give up. We have successfully established something that anybody who's known me for five minutes can attest to. I'm a bad influence.'

'You can say that again,' James says. 'I mean, look at poor Gen, hanging out with this bunch of reprobates on her weekend off.'

My face warms, but in a good way. Even with the

bickering and last night's mess, it's nice to be a part of something that feels a bit like a family, only full of people who have chosen to be together. It makes it special. I shrug and brush it off, unable to come up with anything witty in response.

The conversation carries on like that for a while, carefully diverted again away from the topic of last night. We're getting better at avoiding it, and James seems to relax finally as Kira starts to tell the table about the shots of the island and the lighthouse she's managed to take so far and which ones she thinks she might use for the magazine.

I help myself to a couple of sandwiches and sit munching on them quietly, relaxing slowly as the minutes pass without incident or jab aimed at James. There's still an edge in the air, buried just beneath the surface, so I keep myself to myself in case I somehow unbalance things. It's a stupid notion, but I have a feeling that some of this is my fault. Like me being here is somehow unsettling everybody.

Maybe it's the stories I told Jess yesterday. In fairness, she did ask. I can't help it if I did a history degree, or that I'm interested in that stuff. Lucas is always making fun of me for the books I choose to read, but I love true crime – the historical stories are best. I love unsolved mysteries, especially if they're spooky, and anything maudlin is right up my street.

'Didn't you say something about Monopoly?' James says in response to something Kira's pointed out. 'I thought you wanted to play so I could trounce you.'

Kira's mock indignity is a sight to behold. She puts her hands on her hips and gives him a look that could kill. James only laughs, though, and Lucas joins in.

'You're not allowed to play,' Lucas says.

'Kira told me I have to!'

'All right, but you're not allowed to be the banker. You always cheat, and you're far too good at lying.'

I start at this, a hot feeling settling in my chest. Kira shoots me a glance, and I realise that I've let my emotions show on my face. I pull it back and pretend to cough, putting down my last sandwich half.

'Sorry. Just going to go and get a glass of water.'

I excuse myself from the table and head for the kitchen, less for the water and more for an excuse to give myself a second. What *was* that? My reaction to Lucas saying James is a good liar was . . . extreme? Definitely. But I've always been such a good judge of character. Is there something that James isn't telling us about last night? Is that what Lucas is getting at? Or is it simpler than that? A joke from when the lads were teenagers?

'Hey.' Kira appears behind me, holding her mug as though she's come in for a tea top-up. I know that she hasn't though, as she dumps the mug directly in the sink and turns on me, her eyes narrowed.

'Hey?'

'What was that about?'

'What? I—'

'You can't do that,' she says. She doesn't sound angry so much as alarmed. Afraid, even. 'Please. I told you that stuff this morning in confidence. I thought you could be impartial. Lucas can't find out or he'll lose it. He might . . . He can't know about it, and that means you've got to do a better job of hiding it.'

'I didn't mean . . .' I take a breath. 'I know that you didn't want me to say anything, but are you sure that's for the best?'

'Yes,' Kira snaps. 'I'm sure. I only told you because . . .

99

God, I don't even know why I told you except that I thought somebody needed to know and you were the only one who didn't know us then. What happened between me and James was stupid, but I've thought about it some more and I'm sure there isn't any connection to last night. I guess I just freaked out because we'd been drinking and talking before he wandered off, and he seemed sort of like he was back then. Really deep inside his own head drunk, you know? But last time was my fault.'

'No,' I say quickly. 'That's not on you. I get why you told me, and I understand why you're cautious. But it doesn't sound like any of that was your fault. There are two sides to everything and James should have accepted it when you told him it was over. You said he hurt you—'

'That was an accident,' Kira corrects. 'I told you. He was throwing stuff and he hit me. He didn't mean to. The neighbours called the police, not me. It's not a big deal. Just a stupid fight that got out of hand. I just . . . he was drinking a lot yesterday and it brought it all back. I wish I hadn't told you.'

Now that we're whispering about it – here of all places – I'm grasped by how momentous it must have been for Kira to tell me what happened in the first place. I picture it: Kira and James spending a weekend alone together while Lucas went home to visit his parents and Jess and Moira were on holiday. Kira and James *sleeping together*. Kira regretting it instantly, but James feeling like it was meant to be, because he had fancied Kira for years.

Kira said she ignored him afterwards, instead of talking about it. James, under a lot of pressure, had finally got what he wanted for years, only to lose it all in five minutes. There had been weeks of fraught broodiness and confusion, the two of them dancing around each other under Lucas's nose. When Kira finally told James that it had been a mistake – that she wasn't going to leave Lucas over it – he got angry. He threw things. And somebody called the police.

James, immediately sorry, had checked himself into a hospital where he had stayed until his depression was under control. Afterwards, he went to Nepal, where he had told everybody else he had been the whole time. He travelled. And when he came back, they never talked about it again. The same old mistake: silence instead of communication.

'Let's just drop it,' Kira says wearily. 'Okay? It's ancient history. Like I said, I don't even know why I told you. I haven't told anybody – ever.'

'I have one of those faces.' I smile warmly, but Kira shoots me a look so icy that I wonder if I haven't somehow ruined everything between us.

'Sure,' she says. 'Just keep it *off* your face, please.'

'Hey, you two, are we playing Monopoly or what?' Lucas's voice floats through from the lounge and Kira winces. She eyeballs me for a second longer and then stalks off.

I wait for a second, my stomach churning as I try to gather my thoughts. Kira must have told me about James for a reason. She must have been worried. But . . . the feeling I have isn't like any feeling I've had about James before. It's a bad feeling. Complicated. I think I would feel this way even without Kira's history. It's almost as if James has changed, as if being here, with all of the alcohol and in all of the wilderness, has brought out something in Lucas's best friend I never noticed before.

I push it off and follow Kira into the lounge. All of them are gathered around the coffee table and James is sorting through the properties and money to make sure everything is there. Lucas opens his arms to me and I wander over to sit next to him, grateful for his warmth. Even though the fire is still flickering in the burner, it feels cold in here.

'Hey, has anybody seen my cigarettes?' Moira asks. 'I meant to say earlier. Jess left the packet on the table, but it's gone.'

'I told you *no*,' Jess admonishes. 'I don't care if we are on holiday – you're not smoking.'

'I wasn't going to.' Moira tilts her head back in exasperation. 'I just wanted to put them away in case you change your mind. Did you throw them away?'

'I didn't touch them.'

'Are you sure?'

'Why would I lie? I left them on the table.'

'Ladies, ladies,' Lucas interrupts. 'There's no need to break out the pillows.'

'Oh, Lucas,' I say.

'Gross,' Moira agrees.

'I'm sure they'll turn up,' Lucas continues, completely ignorant of his own horrible taste in jokes. 'Nobody's been in here since this morning.'

I feel the same chill from earlier building in me. I know the ghost stories I told Jess aren't real, but it would be so easy to believe them now. The rain lashes down outside and the fire flickers in the burner behind the glass, casting long, spindly shadows like spider legs. Jess turns her full attention towards choosing her token for the game, shoulders hunched as though she can feel it too. It feels a little bit like we're not meant to be here; like we're intruding in somebody else's home.

# 12

## *Moira*

I get stuck with the racing car for Monopoly. It's not my most hated piece – thank you, iron – but it's definitely down near the bottom of the list. Jess has managed to get the coveted dog and I'm envious with every roll, although a little bit less by the seventh time she ends up in jail.

It's cosy in here, all of us together like this. We talk about anything and everything while we play; Lucas is on about his new boss, who apparently is the world's worst – always said with a smile at Genevieve – but Jess turns quiet as the work conversation moves to me; about how we're coping now I'm back in my office at the auction house instead of at home.

I haven't been working the same ridiculous hours as in my last management role, but Jess still isn't coping. Even though it was her idea for us to try to get back into some sort of normal routine. Though, I suspect by 'normal' she meant I should find a more stable job where I could still work from home part of the time. I've been lucky enough to pick up a position with similar pay to the one I left when we had Emma but it's been a bit of a shock for both of us. Still it's one thing to talk about that between just the two of us and another thing entirely to have it laid bare. Especially with Genevieve listening in. I've got absolutely nothing against her, but it's not the same as it being just us, is it? She's not family yet.

Jess shrugs off the questions about anything except Emma, who she's happy to talk about for hours. I sit back and let her take a break during one of her turns to show Genevieve the picture of Em on the beach in Cornwall with a smear of ice cream right from her forehead down to her chin like some kind of war paint. I feel like I should be doing more. I should be cooing and getting my phone out, telling stories and relating everything back to our daughter. But I don't want to. Is it awful to admit that I've been enjoying not having to talk about babies or children – or even work – for once, until now?

'It's your go, Kira,' I say, passing the dice over Jess's outstretched arm. 'Please, go before you get the whole holiday album and an Instagram tour.'

'Oh Mo,' Genevieve says, 'I'm sure they're all lovely pictures.'

'Doesn't mean everybody wants to see them,' I murmur.

Jess pointedly puts her phone face down on the table and returns her attention to the game at hand with her arms folded across her chest. I can't do anything right this weekend, it seems. I really should learn to just keep my mouth shut.

'Did you hear that?' James asks. He's staring over his head, towards the ceiling. I glance up but all I can hear is the rain, and the crackling of another log breaking down in the fire.

'Nothing, mate,' Lucas says. 'The rain.'

'Wind, probably,' Genevieve says. 'They say that sometimes the wind would drive lighthouse keepers mad, the way it battered at the windows during storms, making noises that would sound like human footsteps, or babies wailing. There's one story about a man and a woman who kept a lighthouse somewhere down south. They lost their little boy when he was very young because he managed to get out and wandered off and they could hear him crying but they couldn't find him until it was too late.

'He'd fallen into a rock pool but he couldn't swim so he drowned as the tide came in. And then every time the wind blew after that, the wife swore she could hear her son crying, until one night there was a very big storm and she couldn't take it any more. She ran out of the lighthouse into the darkness trying to find him, and she was swept away. Her husband went out after her and only survived by sheer luck. People who visit that lighthouse claim to be able to hear the boy sob whenever it storms.'

The room is silent now, everybody looking at Genevieve, who starts to blush. Jess has forgotten that she's mad at me and grips my knee. I wish Genevieve hadn't said anything. James looks shaken, too; pale, and as if he wishes he hadn't mentioned whatever noise he thought he heard.

'That . . . sure is a story,' I say, breaking the silence and ignoring the slick feel of my own palms.

'Sorry,' Genevieve murmurs. 'I just read a lot of folklore. I think it's fascinating – how people lived, but also the stories that survive them. People find ways to turn all sorts of tragic things into stories.'

'It's a good story,' Lucas says. 'It'd make a really cool Netflix show. Like that haunted house one that we

105

watched.' He nudges Genevieve and she just pulls a face, embarrassment making her quiet.

'And on that note,' Kira says, 'I think we should play something else. Lucas is an even worse banker than James.'

'I could have told you that would happen,' I say. 'You should have let me do it.'

'I don't know why I didn't.' Kira shakes her head. 'Who's for poker?'

We pass the next hour or so playing various card games, including an imaginatively titled one Genevieve teaches us called 'Hollow Man'. When we pick teams, Jess chooses Kira in a petty jab that hurts more than it should, and I end up with James instead. He's distracted, hardly even listening when I ask him to choose a card, and then playing spades instead of clubs. It turns out the girls are a really good team anyway; they wipe the floor with the other four of us before declaring that 'cards are boring now'.

'Well what do you want to do then?' Lucas asks. 'We can't exactly go outside unless we want to be blown away. I'm dying to stretch my legs, but I guess we could just start drinking.'

'No,' James groans. 'Please, no. Not yet. It only feels like five minutes.'

'It's too early,' Jess adds. 'At least wait until after dinner, otherwise we'll all be passed out by nine o'clock.'

'We might be already,' Kira says. 'I'm knackered. And hungry again already.'

'Never too early to start drinking.' Lucas slaps his thighs enthusiastically. 'Come on, you were the one offering me a beer earlier, Jess.'

'Only because you brought it up!'

'It's too early,' Kira says firmly. 'Let's pick another game.'

Jess heads over to the rough-hewn wooden shelves. 'Jenga?'

'God no,' Lucas vetoes. 'Nothing that could involve a brick to the face.'

'He's always so worried about his beautiful face.' Genevieve gives the rest of us a conspiratorial wink. 'Maybe we should play Game of Life—'

'Absolutely not,' Kira says. 'I already have real-life stress – I don't need fake life stress as well.'

'Well we've played through every card game in my repertoire,' I say, 'and a few more to boot. What about something like . . .' A spark of excitement shoots through me. 'I've got it!'

'What?' Jess scowls at me. 'Not Cluedo again, *please*.'

'Oh my God that was *one* weekend *five* years ago,' I exclaim. 'Will you never let me live that down?'

'Cluedo twice in one weekend because you got us snowed in? With no WiFi and no mobile signal? And no books, or puzzles, or even *wine*? Never. I will tell that story until I go to my grave.' Jess grins. It's not malicious but she's definitely enjoying herself, and Genevieve is holding back her laughter. 'And I'll probably tell it long after, too, if I come back as a ghost. Especially if I die first.'

James jerks his head up when Jess mentions dying, but covers it with a small throat-clearing grumble. I don't know if he realises that I noticed, but he looks at me as he says 'So what game do you think we should play if it's not Cluedo?'

I beam. I'm really excited now. It's the perfect choice. Active, childish, and hopefully it won't last long. I'm really hankering after an early night and a sneaky pre-bed bath, which means I really don't want Jess stuck in the kitchen until gone seven again tonight.

'Well, go on then,' Kira says. 'Tell us.'

'Hide and seek.'

'Great,' Jess murmurs. 'As if it's not bad enough with the ghost stories, now you want us to find places to hide and then sit and wait for somebody to find us?'

'What, are you scared?' Lucas bares his teeth in a way which I'm sure is meant to be funny, but which scares Jess even more. She puts her head in her hands and does a little whine. I bite back the laugh that builds in me.

'Oh come on, it'll be fun! I mean there's only so many places to hide, right?' I say.

'Yeah but we don't know any of them yet,' Jess replies, her voice muffled behind her hands.

'That's half the fun! What do you guys think?'

I can see that Genevieve is secretly thrilled but won't agree until Lucas does for fear of upsetting Jess further. Lucas laughs and Kira shrugs like she doesn't care much either way but it's clearly better than Cluedo – which I resent, but maybe she has a silent point. James doesn't commit either way immediately, just glances up at the ceiling again and then nods.

'All right,' he says. 'I'm in.'

'Me too.' Lucas pumps his fist. 'Please *please* let me be the finder first.'

'Ughhhh,' Jess says. 'Fine. Whatever. Can we get it over with then? A glass of wine is waiting for me.'

'Hey, you said it was too early.' Lucas mock scowls.

'It was. Now it isn't. So bloody hurry up and let's *go*. I'm far too old for this shit – at least until Emma is old enough for this shit.'

I don't say anything, but I'm pleased to hear Jess swear. It's such a small thing – so stupid – but it feels more like the Jess I married. When we first met she had a mouth like a sailor, but these days she won't even swear when Emma *isn't* in the room in case she gets into bad habits she might pass on. I'm always the one casually apologising about F-bombs, which feels so topsy-turvy that it's like something out of a dream.

There's a flurry of activity as we stow away cards and throw away empty Coke cans, half-drained mugs into the sink; and then there's a sense of something about to happen. It's like we're standing on the edge of a precipice, a feeling building in the air like electricity, all crackles and sparks.

I haven't been this excited about a kids' game in years. Lucas succeeds in nominating himself to go first and he stands in the lounge area with his hands over his eyes – firmly shut, because he absolutely refuses to cheat with these sorts of games, preferring to win the old-fashioned way – while the rest of us scramble about like newly born lambs.

'One . . . two . . .'

Kira races into the kitchen, and Genevieve creeps to a spot directly behind the sofa where Lucas is counting. A bold strategy. Jess grabs my hand and we both run towards the stairs, slowing to a tiptoe to avoid any creaking steps. James comes bolting up behind us and then stops where the frosted glass bricks turn to stone, in the little alcove on the first floor, his finger over his lips.

Jess and I inch up further, right to the top. It's a risk, but we know at least that if Lucas finds James he won't find either of us first. The view is magnificent again now, the sun hidden by thick clouds and the mist on the water in that curious place between heavy and light where everything looks like a mirage. Even the swollen rainclouds are

109

foggy, inconsistent, like a watercolour painting, and the sky is the colour of old bones.

'Where?' Jess hisses.

I glance around. There's less to hide behind in this lamp room than I remembered, but the pillar which holds the light is huge: big enough for two. I gesture that we should hurry over, but Jess has other plans. She picks a spot beside the door, where the lip of the doorway is thick enough to hide her. I can just about make her out, her white jumper and golden hair blending with the small patch of wall behind her.

I stick out like a sore thumb. Dark jacket, dark hair, so I hunch down low, hoping that Lucas won't see me and I'll be able to sneak back down the stairs.

We wait like that for several long minutes. It feels much longer than the seconds ticking past on my watch suggest. I can still hear Lucas counting, I think. Or perhaps that's simply an echo. I didn't realise last time we were up here, but the sound is weird. Every noise from downstairs seems to tickle my skull with a faint muffle. I hold my breath, listening harder, heartbeat loud. I think I can hear Genevieve laugh. I bet Lucas has found her by now. I wonder if he'll go towards the kitchen, and Kira, next or if he'll be coming up the stairs.

If the rain stops it would be fun to try playing between here and the cottage. We'd have even more places to hide. But I also don't like the idea of leaving the lighthouse. It's got its claws in me now. Even as I crouch, body tense and waiting, I'm mentally picking out my next hiding spots. I could try to squeeze under the dining table, or maybe in the small pantry in the kitchen. I wonder if that's where Kira is . . .

Five minutes go by. Then a few more. Jess inches out of her spot, as if thinking she might come towards me. But just as she does it, we hear footsteps creak on the stairs below. Jess lets out a tiny squeak and then presses her lips tightly shut, her eyes wide. I can see the laughter inside her, waiting to spill out. She never could control it.

I can feel it too. It feels like hysteria. God, it feels like being alive, being young. I wonder why we haven't done this before. My knees press into my chest as I crouch lower, my hands planted firmly on the floor to keep me steady.

What's taking him so long?

The footsteps seem to have stopped. It sounds like he's actually going back *down*. I relax a little. Maybe he's spotted James now. I picture him crouching low like me, hidden in the doorway watching Lucas go past, thinking he's got away with it. And then *Boo!*

Except I don't hear anything that sounds like somebody getting caught. And distantly I think I can hear Lucas downstairs again.

'Marco . . . Marco . . .' His voice sounds distant, more like he might be in the kitchen or the sunroom.

Nobody shouts *Polo*.

Jess looks at me quizzically. I shrug. She inches out again and hurries over to me. I pull her in, tight behind the central lantern pillar. She crouches down beside me.

'Sorry about earlier,' she whispers. The laughter is gone from her voice now and she sounds tired. There are frown lines on her forehead, deeper now than the last time I noticed them, but laugh lines at her mouth. It's been a long journey, but I'm grateful for everything we have. 'And I'm sorry I have to keep saying sorry. I've been so on edge since we got here. I don't know what's going on. It just doesn't

111

feel . . . It's not as restful as I thought it would be. I have this horrible feeling – I have done even since before last night. It's making me feel awful. I've been mean.'

'I'm sorry too,' I say softly. 'Always. I know I drive you up the wall.'

Her nose is very close to mine and I have the insatiable urge to touch it lightly with my finger, like I do with Emma. She has Jess's sense of fun – the old Jess. But the new Jess isn't worse or better, she's just different. We have different priorities now. Perhaps the way I fight her is childish, rooted in old feelings. She's right about the island, though. The lighthouse. We've all been rubbing each other up wrong since we got here. Something doesn't feel *right*.

'You don't drive me up the wall. Well, you do, but I knew that going in.' She smiles, and then presses her lips to mine. It's a sweet kiss, comfortable and soft. I feel the muscles bunched in my shoulders relax and I lean closer.

And then there's a loud noise, like a bang, like two feet jumping on the floor.

'Aha!'

Jess and I fly apart like guilty teenagers. My heart hammers as I take in first the hulking shape, dark in this half-light between afternoon and evening, then the change in atmosphere. The rain is coming down harder again and everything feels fuzzy. Panic courses through me as I think of the footsteps on the stairs – uncontrollable panic, wild, inexplicable. I have visions of Genevieve's mad sailors, ghosts with hollow eyes and rotting skin, coiled in generations of seaweed and bloated by black seawater.

But it's only Lucas, a broad grin on his face. He's triumphant, hands on his hips, still bouncing with glee. The loud noise must have been him jumping into the room to scare us. I roll my eyes to hide the pounding of my heart.

'Took you long enough,' I say.

'Hey, I like to be methodical.'

We pull ourselves to our feet and all three of us begin to tramp down the stairs. Every sound echoes. Jess grips my hand and I squeeze it back, glad that we had our moment together, even if it was only a moment.

We get to the bottom of the stairs and Lucas peers around, as though he's still looking for somebody.

'Aren't we the last ones?' I ask. Surely he must have found the girls downstairs first, otherwise it's just lazy searching. Mind you, I dread to think what else he could have been up to if he found Genevieve first. Poor Kira, sitting in the kitchen somewhere having to listen to them canoodling.

'Gen and Kira, yeah,' he says. 'Easy.'

Kira and Genevieve are sitting near each other in the lounge but not speaking. They look up when we enter the room and Kira mutters, 'Finally.'

'Where's James?' asks Genevieve.

We stop, everybody looking at Lucas.

'I haven't found him.'

# 13

## *Kira*

'How can you not have found him?' Moira asks. 'He's the biggest one of all of us. Very obvious. Six feet tall, shaggy hair, least likely to get lost under a table?'

Lucas shrugs, clearly too deep in his own self-importance to realise the significance of what he's said. But he seems to be the only one not bothered. The rest of us are reliving last night: the worry, and that unsettled feeling that Genevieve's stories gave us. Moira and Jess glance at each other, silently communicating something that looks like a question. It makes me start to panic. I heard James follow them up the stairs.

'Are you sure he didn't do the thing where you like . . . creep out of your hiding spot and follow the person who's It, and hide somewhere they've already checked?' Jess asks. She hesitates, then adds, 'I don't want to spoil the fun but we saw him on the stairs earlier.'

Lucas wrinkles his nose.

'Nah, I'm too good for him to do that. I'd find him in a second if he was following me around. He must have picked another hiding spot before I got there.'

'You didn't find us for ages,' Moira points out. 'We thought you'd given up and gone to bed.'

'Who says I didn't find you?' Lucas smirks. 'Maybe I just didn't want to come and get you straight away.' He follows this with a pointed look and Moira blushes. Jess laughs, but it's a breathless little sound.

The faint feeling of something amiss comes back and I shake my head.

'Did you look everywhere down here?' I say. 'Maybe he came back down the stairs before you went up.'

Lucas gestures with both hands. 'Sure, but I'll look again. You can all help me. And then can we *please* have a drink? This is boring.'

I glance at Genevieve but she's already getting to her feet. She has a strange look on her face, as if she's thinking hard: questions flit across her features. I wonder if she's thinking again about what we talked about this morning, about James, or if it's something else.

'Well if this is my only chance to be the finder then I guess I'm game,' Moira says. 'I bet he's found somewhere really stupid to hide.'

'Mmm,' Genevieve says distantly. 'Probably.'

We begin to move into the kitchen, although I know that James isn't in here. He can't be. I'd have noticed him from my spot near the door; he would have had to come past me to get into the room. I wonder if he headed into the sunroom.

'Maybe we should try through there,' I say, gesturing. 'Under the table, or those loungers that look out over the sea.'

Lucas shrugs again. He's lost all interest now, but there's some tension in the air that keeps us searching where normally we'd probably think it was funnier to abandon James to a fate of waiting until he, too, got bored. Normally I'd be laughing. Half an hour ago I might have been. Now all I can think about is his loss of control on that night all those years ago. How his eyes had shone so wildly. How afraid I'd been. And how I'd recognised some of that mania in his face tonight, when Mo suggested hide and seek . . .

We traipse through as a group, but the sunroom is empty, all wavering shadows as the rain runs down the huge sheets of glass. The terracotta tiles seem pale, like the ground is rising to meet me. Perhaps I'm starting with a migraine: my vision is fuzzy as my blood pressure rockets.

'Not here.' Jess shakes her head. 'Kitchen?'

'No, not the kitchen,' I say.

'Might as well check, just in case,' Lucas says, cutting me off. I bite back a retort and let him push past me, heading back into the lounge.

'He could have snuck back in,' Genevieve says. She's trying to be helpful, to soften the slight, but it only makes me angry. She shouldn't have to stick up for me when Lucas is a dick. Lucas just shouldn't be a dick. But at least the dislike now isn't for Genevieve – I just want to give Lucas a good talking to.

'Maybe we should split up,' Moira says. 'That way if he's sneaking around thinking he's being funny we can catch him.'

'No way,' Jess says. 'I've had enough of splitting up, thank you. I don't even have to watch horror movies to know that's a bad plan.'

'We're inside, Jess. How far could he have gone? How far could you get from me?'

'I don't care. He could have left and then somebody will

go outside after him and we'll be combing the beaches again before somebody can say "We're going to have to call their parents". So no.'

'James, you can come out now,' I call loudly. 'We're done. You win. We want to play something else.'

'Or drink our weight in paint stripper,' Moira mutters.

'James?' Jess calls his name too, the shrillness of her voice hammering home how nervous she is. 'Jaaaames?'

The fire in the lounge has died down now, but it's stuffy in there. We're all dressed for the weather and I can feel a prickle of sweat between my shoulder blades. I glance around the lounge again; at the coffee table and the standing lamps, the side tables, the sofa . . . There are only so many places to hide, and we've searched them all.

'Are we even sure he's still in here?' Lucas asks. 'I mean, if I were him I'd have gone to the cottage. We didn't set any rules.'

'Wouldn't we have heard him?' Jess glances at the heavy front door.

'And in this weather?' Moira shakes her head. 'It's throwing it down. Why go out there?'

'I don't know, because he wanted to win?' Lucas's voice raises. He's starting to get angry now, I can tell, though I'm not sure if it's because James has beaten him or if he's worried too. 'He wouldn't want me to beat him.'

'It's just hide and seek,' Genevieve says softly. 'Just a kids game.'

'Exactly,' I point out. 'It's just a game. What does it matter?'

'You weren't saying that when I was cleaning up in poker,' Lucas says. There's an edge to his voice, a coldness that I haven't heard directed at me in a long time.

'That's because you were cheating,' I say, equally cool. 'I don't care about winning.'

We lock gazes. I realise how strange it is, to argue with him while his girlfriend is standing right there. I try to dial it back, but there's something about Lucas's expression that sets a fire burning in me, and I'm not sure if it's anger or disappointment or shame but it's hot and gnawing.

Eventually I look away. This isn't the right place, or time, to address any of that old stuff.

'James?' Jess calls again.

'Wait. Shh.' Genevieve holds both of her hands up. The way she commands the room would make me angrier except that the expression on her face, one of intense concentration, stops me in my tracks. She's got her eyes trained on the ceiling.

'What?'

'I think I hear something.'

'James?' Jess whispers.

We're all whispering now, I realise. A strange sensation ripples through us. It feels like fear. We all stand perfectly still, waiting. And then – there it is.

'Do you hear that?'

It sounds like . . . footsteps. On wood. The floor of the lamp room is concrete, or something hard anyway. You wouldn't hear footsteps. Which means—

Genevieve is already moving. She heads slowly for the stairs, and I follow a step behind. I see Jess grab Moira's hand, and Moira shakes it a little but then lets her hang on. I understand. It's only a game, but we're all on edge. When we find James I'm going to kill him for winding us up again.

He's not in the staircase. The sound has stopped now,

119

or we can no longer hear it, but the echo seems to be in my head forever. Perhaps it's my heartbeat. God, this is so stupid. Frustration boiling over, I march up the steps faster, winding around until I nearly slam right into Genevieve's back.

She's on the first landing, where the steps stop briefly to make room for a door. The door we couldn't open.

'It's locked—' I start.

But Genevieve reaches out and pushes the door and I realise that it's not locked. It's not even properly closed. The door swings open quietly enough, just as the others come to stand behind me.

'What the . . .' Genevieve looks over her shoulder at me and then steps forward and I see what she's seen. It makes my toes curl, questions spinning inside my head. The owners shouldn't have kept this from us. This is – it's weird. It's creepy.

'James, what on earth?'

'The door,' he says. 'It wasn't locked any more.'

# 14

## Genevieve

It's a bedroom. Or it was once, but it looks like it hasn't
been used in a long time.

I step through so Kira and the others can see, too, but
it feels weird to be in here. Forbidden. There's some spice
in the air, a smell like secrets, dust and old fabric softener.
And it's cold, too. Weirdly so. Yet, despite the growing storm
outside the curtains don't move with any sort of breeze,
and the window is firmly shut. *It must only be single-glazed*,
I tell myself – but somewhere in the back of my head I
acknowledge the thought that it's not the windows that
make this room feel cold. It's more that it feels *haunted*.

The grey afternoon light through the windows barely
illuminates the polished wooden floorboards, the single bed
with a white iron frame. The bed sheets are pink gingham,
the curtains to match. There's a bookcase filled with trinkets,
an old stuffed bear with a cracked glass eye and a doll with
a mop of yellow wool hair. To my right there's a dressing
table, white to match the bed, and a wardrobe that looks
handmade, built to follow the shape of the wall.

'Oh, shit,' says Lucas. I wish he'd lower his voice. It feels like standing near a grave.

'It was locked,' Kira says firmly. 'I'm sure it was. Wasn't it?'

'Yes.' I remember checking it yesterday myself. I remember wishing we could get inside. I feel a chill race down my spine at the thought that somebody – that the very lighthouse itself – might have heard me. 'It was locked.'

'How did you get in?' Jess demands.

James is still by the window, looking out over the ocean, moody and roiling. There is nothing peaceful about this room. James turns away and points at the door.

'It wasn't locked. It was open.'

'But how?' Kira asks. 'It *was* locked. Before. We couldn't get in.'

'I know that,' James responds wearily. 'But I'm telling you that when I came up here it was open. I didn't mean to. I leant on it while I was waiting for Lucas and it just . . .'

Moira and Jess exchange another glance. I notice that they do that a lot. There's a lot going on there, under the surface. I wonder if that's what it's like to be married. An implicit understanding. I think of Lucas. Sometimes we can communicate without other words, but sometimes . . .

'Bollocks,' Lucas says, too loudly again.

'Well, whatever,' James says. 'We should go.'

'Agreed,' Jess says. 'I'm getting some serious horror vibes.'

'Wait,' Moira says. 'I just don't get it.'

I'm still searching the room for signs of who it belonged to. A little girl, more than likely. The decor looks like something straight out of an eighties Laura Ashley advert. Patterns everywhere, matching cushions on the bed and shades on the little ceramic lamps beside it. There are a few books on the shelf, too. I inch closer, something telling me to tread carefully, and examine them. A few I recognise from my own childhood, like *The Secret Garden* and *Peace at Last*.

The toys, too, are old-fashioned. There's a little pink plastic telephone with a rotary dial and a tiny plastic bucket filled with marbles. A fresh shiver works its way through me. This whole place has been renovated, right down to the flooring in the lamp room upstairs. Why would they leave the bedroom like this?

'I'm out,' Jess says. 'Nope. This is super creepy and I am not here for it.'

'I'm with Jess,' Kira says. 'Not creepy, but I don't think we should be in here. That door was locked for a reason.'

'It wasn't locked,' James repeats.

'Okay, fine, it wasn't locked. But it's still not for us. Now get out. Come on. All of you.'

I can see that Moira, like me, longs to have a proper look around, but we all let ourselves back onto the staircase, filing down it in silence. Moira lingers a moment, watching James as he closes the door carefully. There's something not right about all of this, but I can't figure out what. It's as if there's an energy here. I felt it before, yesterday, and after my shower earlier. I can feel it again now. As if we aren't alone. I told Jess they were just stories, but I don't know what I believe any more.

'You okay?' Moira has ushered Jess ahead of her, waited for James to go too, and now it's just the two of us at the back. Lucas hits the lounge and starts to talk so loudly I can hear him from here, his voice ricocheting like a bullet.

'I'm fine. It's . . .' I resist the urge to turn around. I don't know if I want to check to make sure the door is still closed or if I'm almost hoping it won't be. 'I know I was going on about ghosts yesterday but this is something else. Right? It's not just me?'

'Not just you.' Moira is ahead of me so I can't see her face, but her posture is relaxed – too relaxed. As though she's trying hard to keep her shoulders loose, her steps carefree. 'But I don't believe in ghosts, for the record.'

'Right.'

Downstairs everybody has gathered in the lounge, except Jess, who brings a six-pack of beers and a bottle of wine through from the kitchen, and Kira, who's carrying glasses.

'I think we need to chill ourselves out a bit,' Kira says pointedly. This is directed at me. I resist the urge to pull a face, but my reaction must still show because she goes on, 'All those ghost stories are just winding us up. James freaked us out last night—'

'I didn't mean to.'

'No, but you did. So I think we need to have a drink and just *relax*.'

'You can't be telling me you don't think something is a bit spooky,' I say, as calmly as I can. Surely they must feel it too? It's like a hand on the back of my neck; a pressure that I can feel everywhere in here. I thought it was just because of last night, James wandering off; but now I'm not sure. 'I only told a couple of stories yesterday.'

'And the one about the missing boy and the wind,' Jess says quietly. She won't meet my gaze.

'Okay, and that one. I can't help that this place really inspires those sorts of stories. But I did dial it back. I wasn't trying to upset anybody.' I try not to sound too apologetic, because I've always hated people who back down the minute they're challenged – it's something I tell my staff all the time: when it comes to advertising, or anything at all, if you're wrong you can admit that, but if you're right and somebody is just uncomfortable then you have to own your decision or what's the point?

'It's not all Gen's fault,' Moira says. 'I think we're blowing it out of proportion a bit. There's a bedroom we weren't told about, behind a locked-not-locked door, and James got drunk and wandered off.'

'And there's the missing wine,' Jess points out.

'I thought you were convinced I'd taken that,' Moira says drily. Jess shrugs, still looking at her knees.

'You couldn't find your cigarettes either,' I say.

Moira's jaw clenches and I wonder if I've stepped in it, but Jess just says, 'I didn't move them, I swear.'

'Okay fine, so we've got a bottle of wine and some cigarettes going for a wander,' Kira says, with a hardness to her voice. 'Big deal. Lucas probably took them.'

Lucas has been surprisingly quiet until now. He's got his phone in his hand, but from the way he's hardly paying attention to it I suspect there isn't any signal. The rain makes it hard to even get one bar. He reacts when Kira says his name, shaking his head.

'Nah, you know I don't drink wine. Vile stuff.'

'This isn't about the wine. Or the cigarettes. I'm trying to talk about ghost stories.' Kira is getting exasperated. She'd perched on the arm of one of the sofas but now she gets up and begins to pour three glasses of wine, her movements jerky. 'I just think we've got this thing in our heads.'

'Maybe Genevieve is right.' James has hardly spoken since we came down from the bedroom, but he's gone pale again. Or maybe that's just the light, ghostly grey through the clouds. I can hear the rain still, lashing against the glass wall of the sunroom. Kira finishes pouring the wine and moves on to turning on the rest of the lamps. She ignores James entirely.

'I think we should have another game,' she says brightly. 'I'll even play Game of Life.'

'What do you mean?' Jess asks, turning to James. 'About the stories?'

James shakes his head. 'No. Well . . . Not exactly. Maybe we shouldn't be here. Maybe there's something . . .' He stops. He's got a can of beer in his hands but he hasn't opened it. 'Maybe there's something about this island that we're not aware of. A history or something. Maybe we should . . .'

'Oh for God's sake,' Kira snaps. 'Will you all just stop it?'

'What if somebody died here?' Jess says quietly. 'What about the stories about sailors who died on the rocks? What about the previous owners who . . . who never wanted to leave? I don't believe in ghosts, but . . .'

'Don't be daft,' Moira admonishes. 'Come on, that's the sort of thing we'd be told about. A couple of things being misplaced is hardly reason to assume the island has a "spooky history".' She draws quotes in the air but it's half-hearted.

'Yeah,' Lucas agrees. 'Not least because it would probably be a selling point for people like Gen.' He grins at me but it's not funny. There's too much tension in the air for the joke to land. I'm starting to feel out of place, as if this is all my fault.

'And they'd have said something to Kira,' Moira adds. 'She's meant to be promoting this place for the magazine. Why would they want to leave out something like that? Seems like a no-brainer.'

I can see that Jess is still brimming with questions, but she clamps her mouth shut stubbornly and goes back to avoiding looking at any of us. Lucas leans back on the sofa and pops open a second can of beer. I'm starting to dread dinner, a long evening with everybody grouchy and argumentative.

Maybe I should agree with Moira and Kira, just so we can claw back yesterday afternoon's air of festivity. Maybe I should take it all back, the stories and the folklore, say that I made it all up to scare them. Perhaps I should tell them that there are no such stories as the one about the crying boy and his mother cursed to madness. I should take Jess to the side and ask her to forget I ever mentioned the Irish bishop who built a chapel on the same island where years later three lighthouse keepers disappeared; she should forget that I told her that even he, a man who would later become a saint, was too afraid to stay on the island overnight.

But I can't bring myself to lie, to tell them that I don't believe there's something to the tales. If anything, I'm desperate to know more. And I can't lie and say that I haven't felt a strange energy here – a presence. Because that's what it is.

The empty bedroom has got me thinking, and now I can't shake the feeling that's been brewing since we arrived: this island isn't ready for visitors.

# 15

## *Moira*

'I'm going for a walk before dinner,' Genevieve says.

Her words are like the spell that finally gives us permission to part ways. We've been bubbling up against each other all afternoon, eager to part and yet too nervous to be the first to leave. Lucas looks like he might ask Gen to stay, but he doesn't, and once she's slid into her jacket and left the cautiously coiled warmth of the lounge the air feels clearer.

James lets out a little breath.

'Phew,' he says aloud. 'Who knew we were all so superstitious?' He lets out a coarse laugh with a nervous edge to it and runs his hands through his hair, then settles back into the arms of the sofa and actually opens his beer.

'Speak for yourself,' Kira mutters darkly. 'I wanted to play Game of Life.'

'I didn't know Gen was so into all this . . . folklore stuff,' Jess directs at Lucas. 'Did you?'

Lucas shrugs and drains his can. 'Yeah but usually it's limited to her fancying going on tours round castles whenever we go away for the weekend anywhere. I think I've been to just about every stately home in the south-east.'

'Do you not think there's something to it?' Jess asks. 'I mean, not like ghosts and stuff, not specifically. But she was talking about energy and vibes yesterday. And we have to admit this place is pretty spooky.'

'We're on a Scottish island in September,' Kira points out. 'What did you all expect? The Bahamas?'

'No, of course not,' Jess back-pedals. 'I just mean that it's a bit . . . You know, with the mist and stuff.' She shrugs hopelessly.

I feel like I should wade in and support her, but Jess has absolutely made her bed and I'm tired. I'm really starting to feel our late night now, and all that running around followed by wine and the warmth in here hasn't helped. My limbs feel like lead.

Kira looks at her watch and Jess takes the opportunity to shoot me a dirty look that is somehow both annoyed and loving. I give her my cheekiest grin. It works and she smiles back. Forgiven. I know I should be more patient, more helpful; but if anything, having Emma has convinced me that we spend too much time as humans pretending that we forget how we really feel half the time, and it isn't worth it. Honesty is a prize.

'Well, as much as I had fun crawling around upstairs, I think I need to go for a lie down before we try to come up with something for dinner.' Jess stretches.

James seems startled by her movement, but he nods too. 'Not a bad plan.'

'I'm in,' I agree. 'That was literally all that was on my bucket list for the weekend beside eating amazing food. *Sleep.*'

James laughs. He starts to wiggle his eyes, but stops and laughs harder when Jess stares daggers. He might think it's funny, but there's no chance of any of that going on when either of us are this tired. That's probably been half the problem since Emma was born.

'Sleep? I just opened another beer!' Lucas says. 'Wish you'd said you'd all be disappearing.'

'I'll stay,' Kira says after a beat. 'We can play snap.'

'The beer will still be there in a couple of hours,' I say.

'Let me go, Lucas,' Jess intones, 'or I'll feed you nothing but Camembert for dinner. Don't think I've forgotten how much you hate it.'

Lucas shudders gamely and then waves us off. 'Oh, whatever. Gross. Go be gross together.'

I wait for Jess to get up and then we both drag on our jackets, still damp from earlier, before heading out into the late afternoon light. The clouds are still thick and grey but the rain seems to have died off temporarily and the air smells fresh and green. I inhale deeply, enjoying the feeling of the cold in my lungs.

'Hurry up,' Jess says. She's at the door to the cottage already. 'I don't like the way the light makes everything look when the sky's like that.'

'What? Why?' I laugh.

'It's too . . . I don't know. Like half day, half night.'

'It's only like twilight,' I say.

'Well, exactly. It's too early for that.'

'You've never minded the rain before.' I kick off my boots in the cottage foyer, really feeling the difference in temperature between the cottage and the lighthouse where we've had the fire burning all afternoon. 'What's different here?'

'It's not the rain. It's because . . . the shadows are just really long, I guess,' Jess says thoughtfully. 'I never noticed it before. And the air seems . . . I don't know. Too . . .'

'Too still?'

'Yes. That's it. It's too still, even with the bad weather. The rain's been battering all day, all that wind, but now it's all stopped and it's just still and quiet. It feels – empty.'

I don't say anything, but I do understand what Jess means. I've felt it too. It's like the island is waiting for something. I won't admit that to her, though, because I know it'll freak her out more. And I don't believe in any of that stuff. I can't. One of us has to be the sensible one.

'I'm so tired.' I rub my hands over my face and knead my knuckles into my eye sockets with a groan. We've reached our bedroom now and I'm looking forward to a couple of hours of blissful sleep, a thick blanket and my fuzzy socks and Jess curled warm at my back.

But then I realise she hasn't started her usual routine; I'd expect her to be shucking out of her jeans, or at least pulling her jumper off, but she's not moved from the doorway.

'What's up?' I ask.

'I . . . I just thought I saw something. Out of the window. It's nothing.'

I turn, taking in the sky, bruised and swollen, and the dark landscape out of the window. I see a faint glimmer of my reflection too, dark hair and bronze skin: all but a silhouette against Jess's pale oval face.

'Just the reflection,' I say.

Jess nods, but she doesn't look convinced.

'Oh, while I remember – I've been meaning to ask you, will you be able to stay home with Em on Thursday night? I got invited to go out for dinner with a client, and I think it'll be really good for Tinleys if we make nice . . .' I start talking, willing myself to fall into home routines even here, just to keep things steady, to keep the world from tilting. But Jess frowns at me. 'What?' I ask again.

'Why do you always do that?'

'Do what?'

'Change the subject.' She crosses to the bed and begins to take her jumper off, but she's doing the hunched shoulders thing which I know means I'm about to get it in the neck.

'I . . . thought we were done talking about ghosts?'

'You did it before, too. Any time I mention how I feel, especially since we got here, you change the subject or tell me not to be stupid.' She throws her jumper down. 'The others are starting to notice.'

'Notice what?'

'That you think I'm stupid.' Now she looks at me and my stomach bottoms out. It's not true – not even remotely – but I didn't want to have this conversation.

'You're not stupid,' I say, as calmly as I can. 'Not at all. I just . . .'

'Just what?'

*I just don't want you to get worked up.* If I say that, she'll absolutely lose it, and it's not a battle I want to have. I sigh through my nose and try to think of something, but she continues speaking before I have the chance.

'You think I'm *unstable*.'

I don't know what to say to that. Of course I don't think she's unstable. She's just been under so much pressure at home lately, and I know since she's been home alone with Emma a lot more she's had to start taking her medication again. She hasn't told me, but I know when it gets bad. And I only want to help.

133

I open my mouth, but nothing comes out. Everything I can think of to say sounds puerile, like I'd be trying to pacify her instead of speaking the truth. Jess tosses her head, golden hair down her back, and instead of speaking I move towards her, kneeling on the bed by her side. I take her hands in mine.

'I really do think Gen is right,' Jess says. Her voice is quieter now. 'I don't want to hurt Kira's feelings, but I don't really think I like it here. No, you know what? I actively *do not* like it.' When she looks up, her eyes seem very dark blue; like two endless pools of worry and fear that I can do nothing to assuage.

It's not relief I feel, though. I'm glad she isn't upset with me – I am – but there's a little pocket of heat in my belly. I am *angry*, I realise.

'Do we have to talk about it?' I say earnestly. 'Please, can't we just relax and enjoy the peace and quiet?'

'Peace and quiet.' Jess pulls her hands back and pinches the bridge of her nose. 'You're always talking like that, too. As if you can't wait to get away from us to go to work. As if you couldn't wait to come away this weekend.'

'I couldn't wait!' I throw my hands up in exasperation, sitting back on my heels as the mattress wobbles. 'It's not about not wanting to be with Emma. It's about wanting to spend some time with you. Just you.'

'There isn't just me here.'

'I know that, but we don't *ever* have it at home. This weekend we have opportunities for time alone. Like right now: a nice nap together, just sleep and nothing else. No worrying about work, or Emma; whose turn it'll be to go if she wakes up; who's going to take her to the park or her play dates. I *love* her, but I love what we have together too. Am I not allowed to miss that?'

Jess doesn't say anything at first, and I can see that she's thinking it over – genuinely thinking – but it doesn't last and seconds later the shutters go down again and I can see that she refuses to admit any of it. She won't tell me how she's been struggling; she won't talk to me about the medication or what I can do to help. And the worst thing is I know I can't ask without her thinking I don't trust her. So I don't push it.

'I just have this feeling,' Jess says. 'About the lighthouse. Or – or I don't know. About Emma.'

'What do you mean?'

'I have this feeling,' she says again, bringing her fist to clench just beneath her ribs. 'I can't describe it. It's a bad feeling. Sort of like when you're worried you left the stove on.'

'Are you still worrying about leaving Em with your mum and dad?'

'Yes, but this feels different.' She blinks. 'I don't know how many times I can say *I don't know*, but I don't. It's just a feeling. Maybe it's the vibes Gen was talking about. Energy. History. Maybe the lighthouse is haunted. Or maybe I just don't like that little girl's bedroom we found. Why would the owners leave it locked away like that? If they renovated it, they could fit more people on the island, make more money . . .'

Jess finally begins to unbutton her jeans, readying herself for a sleep. I think again how tired I am, but now I know I won't be able to sleep.

'It probably just means something to them,' I say.

I just wish we knew what.

135

# 16

## *Kira*

It's a long time since I've been alone with Lucas. When we
first broke up I avoided him a lot, and then, after Lucas
met Genevieve, he started to avoid me. Not in any obvious
sort of way, but I noticed it because I'd spent so many
years noticing him.

It's not like I worried it would be, though, just the
two of us. In fact, it's almost comfortable. Lucas slows
down on the beers once everybody else is gone and I nurse
a glass of wine, and, just as I suggested, we get the cards
back out and Lucas begins to deal for snap. It's a game we
played a lot in the early days, when we were first dating,
but it was never about anything romantic. It wasn't about
winning or losing, either; just playing. Something mindless.

I think of the simple pleasure I take in the setup of the
game, of the fun we had earlier before James ruined it, of
the wine and Jess's fancy cooking . . . Somehow this
weekend we are all trying to prove that we are still capable
of feeling childish delight, while simultaneously we're
desperate to prove that we've grown up, too. Ten years is

a long time. *Look at me, look how far I've come – but I'm still the old me, too.* It's impossible.

'You look like you're in deep,' Lucas comments. He taps a finger to his forehead and then sticks his tongue out at me.

'Just thinking,' I say.

Lucas pauses. 'Am I allowed to ask what about?'

'Of course you are.' I sip my wine. 'I was just thinking it's funny how we're all stuck in this limbo. We are now the adults who long for . . . *adultier* adults to fix their problems. We've become the people we made fun of at uni.'

'What problems?' Lucas begins the game, playing slowly at first as he always does.

'This weekend.' I sigh and toss down a two of clubs. Snap. Lucas wins.

'You don't think people are having a good time.' It's not a question.

'No. I mean, are you? The lighthouse is perfect. It's the best location we've ever had for a get-together, but nobody seems happy here and everything keeps going wrong. James . . .' I trail off, careful not to raise my voice too loud. He left the lighthouse not long after Mo and Jess but I don't trust that he's not lurking somewhere, since that seems to be his new habit of choice, '. . . It's like he's determined to sabotage. I don't know if it's because it's ten years and we're all . . . I don't know, trying to prove something?'

'What could we possibly have to prove?' Lucas genuinely can't see it.

But then, he never could. He's got this amazing new job, a beautiful girlfriend who's an absolute boss – and a bloody nice person to boot – and the rest of us feel pathetic by comparison. Even Moira, who loves her job at the auction house, seems quiet this time, when normally all we hear are stories about her weird and wonderful finds.

'We're not all like you,' I say. 'We don't all have a shiny new job and a pay rise to match.'

'Kira, your job is why we're *here*,' he points out. 'What would the Kira from ten years ago think about that?'

'She'd ask me whether I owned my own car yet,' I mutter. We both play sevens now and this time I win. 'And I don't. So. You know.'

'It's all relative. You live in London, Kira, you don't need a car.' Lucas shrugs in that easy, infuriating way of his, and I find myself wishing I had the joker Lucas here with me right now instead of this blasé, yet somehow sincere, one.

'Whatever.'

Nobody has bothered to build the fire back up again and we've been in here long enough that it's died right down. It's amazing how quickly the heat seems to drain away now I've noticed; as if there's something sucking it right out from around our bodies. The sun has begun to dip beyond the horizon and the windows are dim with the slowly creeping night. I wish, suddenly, that there was some kind of lamp outside the lighthouse, so that when it gets dark we might be able to see the cottage through the glass in the door. Without it, I know it will feel like we might be the only people in the world.

I picture the expanse of window in the sunroom, the porch that wraps all the way around to the ocean just beyond it, and aside from occasional slices of light from the lamp upstairs I know that in just a few hours the glass will be empty and black. The thought makes me feel naked, exposed, and I curl tighter into the sofa.

'Anyway, all I'm saying is that James has more to prove

in life than we all do,' I say. 'Or he thinks he does.' He always has, but I don't say that. Lucas won't believe me; he never does. To him James can do no wrong. But I don't think James has ever really recovered from being the only one of us to graduate with a third. He took that hard, especially after what happened between us, how that affected him . . .

It was as if that was the point when he stopped trying. He never lasted in a job after that; has never earned more than minimum wage. And while the rest of us don't care – we would never hold it against him – he holds it against himself.

'You think he's trying to make us pay attention to him?' Lucas asks. He looks genuinely surprised.

'Well, honestly as far as I see it there are two options,' I say. 'One: James went for a walk last night and for some reason now he suddenly believes in ghosts, just like your girlfriend . . . Which is ridiculous because James does *not* believe in ghosts. Or, two: James – and I don't mean this in a bad way – likes the attention he got last night, hence why he wandered off again today.'

'And conveniently discovered a creepy bedroom from the 19-whatevers,' Lucas says, clearly unimpressed with my theory.

'He didn't magic it out of thin air, but I don't believe that door wasn't locked. I checked it. So did Gen. It's like he's *trying* to find ways to scare us. I bet that's what he was doing while we were playing. Finding something to freak us all out.'

Lucas wins another round, but he's distracted, muttering how he wishes Genevieve would come back from her walk before it gets dark. I say nothing, just push back from the coffee table and wander to the sunroom doorway. I was right about the glass; although the sun hasn't sunk away yet, already the fading evening light and the dark clouds make the glass feel invisible, as if there's nothing to stop us tumbling into the swathe of water beyond.

'I still don't get why James is doing this,' Lucas says, going back to our previous conversation. 'It's not exactly funny. He's always been good at being funny. Surely you get better attention from being a clown?'

All of a sudden I realise I don't have to stand here feeling nervous about the slow, creeping darkness. I don't have to feel naked next to this invisible glass. So I switch on all of the lights, bringing the terracotta tiles and the table which is still a bit messy from lunch back to life. The grey light is immediately drowned in golden illumination.

'Yeah but you're funny too,' I say. A year ago that would have hurt to say, but something this weekend has softened in me. Maybe it's getting to know Genevieve. 'James has competition when you're here too.'

I turn back and Lucas is frowning. 'But it's always been us,' he says. 'Both of us. Together.'

'I don't know then.' I sigh, blowing out my frustration. 'All I'm saying is that things aren't how I planned. And I'm annoyed.'

'Gen didn't mean to upset anybody.' Lucas is on his feet now too. He wanders to the sunroom and peers through, as if wondering what I'm doing. I'm not sure why I'm in here except that it feels dangerous. Exposed. Maybe I want Lucas to see me – but that sounds stupid.

'I wish she'd read the room a bit better.'

'It's not her fault that Jess is so wound up by everything right now.' Lucas folds his arms defensively. 'Honestly, getting freaked out by a couple of ghost stories? We're not children.'

'It's not Jess's fault either,' I snap, suddenly weary. 'She can't help that it scared her.'

'She made herself scared!' Lucas is getting annoyed too. The feeling in the air has shifted, and now it's on a knife edge. Suddenly I can feel that tension again – old resentment bubbling – and I'm getting angry too. 'Talk about people who like attention; all Jess does is try to piss Moira off—'

'What, and Mo doesn't do the same? That's what they *do*.'

'Exactly!' Lucas throws his hands up. 'You can't blame Gen for everybody else's neuroses. Jesus Christ, Kira. I know you don't like her but that's not fair.'

I bite down on my lip so hard that I can feel blood welling there, taste the metallic tang on my tongue. How dare he? I've been nothing but welcoming. I've tried my best, anyway.

'Fuck you, Lucas,' I say, forcing my voice into ice.

Lucas blinks once, slowly, but doesn't respond except to turn around and walk away. His shoulders are rigid, his back straight as a rod, and I know then that I've gone too far. He gathers up the playing cards, places them in a neat pile on the table, and then grabs another beer.

'I'm going to find Gen,' he says tiredly.

I stay in the sunroom, turning my back on the lounge. The anger bubbles, but as soon as Lucas is gone I regret it. I'm not even sure what came over me. It felt like something else – something not entirely *me*.

The clouds are thicker again now, no hints of the dipping sun through a canvas of dark grey and purple, as if another big storm is brewing. The air is cold and I shiver a little. I should apologise to Lucas, but there's only so many times I can apologise for being tired without that just being who I am now. I rub my fingers into my scalp, mussing my hair, and am about to leave when I notice something.

There, on the table, are Moira's cigarettes. The packet is right on the edge, as though it has been placed there in a hurry. I see them hollowly, a prickle of something at the back of my brain. Nothing about this is odd, of course. Except I could have sworn they were not there earlier.

# 17

## *Genevieve*

It's a relief to get outside, away from the others for a minute. I do still feel grateful to be here, but I'd forgotten what it's like to be around so many people all the time. All but one of my brothers live abroad so family gatherings have been small for years. Usually it's just me and Lucas in our little flat, occasionally with another couple of friends round for dinner, or my brother Ted stopping by for a cup of tea. A few hours with James here and there, and even that usually involves me going to bed early. Being around all of Lucas's friends for so many solid hours has already started to sap my energy.

But as I walk away from the lighthouse, the weak sun illuminating my path through the grass towards the small shack, I realise it's not just that. There's definitely something about this island, too. I'm magnetised and also exhausted, in a constant state of alertness that makes me aware of everything here. Every sound, every sensation, every shadow moving between trees, as if my subconscious can never truly relax.

I pull my phone out as I begin to settle into a brisk stride. The rain is spotty still, but it isn't coming down hard enough to obscure my screen. I've hardly had any signal since we got here, but I'm hoping that if I head towards the shack again, and perhaps a little further where the terrain slopes gently upwards, I might be able to get enough 3G to do a Google search or two.

Something hasn't sat right with me today. Or yesterday – but worse now. Since we saw that bedroom . . . I keep picturing the gingham bedding, the worn old teddy bear. None of that stuff looks even remotely new, but it's not collectible either. And that raises some questions about why it's still there.

I know the others aren't as bothered as I am, but it's in my head now and I won't be able to settle again until I find some answers.

The path diverges when it hits the shack. One branch leads right to its door and the other follows the rise of land behind it. I noticed the second path last night but it was too dark, then, to see where it led. Now I realise that it's a good job we didn't head this way looking for James. There are rocks that claw out of the grass: fat grey boulders and some that are jagged and black. If we'd fallen over in the dark, we could have hurt ourselves quite badly.

I pick my way through the rocks, making sure to keep to the dirt track as a hill rises ahead. It's a short walk but I'm soon breathless, the wind stealing my thoughts too until I'm relaxing a bit, enjoying the feeling of my legs and arms and lungs all working as they normally do. A little routine never hurt.

When I reach the peak of the rise I turn to look down the way I've come. The path spills out behind, the shack a dark smudge nestled between folds of green, and beyond that the lighthouse, the lamp a beacon on the cliff. The lights are on in the cottage, too, warding off the rainy dimness. I can see nearly everything from up here: even the start of the path that leads back down to the beach. Distantly I wonder what it would look like to somebody else, somebody who belongs to this island the way we never could. Would we look like intruders? Interlopers wrecking perfect peace? Perhaps, to the ghosts of dead sailors, we'd be a welcome sight: sort of like a search party.

I unlock my phone and grin to myself when I see the little bar icon appear, a spinning circle next to the 3G symbol. Not perfect, but it'll do. I pull up the Google screen and begin to search.

It's over an hour before I start the trek back down the hill, my lips numb from the wind and a glorious sunset beginning between swathes of more dark clouds. My heart thumps as I skid in the dirt beneath my trainers, but I resist the urge to tumble into a jog, although I'm dying to.

By the time I reach the cottage I know I'm flushed and sweaty, my hair wild, but I don't care. I kick off my trainers next to the shoes at the door and I'm already slipping out of my coat as I head straight for my bedroom, hoping Lucas will be there.

'Jesus, you've been gone ages,' he mumbles, rolling upright from a nap I've clearly just interrupted by shoving the door open. 'I tried to find you but then I just needed to rest my eyes. What time is it?'

'Jess hasn't even started dinner yet,' I say. 'But listen, I've just been for a walk—'

'Find any ghosts?' Lucas yawns and stretches, his

expression playful as he pats the empty side of the bed. I sit, but reluctantly, my whole body filled with a fizzing kind of energy.

'No – but listen, I did find something interesting.' I pull my phone from my pocket and wave it at him.

'Is it WiFi?' he jokes. 'Porn?'

'Lucas, will you let me talk?'

His expression shifts from sleepy playfulness to more open curiosity.

'I knew something was weird earlier, when we found that room. I started to think maybe there's a reason for it. And I think I've found it.'

I pause, trying not to wish I had a slightly more energetic audience.

'You got signal?' he asks. 'Seriously?'

'Lucas!' I exclaim.

'All right, all right, go on then,' he prompts without fanfare. 'Are you going to tell me or do you want me to guess? I have about three options, all of which involve the word *ghosts*. But I'm guessing—'

'That's not funny, but you're not entirely wrong. I said there was a weird energy, right? Well I Googled the island and the lighthouse. There aren't many links except for the pages about island escapes and stuff, but most of it isn't about Ora. Mostly if you type in lighthouses you get films and Wiki pages.'

'But you found . . . ghosts?' Lucas prompts again.

'I found out why that bedroom exists,' I say. 'I think.'

Lucas takes a moment while this sinks in. I can see his brain working, his jaw clenching, and then he shrugs.

'Okay?'

'So, I'm assuming the people who own this place now

148

used to live here. At least I think it's the same people, anyway, since there's no discussion about it being sold and usually that would be on the Internet, right? They're presumably the ones who've renovated it and stuff, too, and left that bedroom like it was. I don't think that can be an accident. Anyway, something like forty years ago a family who lived here lost a daughter.'

Lucas shifts uncomfortably on the bed. 'Lost, like . . .?'

'She drowned. She was two years old and she probably went into the water, I think from right off the lighthouse porch as it was then. It was in a couple of local mainland papers at the time and I found a link to somebody discussing it on some weird forum . . .'

'What kind of forum?'

I'd hoped he wouldn't ask, but I scrunch my nose up and say, 'A ghost one. Not one of those creepy ones, just like people talking about hauntings and stuff.'

'And that's not creepy?'

'No, it's all very scientific,' I brush him off. 'There was one guy who mentioned the island by name which is how I found it. He said that he'd been working here last year – I assume he was here as part of the team that did the renovation. He mentioned a property development company – and that everybody got really nervous because stuff kept going missing while they were on site. Sandwiches, jackets, flasks of tea, once even a pile of folded tarps. Anything that was out of place, put down temporarily, was liable to vanish. No rhyme or reason, but half the time it'd turn up later, just in a different place. The boss apparently said it was birds or stuff got blown away or whatever—'

'Well that sounds logical.'

'Yeah but my point is – the thing I've been talking

149

about, the feeling, that vibe I've been getting – this guy felt it too.'

Lucas goes quiet and very still. He's chewing on his bottom lip like he does when he's really unsure about something. I know it's not a lot to go on, but I have a strong feeling about this. I've not been making it up. There is something here that isn't just an old building; there's history, and it's seeped into the earth, the air.

'So you think it's actually haunted,' Lucas says eventually. 'Honest to God *Blair Witch* haunted?'

'Not exactly—'

'Because I have to say I'm . . . not thrilled.'

I don't really know how to respond to that, because I'm not thrilled either; but I'm not afraid. Not really. Still, the thought of ghostly hands moving everyday items is unsettling.

'Do you think the two are linked?' Lucas asks. 'The little girl dying and the . . . other stuff?'

'I don't think there's the ghost of a two-year-old throwing stuff around, no. But I do wonder if the girl's death could be linked . . . I don't know. It's just interesting, isn't it?'

'Do you think we should tell the others?' Lucas leans back on the bed, resting on his elbows. It's meant to make him look confident, I'm sure, but it doesn't. He just looks nervous. 'I think maybe we should.'

'I don't know.' I've been wondering the same thing since I found the information. Is it worth it? It's only little things going missing, and a feeling that's getting stronger. At first I thought it *was* just a 'feeling' – not good or bad. Now I'm not so sure. Now it's more like concern, a growing niggle at the back of my mind. 'Do you think we should?' I ask. 'Really?'

Lucas thinks for a moment. 'Yes,' he says eventually. 'Yes, I think we should. I think everybody will want to know. I'm not sure what it means, but I don't like it. At best it's carelessness on the owner's behalf, not sharing a history like that. And Kira should have researched better. I know we were told to be careful, but if somebody has already died on those rocks . . .' He shakes his head.

'We could have easily had an issue with James wandering off,' I agree. 'It's different if you know somebody's already died.'

'Exactly.' Lucas rolls his head on his neck and then relaxes a little. He pats the edge of the bed. 'I don't want to think about it.'

I quirk an eyebrow at him. He's got that playful look on his face again, although I'm not sure if it's me but it seems hollow now: an act.

The others will be starting to make their way over to the lighthouse soon, gathering the booze and planning what we'll have for dinner. Suddenly I think about earlier, about Lucas messing around before we headed over for lunch.

'How *did* you get over to the lighthouse so fast earlier?' I ask. 'Just out of curiosity. One second you were outside the window and the next you were in the sunroom, like magic.'

Confusion flits across Lucas's face.

'What do you mean?' he asks. 'At lunch? I told you, I walked over. I was never outside any window. Which window?'

'You were waiting to scare me,' I push. 'I saw you. And then you . . .' I stop as the look of confusion grows. 'It wasn't you?'

'No. Everybody was too wound up already. I just went

151

straight over while you were in the bathroom.' He pauses and his face is so earnest it's hard to ignore the way my brain tips all the way into the bad feeling.

It is bad, now, isn't it?

'It wasn't me.'

# 18

## *Moira*

The whole way through dinner everybody is on edge. Lucas keeps glancing at Genevieve as if he's waiting for something, and James won't put his phone down even though the weather has left us with virtually no signal. Kira keeps brightly suggesting that we have a game of charades, desperate to stop the atmosphere from growing any worse. Nobody will officially say no, but it's clear none of us want to play. Jess's meal of pumpkin soup with crusty white bread from the M&S bakery goes down okay, but the enthusiasm we all had last night is gone. Mind you, it probably doesn't help that I caught Lucas stuffing his face with biscuits while Jess was cooking.

It's not until I get up to help Jess clear away the bowls and plates that I realise I've probably had too much wine – maybe five glasses already. We've been sat eating and chatting for a good couple of hours and I haven't been keeping track, just keeping up with the others. I'm unsteady on my feet and feeling a bit sick. The garlic taste in my mouth is too strong and my head too heavy.

Jess is a bit worse for wear too. She laughs as I stagger into the kitchen carrying plates up my arms like I used to when we both worked in the same restaurant during our first year of uni. It was how we met before the term even started. The way she smiles makes me warm right through, but there's an edge to it too, as if she needs to laugh or else she might cry instead.

'You okay?' I ask. 'The soup was delicious.' I kiss her on the cheek and run the taps to fill the sink. Jess slumps against the counter wearily.

'I miss her, Mo.'

'Em? We've only been gone a couple of days, and we'll be back soon.' I don't admit that I miss her too, even though I do. It's like missing a part of myself: a void inside my chest where the rest of my heart should be. But it's healthy to have a break, to reconnect with each other, to spend time with friends, and we haven't done much of that on our own since Emma was born.

'I have these . . . visions. Of bad—'

'Jess,' I say firmly, cutting her off. 'She's fine. They're fine. Come on.'

Jess rubs her hands up her arms, even though it's not especially cold in the kitchen. Gen built another fire in the log burner while we were cooking but it's died again now. The lounge is still passably warm and the sunroom is hot enough with food and booze and chatter to ward off the night.

I take Jess's hands in mine for the umpteenth time this weekend and massage some warmth back into them; the skin around her nails is almost blue.

'I just can't get warm,' she says. 'It's this place.'

'Are you coming down with something?'

154

Jess shakes her head, but without conviction. 'I don't know. We were out late and I'm still tired. It's cold out there. I just feel like I've not been warm since we got here. It's not like me.'

I wrap my arm around her as we leave the dishes to soak and head back towards the sunroom – it's somebody else's turn to wash up. But as we come through to the lounge we see that everybody has migrated in here; the bottles of wine and glasses are piled up now on the coffee table, and Lucas has a fresh can of beer.

'So, what's the plan tonight? I still want an early night,' I say.

Everybody looks at me. It's clear we've interrupted something. Kira looks suspicious and James is twitching his leg nervously, bouncing the ball of his foot on the floor.

Nobody says anything.

'Lucas?' I ask. He seems the most in control, but even he looks a bit shaken. It's the same way he's been acting all through dinner – almost secretive – only now he looks ready to talk. 'What's going on?'

Lucas glances at the others before he says, 'I was telling the others . . . Gen found something.'

Genevieve looks uncomfortable in her spot by the ashy remains of this evening's fire, where she's perched on the small footstool, her elbows resting on her knees and a glass of wine between her feet. She winces as Lucas mentions her name.

'I wasn't sure whether I should say, but . . .'

'Oh for goodness' sake,' Kira mutters. 'All this drama. What's the matter? Have you finally *actually* found something to complain about?'

Genevieve's wince becomes a full-on grimace, but the

way she squares her shoulders makes me think Kira might be close to the truth. I pull Jess further into the room and we perch on the edge of the sofa.

'It's . . . not a big deal,' Genevieve says. 'I don't want to blow anything out of proportion.'

'I'm not sure I agree.' Lucas puts down his can and leans forward intently. 'She Googled the history of the island. Found out about that kiddie's bedroom upstairs. We're thinking there's a reason why it's still there and I really don't like it much.'

Kira starts to roll her eyes as Genevieve says, 'There was a little girl who died here.'

The air in the room seems to crackle with electricity as we all exchange glances. I don't see so much as *feel* Jess shiver against me, and I place a warm hand on the small of her back. She's already rigid, her muscles bunched tight, and I know that this will really upset her. Talking about the death of a child, while she's feeling like this? While she's worried about Emma?

But I still have to ask, for my own peace of mind. I have to know.

'How did it happen?' I ask.

'She drowned,' Genevieve says. 'Back in, like, 1980.' She pulls her phone out of her pocket and holds it between her palms. The screen is dark. No notifications to set it pinging to brightness. I'm suddenly aware again of how isolated we really are here.

'Was it . . . an accident?' Jess asks faintly.

'Didn't say, but I guess it must have been. I think she fell from the cliff, but there weren't loads of details.'

Suddenly we're all staring at James, and he shifts uncomfortably in his seat. I guess it's not lost on any of us how dangerous it was for him to have been wandering around by himself the other night. It's treacherous enough during the day; I've seen the way those waves crash against the cliff, the force that causes the foam to spray feet into the air.

'Well, okay,' Kira says, somewhat put out. 'So there's a reason the island hasn't been occupied for a while, and a reason why they've reinvented the place. Does it matter? The lighthouse is amazing and the cottage is super comfortable. We're only meant to be here for a nice weekend, for a break, and for me to get some bloody photos.'

'Don't you think the owners ought to have told you?' Lucas says. 'Before we came?'

'Why?' Kira lets out a frustrated breath. 'Why does it matter? I'm sure people have died in most of the hotels you've ever stayed in and it's not like everybody gets informed about it.'

'Not usually children, though.' Jess is so quiet even I barely hear her, but Kira gives her a look that is ice, barely coated in a layer of concern.

'No, I agree that's very sad. But what does it matter to us? We're here to have a nice time, not to hunt history. We're staying in a lovely, renovated, historic building. Wouldn't you assume bad things might once have happened here? Or at least some things that you just don't know about?'

'I don't like that they kept it a secret,' Lucas pushes. 'I really don't like it.'

'It's not a secret!' Kira exclaims. 'Your girlfriend found it on Google in hardly any time at all. How is that a secret? It's just that they didn't say anything. Would you want your past spread about like that? Would you want to be reminded

157

about it? Especially if you were still mourning. I don't blame them.'

'It's not just the little girl dying though,' Genevieve says. It's clear she's uncomfortable and really would have rather kept all of this quiet, but now she's going to have to defend herself. I wish I could bundle Jess up – sweep her away before we start the inevitable conversation ahead – but I can't. 'It's the other stuff.'

'Like what.' This is less a question than a pointed statement. A dare. Kira waiting for Genevieve to make herself an outsider, once and for all.

'Like the stuff going missing,' Lucas says, wading in so Genevieve doesn't have to. She's got her mouth open, but he cuts across her. 'Mo's cigs; that bottle of wine these two were going on about. And Gen saw somebody lurking outside the cottage yesterday but then there was nobody there.'

'I didn't – I didn't definitely see anybody . . .' Genevieve trails off.

'Wait, what?' Jess asks, alarm making her voice tight and kind of shrill. I rub her back harder, trying to calm her down before she can get too nervous, but she pulls away. 'What do you mean you saw somebody?'

'I . . . I thought it was Lucas. Outside the cottage. But then Lucas was in here so it couldn't have been.'

'What, and it couldn't have been James?' Kira demands. 'Or any of us? Jesus, this is getting stupid. I wish we'd just booked a cabin in the Lakes.'

'No,' Genevieve says. 'I mean, *no*, everybody was already in here when I looked. I literally just – saw a figure, I thought it was Lucas, so I came straight here to try to prove something, but he was already here. You were *all* already here.'

'I really do not see the problem,' Kira says. 'So you imagined somebody being creepy when it was probably just, like, a branch or a seagull or something, and then freaked yourself out?'

'Are you kidding?' Lucas's eyes are wide. 'You don't see why we're *all* a bit freaked out?'

'For fuck's sake, Lucas. Don't get all high and mighty now just because you're on display. You can stop peacocking now.'

'That's not what this is! I'm just concerned because my girlfriend—'

'Yeah well, both of you were perfectly fucking happy to use me for a free holiday venue, weren't you?'

The words are weighted and the silence that follows is punctuated only by Jess's shallow breathing and the desperate reticence that seems to radiate from James. He's almost invisible from the tension. I can feel a flush in my own cheeks, a mess of emotions in my belly. The air in the room feels too tight, too cold. There isn't enough oxygen for all of us.

I want to defend Jess, to say she has a right to be upset like Lucas. I want to say that Lucas needs to calm down, that Genevieve is probably exaggerating things because we already know she's got this thing about *vibes*, but I can't bring myself to get involved in what is clearly now a slanging match between Lucas and Kira. Not least because I'm starting to get nervous. What if Genevieve really did see somebody? How do we know the island is really empty? But I can't say any of it because I'm the sensible one.

'All I'm saying,' Lucas says eventually, his words serrated, 'is that I think you should have done some more research. That surely *this* is the sort of thing that we should have known before we came here. Alone. With no real way of contacting the mainland if there's a problem.'

Kira stares him down.

'So you're saying that I should have provided you with a comprehensive list of the folklore attached to this random Scottish island, a history of the lighthouse owners, and a detailed examination of any deaths on the property. Is that it?'

'I think we're all getting a bit out of hand,' I say, finally psyching myself up to speak. 'I know why you're annoyed, Kira, but I don't think that's what Lucas wants. I think – I think we're all just surprised by the history, that's all.'

'And it's making us think what else we don't know about this place,' Jess agrees quietly.

'But obviously there's no correlation between what happened in 1980 and whatever we think we've experienced this weekend. It's been too long since we all got together. We're not used to each other's habits any more. We're not used to the isolation, or the quiet, or the weather, and our brains are inventing things to explain why we feel on edge.'

Genevieve doesn't say anything. Lucas looks like he might argue, but instead he slams down his empty beer can on the coffee table and grabs his jacket from the back of the sofa.

'Come on Gen,' he mutters. 'I think we can call it a night now.'

'Aw come on, mate. Don't go,' James pleads. It's the first time he's spoken in ages, and for a second it looks like fear that flashes across his face. But as soon as it appears, it's gone, and he's just regular James not wanting to be left alone with us. 'Why don't we crack out the Cards Against Humanity you brought? That'll be hilarious.'

'Nah, I'm not in the mood. Tired. Let's just sleep it off.'

'Lucas—' Kira starts.

'It's fine. I'm done peacocking.'

Genevieve holds her coat awkwardly as Lucas all but marches her towards the door. I'm sure she'd say something if Kira wasn't here, but she doesn't. The door slams shut with a gust behind them and the lounge is plunged into the kind of echoing quiet that always follows a loud noise, so hollow I can feel it in my bones.

'Well, that was fun,' I murmur.

'Don't you fucking start,' Kira says, but it's soft. 'Shall we all just get absolutely shitfaced now, yeah?'

# 19

## *Kira*

I can feel everybody watching me for the rest of the evening. Furtive glances from James, checking to see if I'm okay, and bemused ones from Mo. Jess is doing the thing where she's pretending not to watch me but it's all she's doing, between every sip of wine and every casual top-up of my glass.

The evening slips into infinity the more we drink. The fire is relit, lamps switched on. Somebody hooks up some coffee-shop music on a portable Bluetooth speaker and I can't tell whether it's Mo or Jess but I know it must be one of them because James, as far as I know, still favours the same shitty dance music we used to listen to when we went clubbing at uni.

The sky is disappointingly dark tonight. No stars now, no beautiful swathes of colour blended into the inky black-ness, just those perpetual clouds tinted silver at the crisp edges as the moon attempts to poke through. I wander into the sunroom two or three times to peer into the darkness, in some attempt to absorb the endless ocean to calm the anger that's still roiling away in my veins.

I can't believe Lucas. Or, worse: it's exactly what I would have expected from him, before Genevieve. It's like we've gone a hundred steps backwards, and tonight is evidence that we just can't make it as friends any more. It's mortifying knowing everybody saw us fight again, but most of all I can't bear the thought that Genevieve saw it. I've been doing so well to rein it in, to keep control, but I'm really, *really* angry.

This wasn't what the weekend was meant to be about. It was meant to be fun, relaxing, a chance to catch up; but instead, all of those old feelings and complexities have boiled over. I should have known better than to say yes when Lucas asked if he could bring his new girlfriend. I should have known better than to agree to organise everything as usual. I always end up so desperate to make things work that I put everything on the line, and that's exactly what's happened again this weekend.

Back in the lounge, James is slumped on the sofa with a red clothbound hardback draped over the arm. He's been carrying it around since we arrived, although he's hardly opened it the whole time we've been here. He's got his eyes half-closed, as though he was in the middle of a cat nap, and he opens them both as I sink down near him. I'm not sure where Mo and Jess have gone, but I can hear the faint hum of what might be the kettle in the kitchen.

'You're really angry at him, huh,' James says.

'I'm fuming.'

'I don't think he meant anything by it.' He chooses his words carefully, as if what he says next is too much to verbalise. His curls are standing on end again and I have the sudden compulsion to fix them. 'It's . . . complicated, isn't it?'

'Me and him?' I ask.

'No, I mean this place.' James gestures. 'I don't know. I don't think any of us have ever been anywhere like it. It's wild. A bit scary. It's a great idea but . . .'

'But?' I prompt.

'Well, you know. We're city dwellers.'

'And?'

'And nature is terrifying.' He laughs, but when I don't respond he goes on. 'I don't think Lucas meant to have a go. I don't think he was saying it's your fault either. And I definitely don't think Gen wanted any of that to happen. Did you see her face? But that story, about the girl who drowned . . . I – I wonder if we should go home.'

'I'm not going home. This is my holiday. Our flight back is all booked and paid for. I've got more photos to take and I'm not going to be cowed by a bunch of stupid stories. I don't care what Genevieve says.'

'They're not all stupid.'

I sigh. He's right. 'Okay, not the one about the kid. That's sad. I get it. It's a bit upsetting. But it happened so long ago that I still don't see how it's relevant. It's not like the island is haunted by the ghost of a two-year-old? And besides, that door was locked. We were never meant to go in there. It's not for our eyes.'

'Isn't that exactly what Lucas was saying?' James presses. 'I do think he's right about that. They should have told us.'

'Why?' I can feel myself getting angry again but I try to hold it in, my fists balled in my lap. 'I literally don't understand what everybody is so annoyed about. Do you know that the last owner of my current house died in the house? In my bedroom? Do you know how common that is?'

'Yes, but you're *aware* of that.'

165

'So? Are you honestly telling me that if you'd known a tragic accident had happened here *forty years ago* you wouldn't have come?'

James thinks about this for a second, his expression flickering with indecision.

'No,' he says after a moment. 'I guess you're right. I would have said it wasn't a big deal.'

'Exac—'

'Not now, though. Now I'm here, now I've seen the place and felt . . . I don't know what I've felt. But having felt it? I don't know if I'd agree with myself. I still think that I would want to go home early. I'm unsettled. I've never felt like this, and everybody is being affected. I'm not sure it's . . .' He trails off.

'Not sure it's what?'

'Nothing. I don't know.' James picks at the skin around his thumbnail. I can tell that he's drunk, but I don't think that's where this is coming from. It feels like there's more he's *not* saying; some other reason that he won't share for wanting to leave.

'Did something happen?' I ask. 'Did we upset you after last night? We didn't mean to have a go, it's just we were so worried about you . . .'

'It's not that,' he says, unconvincingly. 'Let's just forget it, yeah? I'm really tired.'

I lean back and kick my feet up, hoping that pretending I'm relaxed will calm me the rest of the way back to normal. A symphony of shrill laughter floats through from the kitchen; Moira and Jess have done their usual trick of wandering off to be alone as the gathering winds down. It used to be in dark rooms, smoky corners. Now it's the kitchen. Normally this would make me happy – I'm so glad they found each other, found balance in each other – but not tonight.

Tonight I watch James from underneath my lashes as we both pretend to doze. I know he's not asleep. He knows I'm awake too. Yet we both sit here, pretending that the booze is enough to numb the feeling that creeps around the edges of everything now. I wish we could rewind to yesterday morning, to do this all again.

To be honest I wish we could rewind further than that. I'm starting to wish we'd never come here. At least then all of this would be somebody else's problem.

The wine and the exhaustion from last night slowly seep into my limbs and before long I'm not feigning sleep so much as properly dozing, caught in that liquid state between sleep and waking. I have half-dreams of losing James to long, coiling shadows, watching as Genevieve yells *I told you so* and Lucas hauls her away.

A slamming door drags me back to wakefulness and for a brief, cold second, I can't remember where I am. My feet are cold even in my shoes and my arms bristle with goosebumps. Groggily I peel my eyelids open, the beginning of a wine hangover already brewing behind my eyeballs.

'Oh,' I say, mouth feeling too full of teeth. 'It's you.'

'Sorry, were you asleep too?' Genevieve kicks off her shoes and pads over to the spare armchair next to the sofa where James lies sprawled, snoring gently. It's darker in here than it was – somebody has turned out several of the smaller lamps and with the fire no longer kicking out heat it's pretty cold. I've got no idea what time it is.

'Just resting my eyes.'

Genevieve doesn't look like she believes me, but it doesn't matter. I reach blindly for a drink, finding only my glass still half-full of wine. I swig it and grimace as the white wine does nothing to alleviate my dry tongue.

'Where are the others?' I ask. I've sobered up a bit but my vision still tilts when I move, so I grip the edge of the sofa as I haul myself further upright.

'Lucas is passed out in bed. Moira and Jess are . . . I don't know.' Genevieve squints and I laugh in spite of everything.

'Oh, yeah. They're pretty loud. I'm glad they finally . . .'

'God, don't.' Genevieve puts her hands over her eyes but I can see that she's blushing a bit.

I wonder what it is, exactly, that Lucas likes about her. She's very pretty, athletic, and very clever, but she's not at all what I thought she'd be like. When Lucas joked that he'd seduced his boss I pictured somebody straight-laced, assertive, the kind of woman I knew from the magazines I've worked for over the years.

Genevieve isn't like that. She's strong – definitely has a backbone – but she's soft, too. I don't really know what's going on beyond the surface, how much of what we see is an act. She's not the sort of person Lucas normally goes for. Normally he picks the scrappy ones, the ones used to rejection, so he can play the white knight. Like he did with me.

'Why aren't you in bed?' I ask to change the subject. It comes out sharper than I intend but Genevieve answers anyway.

'Can't sleep. Can't even think about trying.' She reaches for one of the wine glasses, picking carefully and topping up with the dregs of the bottle. 'I kept thinking about earlier.'

I don't want to talk about earlier. 'Let's not—'

'No, please. Let me apologise. I didn't want to upset you.

I know that you probably feel like I'm ruining everything and I really don't want that to happen. I don't want our differences to stop us from being able to be friends.'

I stare at her. It sounds like an apology but it's the worst one I've heard in a long while.

'I don't *feel* like you're ruining things,' I say. 'You are. It's a statement of fact.'

Genevieve looks taken aback, but I've had too much wine and too little sleep to be gentle. I'm still pissed that she's even here, never mind freaking everybody out to the point that James – *joker James* – wants to go home early.

'It's not funny,' I continue while Genevieve opens her mouth and closes it again. 'All these stories. You could have stopped when you upset Jess but you kept going. I don't know what's going on with you and James either, but – but it's obviously something.'

'Wait, what do you think is going on with me and James?'

'He's never like this any more,' I say, suddenly realising the truth about what I'm saying. It's been there the whole time and I haven't noticed. 'The way he's behaving this weekend. He doesn't act like this now. And when I told you about him – about what happened – you weren't . . . You were surprised, but not how I expected you to be. Like you didn't believe me. Like somebody told you differently. Did James tell you about what happened?'

'No, that's not true. I—'

'You weren't surprised the way I expected, but to you maybe this isn't weird. He's so down and so unpredictable. And he only gets like this when he's stressed, when – when . . .' I trip over my words. 'When he's conflicted about somebody.'

Genevieve makes a show of putting her wine glass down slowly, carefully, silently. She glances at the sofa, but then when she stares at me I'm shaken by how much feeling she shows.

'Are you insinuating that there is something going on between me and James?' she asks.

The silence in the lounge feels very loud. James has stopped snoring but he's twitching. I know we should move so we're talking somewhere else – that we can't wake him up – but I'm too drunk to think beyond the words gathering under my tongue.

Is this what I really think? Do I think there's something between them that's more than friendship? The thought is tawdry, not even worth giving a second of attention, and yet . . .

'Something is going on,' I say coldly. 'I don't know if Lucas is doing his usual trick, being *too much*, and you felt like you needed to talk to somebody else, or—'

'It's not like that,' Genevieve snaps. It's the most anger I've seen from her yet. 'I mean yes, I know Lucas can be – overzealous. But my God, cheating? You don't know anything about me.'

'That's the problem!' I exclaim. 'I don't know you at all. None of us do. All I know is that James hasn't been himself since last night when he wandered off, and *you* spent time with him before he went.'

'So did you.'

'I didn't make him do anything stupid.'

'Neither did I?'

'You were the one who wanted us to build that bloody fire in the first place.'

'I—'

We both stop as James shifts, letting out a low groan that is so guttural, so twisted that it sounds like pain.

170

Then he begins to thrash, his whole body convulsing as he shouts out. It's a wordless yell and it cuts right to my core.

'Shit,' I say. I jump off the sofa and stumble to where James is sleeping. He didn't tell me he was having night terrors again. The ones he had when I first knew him were debilitating, would knock him out for days. Everything scared him. We used to hear him in the night sometimes, shouting. Lucas always made me roll over and go back to sleep because James wouldn't want to be embarrassed by us admitting we'd heard, but after the hospital James confessed he'd always wished somebody would wake him up. I spent most of our third year of uni in that rented house pretending to sleep, knowing I wouldn't be able to, and all along he'd wanted help.

'James?' I say, softly at first. He doesn't hear me. 'James, you've got to wake up.'

His eyes snap open and they're wild. He scans the room, his glance leaping from me to Genevieve and then back, alarm ringing between me and him as I realise I'm holding his hand. The way he looks now reminds me of that time – that day when he lost control – and a spike of fear shoots through me. I want to snatch my hand away but I don't want to scare him more.

'You're safe,' I say. 'It's only me.'

James lets out a breath, a snort that could be relief, but it's tinged with something else. Something like hysteria.

'Thank God,' he mutters, sinking back onto the sofa. 'You're not her.'

# 20

## *Genevieve*

The quiet in the room reverberates around us as James slips, panting, back onto the sofa and Kira holds his hand. She's trembling. I realise I'm shaking, too, and I pull my hands into my lap, willing my pulse to return to normal. It's just James. Just a nightmare.

'Are you . . . Is he . . .?'

'James, you should get up,' Kira says. 'Stretch or get a drink or something.'

James mumbles something nonsensical and pulls his hand back before rolling onto his side. He draws his knees up to his chest and closes his eyes, but I can tell from his breathing that he's still awake.

Kira glances back at me, a blackness in her expression that cuts me. The argument is still there, still bubbling just below the surface, but neither of us will say more while James can hear. I can't get over her accusing me of *cheating* on Lucas. It's ridiculous. And there's absolutely no evidence for it.

*I hardly ever see James*, I want to say to her, even now.

173

I need to defend myself. *Lucas doesn't want to spend time with him as much as he did six months ago.*

And then I realise that maybe that is half the problem. There's probably resentment there, even though James won't say it. I've come in and taken Lucas's attention away – he already lost Kira to Lucas, and now he's lost Lucas to me.

'James,' Kira says again, but weaker this time, the fight gone out of her. 'Come on, at least go to bed.'

James groans and scrunches his eyes shut tighter.

'Go away,' he says. 'I'm tired.'

'Go to bed.'

'I don't want to. Leave me alone. I'm fine here.'

Kira sits back on her heels and lets out a sigh. It's a long one, full of heaviness, and then she scrambles to her feet.

'Fuck you, then,' she says fondly enough. 'You do whatever you want but *I'm* going to bed. I've had enough of this shit for one night, thanks.'

She starts struggling into her jacket, although it's inside out and she gives up eventually with a grunt. She's still drunk. I can tell from her sloppy movements, the way her gaze seems to list back to James whenever she moves. But he's not playing; he won't acknowledge what happened.

'Well?' Kira says. I glance back at her. She's at the door, phone in one hand and a glass with a little wine still in the bottom in the other. 'Are you coming?'

I look at James, then back at the door. The thought of going back to the cottage and lying there with Lucas, pretending to sleep even though I'm absolutely buzzing with questions and will never be able to sleep at all . . . It's no good.

'No thanks. I'll stay here a bit longer. Read a book maybe.'

Kira stares for a moment and then shrugs. 'Suit yourself. Good night.'

As the door to the lighthouse slams shut, blown by an autumn-scented gust of wind that wraps around my bare wrists and ankles, I wonder if I'll ever get to the bottom of why Kira hates me so much. Is it just because of Lucas? Or is there some reason that's more *me*? I'd thought we were getting somewhere, but not after tonight.

James rolls over again, pulling his collar up to cover his bare neck as he turns to face the back of the sofa. I debate whether to just sit here, basically by myself, but after Kira's argument it feels weird to be here with just James, *especially* if he's not talking to me.

So I get up and start to stretch. My knees and my ankles feel tight. At home I do yoga twice a day. Although I went for my walk earlier I spent most of the time messing around on my phone and I'm not used to evenings spent playing games on the sofa. Lucas says I fidget. Even at work I'm always moving. I've got a standing desk which I love – and which Lucas teases me about mercilessly – but I've always been a pacer. I pace in meetings, while I'm on the phone. As much as I love yoga, there's a time and a place for sitting still.

It's too late, or too early I guess, and definitely too dark to take another walk now, but I'm too antsy for yoga so I decide to stretch my legs by climbing to the top of the lighthouse.

I haven't been up here alone, and the cooler air hits me as I begin to ascend. James doesn't move, and I can't tell if he's planning to fall asleep there or just avoiding me, so I'm glad to get out of sight.

It's dark up here, and there aren't any electric lights on

the stairs except for a strip of LED that somebody has placed under the handrail that curves around the outside of the staircase. It's a white light, like the kind Lucas has around his bar in the shed in the garden we share with Anna and Derek downstairs, and it casts everything in ghostly silver. I'd not noticed it before, but it's a nice touch. Or it would be if everybody wasn't so shaken.

I stop at the first landing. It wasn't my intention to stop here. But now that I'm in the alcove with that wooden door right there, I find that I can't just walk past it. I know Kira didn't want us in here – didn't think it was appropriate to snoop – but now that I know what I know, about the family who lived here before, I have to see it again.

As I open the door and step into this time capsule of a room I realise that nobody, not a single person, has asked me for details about the little girl who died. Nobody wanted to know what I'd found out about her except that she died. They didn't want me to tell them that the parents were so sad, so distraught about what happened, that they left the island soon after and that the lighthouse has been empty since. Nobody even asked the girl's name.

'Samantha,' I say. My voice is quiet but it feels impossibly loud, as though the word itself is a ghost I've disturbed. 'Samantha Buchanan.'

It feels, somehow, like a summoning. Like a ritual.

I step further inside and close the door quietly, careful not to let it slam. I don't know if James will figure out that I've come up here, but I can't imagine he'll want to join me given how it shook him up before. But there's something about this room that feels warm, to me, as well as cold. It's cold because it's empty, because it's abandoned, but it's warm because it's still here. This room is filled with love.

I wander towards the window, where the gingham curtains hang in perfect pleats, still held with matching tiebacks. The windowsill is narrow, curved ever so slightly like the window itself, and on it sit three little ornaments. A small bear reading a book, so dusty it looks grey but it might have been brown once; a little rabbit bending down to tie a red shoe with a racing stripe down the side; and a tortoise with a white racing stripe of his own down the back of his shell.

The sight of them is odd, and sad. They remind me so much of things I would have had as a child; things I had long forgotten about until now. If I lost a child, would I be able to leave her things as they are, locked in stasis on an island somewhere far, far away from me? Wouldn't I want to keep them close?

Perhaps it hurt too much to keep these things, but hurt even more to throw them away as though Samantha Buchanan's life meant nothing. So they decided to keep it all here, preserved in time. Like a memorial.

Suddenly I have visions of the island as a graveyard, bleak and silent, and the towering lighthouse as a tombstone to mark their daughter's passing. The thought is stark and sad, prickling the skin on the back of my neck.

I turn back to the room and appraise it with new eyes. Now that I have time, now that I'm not distracted by everybody else, I notice the little touches of love dotted here and there. Stencils on the walls above the single bed showing rabbits and elephants and birds all having fun together. A lamp in the corner with a frothy pink fringe around the edge of the shade, a few pieces still stuck together as if grabbed by grubby hands during a night-time tantrum.

I wander back over to the bookcase to explore the titles,

careful not to touch anything out of respect. I can feel that same energy again, the same feeling I've had the whole time, but in here it's not quite as strong. Almost as though it's buried under a layer of old love, family life; a cotton blanket wrapped around the history of this island.

Whatever happened to Samantha – however it was that she came to fall from the cliff and drown like she did – is it *that* outlandish to think it had something to do with the island itself? Could the same thing have happened on the mainland? I can't help but think of those stories, the folklore that always surrounds lighthouses: the tales of treacherous rocks and sorrowful ghosts, of grief and isolation and torment. There's truth in all of them.

I wonder if the Buchanans thought about the stories when their daughter died; if they wondered if things might have been different if they'd decided to be mainland teachers or farmers or accountants. If they wondered, however briefly, whether ghostly hands might have guided their daughter out of their house, away from their garden and towards the cliff. Towards her death.

I wonder, too, if ghostly hands aren't the only thing we have to worry about. I'm thinking again of Lucas's prank outside the cottage, and how if it wasn't him – if it wasn't a prank – then . . . who was it? I know I saw something.

A shiver climbs my spine.

My eyes are drawn to a photograph I didn't see before, sitting on the top shelf of the bookcase. It's in a pink butterfly frame which has been badly faded by the sun. The photo itself isn't in great condition either, so I peer closer for a better look. It's of a family: mum, dad, and curly-haired toddler. I don't know much about children but she looks to be maybe old enough to walk, that kind of chubbiness in her cheeks that they get when they've started to feed themselves, a small, dark mole on her cheek like a smudge of chocolate.

The parents are grinning at the camera and their expressions aren't staged at all, just happy faces as the baby raises a fist to the sky and the dad struggles to aim the camera back at himself. I think it's the lighthouse behind them, grass at their feet and white at their back, the sun bright in the mum and the baby's blue eyes. They're very blonde, both of them, the dad with darker hair that is swept by the wind to reveal the beginnings of a bald spot.

It's such a normal photo that my heart squeezes. I'm sure they had many like it, but this was the one they chose for their daughter's bedroom, to remind her that they loved her. It was the one they chose to leave behind, to remind her spirit that they never *stopped* loving her.

There is something about this room that feels like unfinished business. I realise that I'm starting to get choked up and I have no idea what time it is. When I fish my phone out of my pocket the battery is dead, so I'm guessing it's late. I rub a hand over my nose, massaging some warmth into my skin and pretending that the tears there aren't real. I'm just tired. I don't know why I came up here anyway.

Except now I'm thinking about Kira again, how much she seems to hate me sometimes. I'm thinking about James, and the awful things she said to me about him. I'm thinking about how, whenever I'm around Lucas's friends, I can't seem to do anything right.

I let myself out of the bedroom, silently stepping from the wooden boards onto the concrete stairs. There's anger in me now, fizzing. It's not a feeling I'm used to. I'm used to being annoyed, yes. Frustrated. But not usually *angry*.

It surprises me, but I think there's fear there too. What if Kira says something to Lucas about me and James? What if Lucas believes her? He's been so odd with me lately that I wouldn't be surprised.

The lights on the staircase are out now, and when I reach the lounge it's empty and dark: no sleeping shape of James on the sofa, no light in the kitchen or the sunroom. It must be close to three in the morning and I'm so angry now that I'm even more awake than before.

I don't bother putting my jacket on, just sling it over my arm. The night air is freezing, the coldest I've felt yet since we arrived here, but it does nothing to calm me. In fact, the anger burns brighter the closer I get to the cottage, the closer I am to Lucas and James and Kira. I'm angry with Jess, too, for the way she has behaved since I told her the stories – harmless bloody stories. Rationally I know that it's not fair for me to lash out, and it's not their fault. But I don't belong here. I never belong anywhere, and no reunion holiday on a remote island is going to fix that.

The cottage is completely dark. It feels almost empty, except that I can hear Lucas snoring down the hall. I'm angry with him, too. He could have stuck up for me more, or at least he shouldn't have forced me to talk to the others tonight. I should have kept it close.

The door to James's room is slightly cracked and I can see a faint blue light shining through the crack, probably from his phone. I make myself walk straight past, even if in my current mood I'm desperate for confrontation. Now isn't the time.

Instead I head for the bathroom, where I don't really try to be quiet. I bang doors, the cupboard, the medicine cabinet. Then I realise that I'm being childish. There's a better way to deal with how I'm feeling, and it's not by waking everybody up in the middle of the night.

I finish up, taking my time, letting my anger simmer away. And then I go to bed.

# SUNDAY

# 21

## *Moira*

After Jess finally falls asleep I toss and turn all night. For the first time in weeks she's out like a light, snoring a bit with her mouth open, her hair spread across the pillow. And for once it's me that can't switch off. I'm sure the wine has something to do with it, but I have to admit I'm a bit envious of the way Jess has managed to pretend nothing happened today. Instead of sleepy, all I feel is sick, my head already woolly with the headache I know will hit me hard tomorrow.

I turn onto my side. The curtains are slightly open where I was a bit slapdash with them earlier, a slim band of silver moonlight striping directly into my eyes. I wince, closing my eyes, letting myself drift into the memory of a couple of hours ago, of Jess's lips on mine, skin to skin. It's been a long, long time since we've had that sort of frenzy drawing us together.

It's the island. It must be. It's the tension of earlier. The alcohol and that fizzing sense of something rumbling barely under the surface. I know the others aren't enjoying themselves, but I'm still stuck on the relief of getting Jess out of London, away from home for a bit. It's been easier tonight to push all of that away and try to think about something else.

The moonlight on my face feels calming now. I crack one eye open slightly and shift so the beam of light doesn't blind me. It feels like the whole world is shattered: silver and black. For a second it looks as if the world is tilting, like there's something moving across the surface of the window. My heart leaps, but it's only a shadow, only a bird or the wind blowing a leaf against the glass.

I sink back and play over what Genevieve told everybody earlier. Now that I'm trying to sleep I keep returning to it, the sleepy heaviness in my limbs still not enough to switch off my thoughts. I can't help but compare the girl who died here to Emma. They were the same age. I've been trying to avoid thinking about what it would be like to bring Emma here. I can't think of a scenario where I would ever feel safe with her that close to a cliff, to those crashing waves and a ten-foot drop . . .

Then I realise. That's how Jess feels all the time. The dangers I can see here, the situations my mind can conjure when I think of Emma here – that's what Jess sees whenever she leaves the house. Sometimes it's small things – doors slamming on little fingers, soft palms pressed against a hot iron – but sometimes it's more. Too many cars on the street, pedestrians pushing at a crossing; a stranger in the park pretending to be a lost tourist. I've avoided thinking about Emma here because I know I wouldn't feel safe bringing her here. Jess can't turn those thoughts off.

It's like a switch has flicked in my brain and suddenly I understand. The world has, to me, always seemed like a series of problems to solve. It's how I approach everything: methodical, systematic. Jess isn't like that. She has the burden of creativity, imagination. She pours her energy into cooking and baking because it's got a formula but there's art there too, in the exotic flavours and blends of traditions. And that's why she's afraid. Raising a child isn't like baking a cake. It's not like assembling ten ingredients and artistically blending them to a set of instructions – and only having to wait a couple of hours for the results. Raising a child is terrifying, and you never seem to know you've fucked up until it's too late.

I roll away from the moonlight and the shadows on the glass, feeling something prickle at my back as I do; some sense that I'm exposing myself, which is ridiculous. There's nobody out there, nobody except us and Genevieve's ghosts. I loop an arm around Jess's warm waist and hold her tight.

Slowly I begin to drift to sleep, but my thoughts have been so jumbled that I immediately start to dream. I see shadows when I open my eyes, and a murky underwater world where the outline of a child that looks *just like Emma* floats below stormy waves. I reach for the child, desperate fingers clawing. My fingers lock around her, both of us freezing and salt-slick. Rocks are jagged underneath, closing in around me, and the cliffs, when we finally surface, icy sea spray in my lungs, are so high that the tops brush the bruised sky. The lighthouse beam searches, pounding, across the water.

I scream. *We're here! Help!*

But no help comes. The waves are too much. I'm losing my grip.

*Hold on!*

But she can't hold on. I can't hold either, my fingers too numb. I can't even cry as the child is tugged from my grasp, the water flooding in where moments before I held her arm tight. I kick and kick, arms propelling me onwards against the waves. I won't give up. I won't . . .

She's gone.

The water closes in around me. It is heavy, lung-crushing, breath-stealing, as if somebody – something – is sitting on my chest. I cough it in, and it's not just water; it's like tar. It is brine and honey-brown sap. I blink. The water is not water any more. I see trees, winter-skeletal. There are secrets within their branches. Suddenly I'm standing below them, the trunks so thick and close together they block out the black sky. My legs are jelly and my lungs ache.

*Jess?* I call. *Are you there?*

There's a figure ahead. I claw my way through between two trees, the bark cutting into my palms. The figure is hunched in the leaves, which are red as blood, oily and multiplying beneath my feet. I glance down and notice that I'm not wearing any shoes – but I can't feel anything. My whole body is numb.

*Jess?*

When the figure turns it's Jess's face I see, but it's not her. It's somebody else wearing Jess's skin. She holds a pile of books in her hands, even as she crouches in the leaves, even as they twist and slip beneath her feet, rising around her. Are they journals? Recipe books? I can't tell.

*I can't stay,* Not-Jess says. Her voice is car tyres on gravel. The sound of an exit. *I can't be here any more.* Tears stream down her face. I'm crying too, big gulping sobs that feel so real, even as I know in the back of my mind that they aren't.

*Don't go. Stay. Please.*

The Not-Jess opens her mouth then and it's yawning, gaping. The sound that rips from her lips is a sharp knife on a glass cutting board, a wrenching so deep my heart trembles. And then she screams.

My limbs go liquid as I pull myself back to waking. I claw at the buttery sunlight, feel my eyelids peel open as if through glue. My mouth is dry, tongue stuck to the roof, my throat tight with unshed nightmare tears; my head pounds with the racing rhythm of my heart. I have no idea what time it is but I'm sure it must be late. I feel the soft mattress under my body, the duvet heavy over my knees, and finally, finally my aching lungs release and I draw in a sudden rush of freezing air.

It is so cold. My limbs are numb with it, the terror of that dark, frigid water refusing to leave me. I try to relax but my body is so tense, muscles taut like bowstrings ready to snap, my skin prickled with goosebumps. Why is it so cold? The window is closed, and yet there is an unmistakable draught, icy fingers tracing my spine, the sensation so much like a ghostly presence at my back that I have to move, have to roll over just to check.

I reach back, expecting to find the solid warmth of Jess's body, soft curves I can wrap my arms around to chase the chill away. But the other half of the bed is empty.

And then the scream happens again.

Pulse thrumming, I haul myself out of bed, legs tangling in the covers, landing on my elbows before I manage to drag myself to my feet. I can't find my dressing gown so I stumble into the hall still wearing little shorts, my vest top twisted indecently, and I'm still cold. I'm tugging my top round as another scream, more like crying, echoes down the hall.

A bedroom door swings open behind me. And then another. But I'm too busy following the sound of the sobbing to pay attention. I know that sound – would know it even if I hadn't heard it on and off over thirteen years; I always say our daughter sounds just like Jess when she cries.

The bathroom door is locked. I twist the knob fruitlessly and then bang my palm on the door. Jess lets out another cry.

'Jess?'

There's a rattle as she fumbles with the lock and then the door swings open. I tumble inwards as Jess falls towards me and into my arms. She's rigid, her skin hot – feverish almost.

'What's the matter?' I demand. 'Jess, what's going on?'

I'm so focused on checking her over for injuries, that I don't see it. Her hair is a mess, her skin is pale and her eyes are bloodshot; all of a sudden she looks too thin, like I've missed something while I've been sleeping. For half a second I wonder if she felt that strange coldness too, if she felt its hands on her spine and if she, too, was indescribably afraid. But then Jess lifts her arm up, finger outstretched, and points, and I realise why she is so scared.

The mirror.

The wall.

'Come away,' I say. I've got an arm around Jess's shoulders and I pull her firmly out into the hallway. She stumbles but doesn't argue, wandering in a daze like she's been drugged. My chest still aches, as though somebody has been sitting on it all night, but I push the feeling away.

'What's going on?' Kira is standing outside the kitchen in an oversized hoodie. She looks pale, hungover.

Lucas is halfway out of his bedroom and I can see the

shape of Genevieve moving somewhere inside. She stumbles out next. James is the last one into the hallway and he looks at me questioningly.

'Go and see for yourself,' I snap.

Jess is still crying but it's a whimper now, more shock than anything else. I lift her chin and force her to look at me. She doesn't look injured, just scared. Her pale face is even paler than usual, dark smudges under her eyes despite the heavy way she slept last night. I find myself thinking of my nightmare, of the Not-Jess, and I have to fight to force it back.

'Are you okay?' I ask.

Kira pushes past us, marching into the bathroom with her hands on her hips, no doubt ready to curse us out for being melodramatic. But then she sees it too and her whole body tenses with anger.

'What the fuck,' she says. Not a question.

'What is it?' Lucas asks.

'Was it like that?' I say to Jess, gently. 'When you went in?'

She nods. There's a glassiness to her eyes but she's not crying now, just letting the truth of it wash over her. I need to take another look. To see it again.

I leave Jess in the hallway and follow Kira back into the bathroom. It's blindingly white. White tiles, white bath, white sink basin and toilet and walls. The decorations are all twee and seasidey: a little statue of a lighthouse in white and navy stripes and some seagulls on the windowsill; a painting of Ora lighthouse itself, tall and white and brutally gorgeous on the wall. The vibe is so kitschy, so perfectly *holiday*; that's why it looks worse, here of all places. Just as bad as when I first saw it.

The mirror is smashed, a spiderweb pattern of destruction across the medicine cabinet. And on the wall, in what looks like chalky-matte Malbec-red lipstick, somebody has scrawled one word.

*LEAVE.*

# 22

## *Kira*

For a second I honestly can't believe what I'm seeing. This kind of behaviour . . . It isn't a joke. It's not even remotely funny. I turn with my mouth open and see my expression mirrored in Moira's face. Anger and confusion, but most of all a horrible sickness in my belly, because I know that one of us did this.

I march out into the hallway, carelessly shoving Mo out of the way. I don't care as long as I haven't hurt her. Jess is still standing with her hands over her mouth, her eyes shining. I march past her too.

'Everybody,' I order once they've all had their fill peering into the bathroom. 'Into the fucking kitchen. *Now.*'

'Can we just – put some clothes on?' Lucas asks. It's the first time I notice that he's in a T-shirt and boxers.

'No,' I snap. 'Kitchen. Now.'

James makes it in there before I do and flicks the kettle on but I turn it off with an unnecessary slap. He makes a noise – an exclamation of sorts – but quickly realises that

I'm not about to apologise and heads towards the table with his shoulders up near his ears.

'And the rest of you, as well. Sit.' I point at the table, and slowly it fills. Too slowly. By the time Genevieve sits down, rubbing at her eyes as if I've been rude to wake her even though it's gone midday, I'm overflowing with rage. It's white and hot and blinding.

'So,' I say, as calmly as I can. 'Anybody want to explain?'

I feel like a teacher and I hate it. Why do I always have to be the one responsible for everybody else? Why is it always up to me? We're only here because of me, and it's my name that's on all of the paperwork with the owners and the magazine. The damages alone . . .

The silence is deafening.

'Well somebody must have done it,' I say. 'So either you can tell me what happened and we'll sort it out together or . . .' I trail off, waiting.

'Or what?' Lucas pulls a face. 'What's going to happen, Kira?'

'Why are you being so defensive?' I turn on him. He's sitting back in his chair, his arms crossed over his chest like it's not even a big deal.

'Hey, this has nothing to do with me.' Lucas doesn't even bother to shake his head. 'Why the hell would I do that? I like it here.'

'This is exactly the sort of thing you'd do,' I push. 'Did you think it would be funny? To freak Jess out?'

'Oh come on. If I wanted to scare Jess I could do it any number of ways – I wouldn't be writing on walls. And anyway, how would I know Jess would be the first one up? I'm not a child and I resent the implication that I'm the only one who'd do this.'

'Well who else is it going to be?'

I glance around the table. Nobody will meet my gaze, but none of them look guilty, either. I don't know what's worse: knowing somebody deliberately damaged property to score a few funny points, or that they're refusing to admit it.

'Hello?'

'It wasn't like that when I went to bed,' Moira says. 'That was at like . . . two-ish?'

Jess nods slowly. 'Same.'

I turn to James and Genevieve, both of whom are staring at the table. James looks confused and Genevieve looks angry. I'm shocked. I don't think I've ever seen her face look so dark and it unsettles me, as if I've been knocked back by a gust of wind.

'Guys?' I say. 'You both went to bed after me.'

James shrugs. 'I don't know what time it was. But . . .' he trails off.

'But?' I prompt. I feel like my mother and I hate it. This shouldn't be my goddamn place, and yet here I am.

James hangs his head, dark curls falling forward so that he looks a bit like a child, but that's where the similarity ends. His stubble is dark and it looks like he didn't sleep well; he has dark crescents under his eyes. He picks at a bit of skin on his thumb nail awkwardly.

'Gen was the last one up,' he mumbles. 'She was the only one still awake when I went to bed. Well, aside from Mo and Jess but they were busy.'

Genevieve stares resolutely at the table, not even blinking at the accusation. But she's fuming. I can tell it from the set of her shoulders; the way she's breathing. I can't tell if it's anger at the accusation, though, or at me. It feels pointed, either way.

Lucas sits bolt upright.

'Oh for God's sake,' he snaps. 'Really? Jay was the one on about leaving the island. You think Gen did this? Why on earth would she?'

'I don't know!' I throw my hands up in exasperation. 'Maybe she's pissed off about everybody telling her to stop going on about folklore and spooky stories? Maybe she's bored of being here and wants a way out? Or maybe she was trying to scare us.' Even as I say the words I don't know if I believe them. I don't like Gen – haven't liked her because of Lucas, and because she always seems so perfect – but is that any reason to think she'd do this? But I don't know her. *We* don't know her, not really.

'Are you fucking kidding me?' Lucas says.

Genevieve stays quiet, eyes still trained on the table. I glance at Moira and Jess, imploring them to say something, but Jess just opens and closes her mouth like a fish.

'I don't think we should jump to any conclusions,' Mo says slowly. 'I mean, there has to be a rational explanation for it. I understand that maybe it seemed funny – when we'd had a drink – but it really isn't. Genevieve, did you write on the wall? It's in lipstick—'

'What's the use in saying I didn't?' Genevieve mutters. 'You're all so eager to believe it was me. Why should I waste my breath? You've all been talking over me like I'm not here. I would never want to hurt or upset any of you like that.'

'So it wasn't you?' Lucas asks.

'No,' she says. 'It wasn't me. But Kira's quick enough to believe it, so why not the rest of you? You don't know me so it's easy enough to believe. Point a finger at the newbie.'

'That's not fair,' I snap, even though it's true. 'You were the last one in the bathroom.'

'And it was exactly the same as it's been the whole weekend when I left it.' Finally Genevieve looks up. Her eyes are filled with a calm rage. I imagine the vortex of anger swirling inside her. I know it's there, but I can't see it now. It scares me that she can bury it so deep. 'I got ready for bed at about three-ish. I'm not sure exactly, but it was late. I cleaned my teeth and washed my face and went to bed.'

And still I don't know if I believe her.

'Well did you see anything?' James says.

'Your door was open,' Genevieve shrugs. 'For what that's worth.'

This feels like the truth – but does that mean anything?

'James?' I ask.

'Yeah, my door was open. I was still awake, I think. I heard somebody knocking about in the hall but I didn't check who it was.'

'And you didn't go back into the bathroom?'

'No!' James exclaims. 'I didn't do it.'

'This is fucking stupid,' Lucas mutters. Jess starts talking to Moira in a hushed voice, so quiet I can't hear what she's saying over Lucas and then James repeating himself.

'I didn't,' James says again. 'If there was a way to check, you'd see that I'm telling the truth. I don't see why *any* of us would do it.'

'You've been scaring us this weekend, though,' Jess says, a bit louder than before. 'You've been acting weird.'

James baulks. 'Why would I smash a mirror? And where the hell would I get lipstick?'

'You said yesterday that maybe we should leave,' I agree. 'Did you mean it? Do you really think we should go?'

'Yes but I wasn't going to resort to that sort of thing! Jesus, I just felt uncomfortable, that was all.' James is sweating, and if I didn't know better I'd think his hands are shaking because he is nervous. But then he gets up and puts the kettle back on again, as though he needs to keep them busy, and I realise that he actually probably just needs a cigarette. I hadn't realised I'd not seen him smoking, but now it seems odd. Perhaps he's been trying to quit and that's why he's been so weird.

'We all need to calm down,' Moira says.

'Oh fuck you, Mo,' I say tiredly. 'I mean that in the nicest way possible but we need to get to the bottom of this. I'm not about to lose this job because one of you knobheads didn't think a prank all the way through. We're not twenty any more. This is a big deal. And it's not just about a broken mirror and a stain on the wall.'

'I'm not saying we are still kids,' Moira says calmly. 'I'm saying that we're not going to get anywhere like this, arguing amongst ourselves and flinging shit.'

'Well we're not going to get anywhere at all until somebody confesses.'

'I know I'm not going to convince anybody one way or the other but I swear I didn't do it,' Genevieve says. 'I can't think of anything I'd want to do less. I love this place! You all know I do.'

'Truer words never spoken,' Lucas mutters. 'You've not shut up about it since we got here.'

'Exactly. Why would I want to leave? Why would I want anybody *else* to leave?'

'Well we're not going to leave, are we,' Moira points out. 'Not over this.'

'I'm not sure.' Jess shakes her head. 'I'm not sure I want

to stay any more. This is – it's stressing me out. And with Emma at home . . .'

'Jess,' Mo says, wincing. 'Come on. It's got nothing to do with Emma.'

James starts to hand out cups of tea and the feeling in the room has shifted perceptibly. Lucas cracks open yet another packet of biscuits and begins passing them round. I'm hungry but I don't take one when it's offered. Instead of relaxing us, this familiar tea ritual is making everybody even more antsy. Mo and Jess keep exchanging glances that could mean anything, and Lucas is staring daggers at me.

I want to sit down, to become one of them. Somehow I'm on the outside again, and this time I know I've put myself here, standing awkwardly leaning against the counter while they all sit at the table like scolded children. But I'm even more confused and angry now than I was ten minutes ago.

'So, are we just going to carry on and pretend that this didn't happen?' I say.

'Kira, drop it,' Lucas says through a mouthful of biscuit.

'How can I? There are shards of mirror on the floor. Jess could have hurt herself! And not to mention we're going to have to explain this somehow. Or did you all bring some bleach with you that'll get red lipstick off a wall?'

'I'm less concerned about the damage than I am about finding out who did it,' Jess says. 'I'm not being funny but I'm really, *really* freaking out now. James, are you sure you didn't?'

'Jess, I wouldn't do that. I'm not that much of an arse. Do you really think I am?'

'No, it's just . . . I don't know! Okay? I'm scared. I don't care if that makes me a baby, but this is all making me feel super weird. Can we all agree that it's weird? It's like this place is *haunted*.'

'Mo,' I implore. 'Help me out here.'

'I can't make somebody confess,' she says, an expression I don't like flitting across her face.

'*Mo*.'

Moira holds up both hands in a soothing gesture and instinctively we all turn to look at her. She's the level head, the one who always has an answer. But even she looks stumped.

'Okay,' she says. 'Look, let's just calm down. Say, for a second, that none of us did it. Nobody got up in the middle of the night and thought *hey, this'll be funny*, or did it in their sleep. Is it possible, then, that . . .' she trails off.

A collective breath, all of us quiet. We are all waiting to see what Moira will say next, because we can see her working up to the words, feeling them out with her tongue.

'Is it possible that it was somebody else?' She pauses again. Jess presses her palms firmly against the surface of the table as if it's sliding away from her and she needs a tighter grip. 'Is it possible,' Mo goes on, 'that somebody *else* was – playing a prank?' She's looking at me now, as if I know the intricacies of the island. I suppose that's my job, but nobody cared one way or the other two days ago what I knew. It was just a cheap holiday to them then.

'There shouldn't be anybody else here,' I say. 'It's just us. The whole island is privately owned. There's only the guy who runs the boat but I've not seen him, have you? And he doesn't live here.'

'He could have been here without us seeing him. It's not like we've been on the beach,' Lucas says. He hands the biscuits to Moira and she takes three gratefully.

'He did tell us he'd be here with the tide if we needed him.' I grip my mug tightly, feeling the heat gently scald my palms.

'Yeah,' Genevieve adds, 'but *have* you seen him? At all?'

'I . . .' I think about it. She's right that we haven't been on the beach a lot, but you can see the path across the water from the window and we've never noticed him come back. I'm not sure what worries me more: that he could have been here the whole time or that he's just left us here, totally stranded.

'He'll have to come back for us though,' Moira says, filling the gaps left by my silence.

'Tomorrow,' Genevieve adds. 'Not today. There's no boat on Sundays.'

Jess lets out a little breath that's filled with more emotion than most words are. I can feel it too, now. The more we talk the more I'm filled with a strange feeling of panic. Of actual fear. The boat *should* have come with the tide and we *should* have seen it. But we haven't.

'Have any of you even spoken to anybody off the island while we've been here?' Jess asks. 'The signal is so bad I haven't managed more than sending a text to my parents. What do we do if the boat doesn't turn up tomorrow?'

Lucas shakes his head.

'Look,' Moira says, always the sensible one. It makes me hate her now, just a little bit. That she can be so confident and make us feel better so easily. 'If we haven't seen the boatman, then he's not here. There's nobody here but us, until tomorrow when he will come back to take us home. This mirror business isn't somebody else playing a prank, because nobody else would need to be here.'

No, this is worse not better: there *shouldn't* be anybody

else here with us. It *should* just be the six of us. But the
island isn't that small. We haven't covered the whole of it.
And somebody damaged the bathroom. Maybe not one of
us – Moira can't prove otherwise.

'Which means maybe it's one of us, after all,' she says
firmly. 'I bet somebody did it in their sleep. Lucas, you used
to sleepwalk. We all had a lot to drink. I'm sure we can
work it out. And between us, we can pay to fix it. It's not
like anybody else would even want to scare us since we're
here to promote the place. Right?'

But I don't believe that. Somebody wrote that message.
Somebody wants us to leave.

What if we're not alone here?

# 23

## *Genevieve*

I need to get out of here. The pressure of all these eyes on me, even with Moira's subtle attempts to draw them away, is too much now. I'm angry. So angry that I can't verbalise it. That's how I know I need to get out. I've been in a hundred situations where I've had to handle my anger; it happens often in boardrooms filled with men who won't listen even to their boss, but I haven't had it happen amongst friends in a long time. It has taken me by surprise.

Kira is still on the war path, but I'm done listening. I don't care that we are going to have to split the cost of the broken mirror and any damage control. I don't care, even though I had nothing to do with any of it. I don't care that I'm starving. I push back the tea James put in front of me untouched, and get to my feet.

'I'm going for a walk,' I say. I'm calm, but firm. Kira looks as though she's going to stop me, but she doesn't say anything as I head for the door, my chin held high. I don't have anything to prove, but it's still hard knowing they will all watch my back as I leave.

I dress quickly in a clean pair of leggings and a big sweater, and I'm just lacing my boots up when I hear footsteps at the bedroom door. I glance up, expecting to see Lucas, or maybe even Kira. But it's Jess. She's brushed her golden hair back into a plait and is now wearing jeans and walking boots, her jacket slung over her arm. In her free hand she holds a croissant wrapped in a napkin and she offers it to me.

'Do you mind if I come with you?' she asks.

I'm surprised but I try not to show it. I take the croissant as my stomach lets out a loud rumble.

'It's a free country,' I say. It's not like me to be snappy, but I can't control it now. It feels like they're all against me, even though all I've ever tried to do is be nice to them. It feels petulant. 'Sorry,' I add. 'I'm just – so wound up by all of this.'

Jess lets me go first out of the cottage – I can still hear the others deep in discussion in the kitchen – and I breathe a grateful sigh as we step, one after the other, into the cold air. It's not raining but the sky is the sort of purple-grey that blankets everything, and the light seems heavy.

'Me too,' Jess says, once we're outside. 'But I'm sure I don't need to tell you that.'

I don't say anything in response. I'm not really sure what I'm *supposed* to say. Is this an apology for overreacting? Is it a dig at me for telling her the stories on Friday? It seems stupid. They're just ghost stories, the sort of tales my brothers used to repeat to me before bedtime when I was a kid.

'Where did you want to walk?' I ask eventually. I realise I've been leading Jess towards the shack, the one we found on Friday night, but I'm not so sure that's a good idea if she's liable to freak out again.

'Wherever you want to go.' She goes quiet for a moment and then says, 'I was wondering if you'd show me where you found the signal yesterday. And I actually wanted to talk to you, too.'

I stop. 'You did? Why?'

For a second I think she's going to say that she thinks James and Kira are right. It must have been me who broke the mirror. But then I swipe my hair out of my eyes and realise that her face isn't accusatory. She looks nervous.

'I . . .' She starts to walk again and I have to hurry to catch her up. Looks like we're heading towards the shack whether I like it or not.

'Jess?' I prompt.

'It's just – all of this.' Jess waves her hand in the direction of the lighthouse, which seems even taller and whiter than it did yesterday. 'It's really getting to me. I needed some fresh air. And . . . and I wanted to say that I'm sorry.'

'Why are *you* sorry?' I ask. 'I know that my stories scared you and I've apologised for that, but—'

'It's not just about the stories,' Jess says. 'Everybody's been going on about them and, like . . . Yes, okay, they unsettled me. I really didn't like the one about the lighthouse keepers who just – vanished. The idea of being swallowed by the sea . . .' She shudders. 'And, actually, the one about the boy and the wind howling at the door and his poor parents . . . But that's not your fault.'

'I honestly didn't think they would scare anybody,' I say earnestly. There's some relief in saying it again, as though maybe out here I can explain myself better, with the wind to back me up. The grass is wet and fragrant underfoot as we begin to follow the tangled path along the cliff. I feel lighter than I have in hours, glad to be out of the confines of the cottage, away from everybody else. I thought I wanted to be part of something, but maybe what I want is to be out here, free from judgement.

'No, no. I know. I didn't expect myself to freak out, honestly. I always liked scary stories as a kid.' Jess burrows her hands deep into the pockets of her coat and hunches her shoulders into the wind. 'That's – I guess it's on me. I've got my own issues, you know? I mean, I'm sure you've noticed. Everybody's noticed.' She stops to pull a stray strand of hair from her mouth and winces. 'But you have to admit that it's . . . There's something here that really amplifies that sense of spookiness, right? Like there's this . . . this energy. This – this vibe. I don't know. It's almost like we're not . . .'

She stops, but I think I know what she was about to say.

*It's almost like we're not alone.*

I glance out over the grey water. I can still feel the lighthouse behind us. It's a presence there, a fingertip pressed into the base of your skull, begging you to turn around and look. I've always believed buildings held energy, but this is something else.

'Yes,' I agree. 'You're right. It's definitely strong.'

'I don't like not being able to call home. I just feel so *isolated*. So out of control, you know? If something goes wrong, here or anywhere else, there's nothing we can do about it. That feeling got worse after James wandered off, like there was this reminder that if he was hurt, if he'd fallen or whatever, we couldn't help him. We couldn't even call somebody without a great big stroke of luck and the wind blowing in the right direction. And I don't think it's like him to act that way, either. He was so – so weird. And that scared me too. It looked like he'd seen a ghost.'

I turn this over. I still haven't decided how I feel about James, about Friday night and about his behaviour since. Or about what Kira told me – about the two of them, the way he lashed out at her and how unwell he'd been afterwards. How much of his wandering off on Friday was already there, waiting to come out when something stressed him out? How much of it was the alcohol in his system? How much of it was prompted by this place?

'You've done a lot of research, haven't you?' Jess continues. 'About the island? That's how you found out about the – the little girl who died.'

'I tried, yeah. I'm not an expert by any means, but—'

'Did you find any other stories?' Jess asks. 'About this island specifically, I mean. You told us before about like . . . general stories. But . . .'

I stop again, forcing Jess to stop with me where the path is narrow and uneven. From here we can see the shack ahead, tucked behind its little rise, although I'm not sure Jess has noticed it. Instead we've turned to look inwards, where the island stretches from grass to trees and then to ocean again beyond. It feels open and yet at the same time enclosed, like a secret. Like something that should be hidden.

It feels like we shouldn't be here.

'Are you sure you want me to say anything at all?' I ask, hesitant. The last time she asked me for stories it ended very badly. 'I don't want to scare you.'

'So you did find something about the island then? Is it . . . haunted?'

I sigh through my nose, running my lip between my teeth. I know what Lucas would say. He'd tell me to be the bigger person, to refuse to say anything that could upset her. But I also know what Lucas would *do*, and there is a reason we get on so well, after all.

'Well, not anything specific. Not any one story. But there are a few little incidents, which is probably more to the point. Nothing, like, *obvious*. No sightings of ghosts or anything. And honestly that makes me think it's more likely to be true.'

'What kinds of incidents?'

We start walking again, this time slower. Jess registers the shack on the path ahead when it appears taller once we crest the rise. I see her face form into a question but she doesn't say anything. I wonder if I'd feel the same energy this time as I felt before, that same sense of waiting, of foreboding, and I wonder if we should go inside.

'There were a few things that cropped up when I Googled the island. And I had actually already heard of a few before we came, but I didn't put the name to the stories until later on. I have a lot of books at home, different kinds of folk tales, true hauntings. You know.' It sounds stupid when I say it aloud.

'Are they bad stories?'

'They're not *good*. A selection. They might not be supernatural, obviously. Nothing to say the island has anything to do with it more than the fact that island living has always been hard and dangerous. I mean, you're cut off from the mainland for a lot of the time, and the cliffs and tides are dangerous whether you're experienced or not. There's also the isolation to consider.'

'Isolation?' Jess turns back to the ocean, shielding her eyes against the light that is still heavy, slanted, slicing through thick clouds. The wind smells very much like rain and I'm not loving our chances for escaping back to the lighthouse unscathed. 'Yeah, you're right. It must have been much worse back in the old days. Being here, by yourself, not even a mobile phone to attempt hotspotting.' She laughs nervously. 'Nobody else except you and your family. That's a bit much.'

'Yeah. So you have stories that kind of make sense. Another child that died years ago after falling from the dock; a young mother who was swept into the sea when she went to chop wood. That one was very sad because they couldn't work out how she ended up falling in the first place since she was on her own, the weather was fine, and there hadn't been any reason for it that they could figure. I do wonder if that was suicide.'

Jess has paled.

'Do you want me to stop?'

She shakes her head.

'There was an incident on the beach on the far side of the island where it was rumoured that a boat crashed in, like, the 1800s, leaving three men dead and another injured. And in the twenties a fisherman was caught in a net he was trying to pull in and drowned and he washed up here on the island, though I suspect he actually went under further from the shore. And—'

'Okay,' Jess says in a big rush of air. 'You can stop for a second.'

'Sorry.' I wrinkle my nose. 'All I'm saying is, the little girl who died here in the eighties – it's not that unusual. A lighthouse isn't really the sort of place you normally decide to raise a child, at least if it's this isolated and you haven't got any help. I think if it was me I'd consider some live-in nanny situation; or I guess other staff nearby who could help, like groundskeepers or whatever . . .' But Jess isn't listening to me any more.

She's staring down the hill, towards the tree line that runs behind the cottage. Everything looks smudged and grey, the trees dark against the grass yet barely visible against the bruising sky. The wind picks up and I feel an icy breath on my neck; I wish I'd put on a scarf or some gloves.

'You okay?' I ask. I follow her gaze, but there's nothing there except grass and trees and sky.

'What?' Jess blinks, startled. Suddenly I realise she's shivering. 'Oh. Yeah. I just thought I saw something . . . someone. I don't know. See, this is the problem. I'm really freaking myself out over this, getting in my head, and now my brain is playing tricks on me. I shouldn't have asked.'

I glance towards the shack. It probably won't be warm inside, but perhaps we can head indoors until Jess feels more like herself again. I'm not sure that it will help, but perhaps I can take her mind off things.

'Let's go in here,' I say, taking control. 'We can get in – we checked it the other night, when we were looking for James. The door is unlocked. It's a bit grotty inside but it'll probably be warmer than out here and you can try calling your parents again.'

Jess glances at the shack and then at me, and I can tell the idea tempts her because she's still shivering – I'm not sure it's entirely from the cold but I'm certain that being cold won't help. So I start walking, not waiting for a verbal response, and make it to the sagging porch before Jess reaches out for me, grabbing my elbow.

'Do you think . . . Are we allowed in there?'

'I don't see why not. It looks like it's been abandoned for years. Come on.'

I finish climbing the steps to the little porch and push my way into the cottage. The floor creaks just as loudly this time, and the door sticks halfway open, but I was right about it being warmer in here at least. Jess steps in behind me and closes the door – although I notice that she doesn't let it shut all the way.

'What is this place?' she asks, peering around.

'We wondered if it was a groundskeeper's cottage. Or maybe a really old lighthouse keeper's cottage, although I can't imagine anybody would fancy trekking from this place to the lighthouse in the middle of the night if the lamp went out.'

Jess shudders.

'Sorry,' I say. I wander over to the wooden table, whose surface is scored with a thousand tiny lines from many years of hard use. I rub my fingers over the divots and whorls absently. 'It seems like I'm always saying things that upset you. I really don't mean to.'

Jess lets out a huffing sigh that's half laughter.

'It's not your fault I'm apparently the world's biggest wuss now.' I hear the soft rustle of her jacket as she pulls her hands out of her pockets again and begins to rub them together. It's so dim in here: the grey sky outside and the filthy windows make everything seem grubby and old – more so than age alone.

'I don't think—'

'I wasn't always like this, you know.'

I turn and Jess is staring at the stone fireplace. There is still an old pot hanging over it, rusted in places, and covered in a fine layer of dust. I wonder if she's imagining the kind of people who used to use it. Whether they cooked family dinners or ate alone. How they died, or why they left, and why the pot came to be left here untouched.

'I never used to be scared of anything.' Jess shrugs. 'And then . . . We had Emma. Everything changed. Now I'm scared all the time, of everything. I won't even leave her with my parents so we can go out to dinner together. It's so stupid, isn't it? Mo hates me for it.'

'She doesn't hate you,' I say earnestly. 'I've never seen anybody love anybody else more.'

'I'm sure she loves me. I just wonder if she hates me too.' She shakes her head. 'Sorry for dumping on you. It's just – I thought maybe you'd understand. You're sensitive, like me, only . . . not the same kind. You can feel things. That's why I asked if you thought the island was haunted.'

Slowly a realisation starts to form, a cold feeling in the pit of my belly.

'You're not just asking because of the stories, are you?' I say. 'Is there something else?'

Jess purses her lips. 'It's – it's a lot of things. We already talked about the wine that went missing. That wasn't right. And James being so distant. I don't know if he senses it too. But when we found him yesterday morning, sitting on his own like that . . . Whatever happened to him – because something did, you can't tell me otherwise – it really shook him up. It's not just that, though. Things have been disappearing all weekend.'

As Jess talks, my eyes rove the shack. And now I'm starting to wonder if Jess is right about more than she thinks. My gaze drifts back to the table, scored with age.

'And I've had the same feeling a couple of times now. When we've been outside, or when I was alone in the kitchen in the lighthouse . . . It's like eyes on you. Like somebody watching you. I keep thinking I'm seeing things;

dark shapes, figures drifting. Just – just now and again, always out of the corner of my eye.'

Jess turns to me fully now and her eyes are bright and wet. She has pulled her phone from her pocket and she grips it tightly. I drag my gaze away from the table.

'I feel like I'm losing it,' she whispers. 'God, it sounds so weird when I say it out loud. Mo would think I'd absolutely lost the plot if I told her, and I really don't want her to worry any more than she already does. But I've tried to ignore it and I can't. I really can't. I just want to go home.'

She's crying now, proper tears on her cheeks. I feel a surge of sympathy, but it's dulled by what I've just noticed.

When we were in here the other night, I could have sworn there was a candlestick on the table. Right in the centre. I remember it because at the time I thought it was out of place, too nice to have been left here when whoever lived here left. And there was still a candle in the stick, waiting to be lit again.

If Jess is losing the plot, then maybe I am too.

Because now the candlestick is gone.

# 24

## *Moira*

'Look, this is just going to keep going in circles and we're not going to get anywhere.' I push back my empty mug and sigh. The kitchen is hot – too many bodies crammed into the space – and I'm desperate to get up and open a window. 'I think we're just going to have to put a pin in it. It doesn't have to be a big deal—'

Kira starts to interrupt but I talk over her.

'I know that there's damage to the property, and that's shit. And somebody is going to have to pay for that, but we'll make sure it isn't you. I can't think of any other way around it.'

Lucas is slouched at the table like he doesn't give a shit, only the tension in his shoulders and the abandoned packet of biscuits betraying the fact that he's pretty upset about this whole thing too. But I can't tell if he's upset because Kira thinks Gen had something to do with the damage, or if it's simply because he thought it would be funny and now nobody is laughing.

'Are we just going to ignore the fact that we have no

clue who did it then?' James asks. If it was anybody else I'd assume sarcasm, but James has an openness to his face that means he's genuinely asking.

'I think we have to. If nobody will admit it was them . . .'

Nobody says anything. I sigh again. But the frustration is better than the niggling thoughts in my head – thoughts of my nightmare, of that dark water closing overhead, the sensation of drowning. And of the freezing air when I'd woken up: those icy, prying fingers on my spine. I didn't want to think of it, as if thinking hard enough might conjure a ghost.

'Right. Exactly,' I say, channelling my frustration. 'So yes, I think we're just going to have to move on. Look, we've got one day left here to try to recover this a bit. We might as well try to spend it relaxing; or at least – try not to bite each other's heads off.'

Kira glares at nobody in particular, fiddling with the handle on her mug.

James goes back to looking at his hands. His face is shadowed, but I can't tell what he's thinking. I've lost touch with him over the years; lost the way to read him like I used to. He's not quite an enigma, and I think that's worse; there are shadows between us of the close friendship we used to have, an understanding that has peeled away year by year, and now there's just a question.

'Well, if we're finished with the witch hunt, I'm going to get dressed,' Lucas mutters. 'I'm dying for a piss.'

Kira shoots him a dirty look, but he doesn't care. He scrapes back from the table as loudly as humanly possible and then wanders down the hall with a careless gait, not in any sort of hurry.

'Arsehole,' Kira whispers.

But James doesn't smile like he usually would. Kira doesn't notice, collecting up the mugs and depositing them in the sink more loudly than is strictly necessary, but I realise that James isn't just staring at his hands: he's frozen in place. Almost like he can't breathe.

I wait until Kira, too, leaves us alone; until it's just the two of us. I sit in silence. I wait. The old James would volunteer something after a while. The old James hated awkward silences; hated feeling like he was holding people up. He was always the one who had to fill the pauses. But we're not the same as we were, and James continues to sit quietly, almost as if he doesn't notice I'm still there.

Eventually I can't stop myself.

'What is it with you this weekend?' I ask. It comes out more aggressive than I mean it to and I try to soften it with a smile.

James looks up in surprise.

'What do you mean?'

'You know exactly what I mean. All this brooding, wandering off. You've not been yourself. Are you . . . okay? It feels like – like there's something going on.'

'I . . . I don't know. I thought I was doing okay. But it's been hard since we got here. Seeing everybody together.' He frowns. 'I lost my job. I don't know if you know. It happened recently. It's not a big deal. I mean . . . it wasn't a surprise. And I thought that was okay. But now I'm starting to feel like . . . maybe I'm not as okay as I thought. I was going to do something different, try to change direction or whatever else you say when you're bottomed out, but being here makes me feel like a failure. You're all so – so put together.'

I laugh and it surprises both of us: a barking, cynical sound.

'*Put together*?' I say. 'Have you seen us? Jess is living on the edge of Meltdown City, and Kira's never got over – any of that.' I wave my hand towards the door in the direction of Lucas and Genevieve's bedroom.

'Yeah, but . . .' He trails off and his face gets that haunted look again.

'There's nothing else going on?'

'I can't . . . I don't want to talk about it. And anyway, you wouldn't believe me.'

'Try me?'

'No.' Suddenly James is emphatic. He shakes his head, hard, and starts to scramble back from the table. 'Thank you, but . . . I – I can't. I think I need to go and get some fresh air. It's so hot in here. I'm melting.'

'James, wait, I'm sorry—'

'Nah, it's cool. I'm just gonna pop over there for a bit. The lighthouse. Go look and see what I can spy from the top. Maybe spot the boat that's never gonna turn up. Maybe eat some actual lunch or read a book. Actually, have you seen the one I was reading? The Agatha Christie? I could have sworn I left it in my bedroom but it's not there this morning.' He tries to turn his expression into a smile but it's hollow, more like a grimace. 'Anyway, it doesn't matter, I'm sure it'll turn up.'

I don't have time to say anything else to him before he's out of the kitchen door. Not two minutes later while I'm putting away the mugs I've just washed and dried I hear James head out of the cottage, shoulders hunched against the wind. I watch through the kitchen window as he crosses to the lighthouse. I wonder if it's just the job

218

situation that's making him act so strangely, or if there's something else.

The clouds look heavy out there now. It's probably going to rain. I had so many plans this weekend of switching off, enjoying my child-free time with Jess. But now she's off with Genevieve – I didn't question it, even though that seems like an odd pairing to me – and I don't fancy spending time with Kira, given her attitude earlier.

I'd brought a book with me but I don't fancy it now. Perhaps something spooky wasn't the best plan knowing I'd be on an island all weekend . . . Still, there isn't much else to do apart from picking my way through two of the croissants Jess left for me. Eventually I go back to my room and grab my phone so I can play a few rounds of Candy Crush, which is a habit I'm still desperately trying to kick, and find that games are about all it's good for anyway. There's virtually no signal now, not enough for a text home to send and certainly not enough to get on Facebook or Twitter. And anyway, I told myself I'd take the weekend off social media.

'You look like you're missing civilisation as much as I am.' Lucas appears in the kitchen doorway, dressed and looking a bit more awake now. He hasn't shaved – probably because of the mirror situation – but the stubbly look has always suited him.

I click my phone off and put it face down on the table. I try to avoid staring as I try to figure out if Lucas had anything to do with what happened in the bathroom, but he pulls a face immediately.

'Oh, give over, Mo,' he says tiredly. 'As if I don't know what you're doing.'

'What?'

219

'Trying to see if I'm guilty? What, do you think I'd have it written on my forehead?'

I let out a surprised huff of breath and Lucas only laughs, a cynical sound that is the same old Lucas. He's always been able to crack me better than the others, which has always surprised Jess. But still, I remind myself, somebody broke that mirror. It didn't just happen. *Somebody* did it.

'Well you can't judge a girl for trying,' I say, quirking an eyebrow. 'You forget I'm a boss now too, dealing with unruly clowns like you every day.'

Lucas comes to join me at the table. It would make more sense for us to move to the lighthouse: to sit somewhere more comfortable, get the fire going and try to pretend that everything is normal. Maybe eat again. But I don't want to. I don't want to intrude on James's solitude, sure, but it's more than that. I don't really want to go into the lighthouse again – at all. I keep picturing that little girl's bedroom and it makes me so unbearably sad. I keep thinking of Emma, of my dream. I can't shake it.

'So you think I did it, then?' Lucas asks. Straight to the point.

'I didn't say that.'

'You didn't have to.'

I purse my lips. 'It's not that I think you did it,' I explain. 'It's more that it's exactly the sort of thing you'd do. You know. Thinking it was funny?'

'You saw me last night though,' Lucas says. 'I was, ah, not even slightly sober.'

'That's kind of my point?'

'No. I mean, I passed out in bed—'

'Well I know that's where you said you were, but I don't

have any first-hand experience of that,' I shrug. 'Kira doesn't think it was you.'

'No, she thinks it was Gen.' Lucas's expression turns dark. 'It's bullshit. Have you ever met a person as nice as Gen? All she's tried to do all weekend is make people happy. She was so excited to come and spend the weekend with everybody.'

'We hardly know her though,' I say. I understand where Kira is coming from. 'I'm not saying I agree with any of it. I really don't see what she'd have to gain, honestly. But it's not like we know her very well. She might have had a reason. You could have put her up to it.'

'She didn't. She wouldn't.' Lucas is emphatic. I can tell that he really believes it, and now I honestly don't know what to think. Until now I guess I half suspected that Lucas really did think it was funny. A way to freak out Jess, just like he used to.

'So, who did?'

'I'm sick of going round in circles.' He shakes his head.

'You're the one who brought it up.'

'No, I didn't – you—'

'All right,' I say quickly. 'Just drop it. Anyway, I half suspect James did it. You guys were always the prankmasters. Guess it would be kind of appropriate if he tried to scare us again after Friday night.'

Lucas goes quiet at that. I tilt my head and try to catch his attention, but he's staring past me, towards the kitchen window.

'What?' I prompt.

'Nah, it's nothing. Just thinking about Friday, I guess. That was so fucking weird.'

'I've been saying that all along. It's what we've all been saying. Has he spoken to you about it at all?'

221

Lucas rubs his bottom lip between his thumb and fore-finger, thoughtful. He doesn't move for a moment, lost in whatever place he's drifted off to. I'm just about to pick my phone back up to play another Candy Crush round when he speaks.

'No, but . . . do you think it has anything to do with all of us being here together?'

I frown. 'What do you mean?'

Lucas leans forward. 'James,' he says. 'Do you think it's too much for him? Last time we were all together . . .'

'What?' I ask. I try to remember. It was a long time ago, and Jess and I – we were busy. Probably too wrapped up in our own lives to notice if anything else was going on.

'He had a bit of a – a blip, I guess.' Lucas looks uncom-fortable, like he doesn't want to say it. 'He kept going on about his job, as if he was trying to prove something. Telling all those stories. Bragging. I don't know. And this time . . . Did you know he's los—'

'I don't fucking believe this.'

Lucas and I both jump as Kira swings into the doorway. She's livid, standing in that tense way I recognise from earlier. This isn't the same rage as before, I don't think. It can't be. Lucas glances at me at the exact same moment I say, '*What*?'

'What did we do now?' Lucas mutters.

'Have you seen the others?' Kira demands.

'Gen and Jess are still out,' I say. 'And James—'

'Fucking *James*,' she swears. 'We need to have a chat. All of us.'

'Kira, what's going on?' Lucas says. 'For God's sake.'

'It was him,' Kira snaps, lifting up what looks like a

bundle of clothes, her fingers like claws. I'm trying to figure it out, but my brain stutters and stutters and I don't understand what she means. 'It must have been him. This is proof.'

# 25

## *Kira*

It's always left to me to clean things up. After Genevieve and Jess leave the cottage I wait a solid five minutes before I can trust myself to leave my bedroom. I know some people are still in the kitchen, and I've heard a couple of sets of footsteps come and go, but I sit on the end of the bed and press my hands tightly between my knees.

I'm trying to decide if I'm overreacting. It's just a broken mirror. Just a bit of graffiti. Oh, who am I kidding? Even when I say the words in my head they sound hollow. It *is* a big deal. Somebody – and I've got no idea who – damaged the house. To what? To get at me? To play a joke?

The longer I sit here, the worse it feels. It's ridiculous. I can't let it get to me. I've got to do what I always do: take control; be the bigger person. So I get myself dressed in proper clothes, jeans and trainers and a hoodie, and head for the bathroom. As I walk past the kitchen I hear the murmur of conversation: Mo's voice and maybe Lucas's too. That only makes me angrier.

I've realised something earlier: I don't trust any of them not to lie.

In the bathroom everything is as I left it. White, everything white, the pale afternoon sunlight filtering through the misted glass of the back window. The window itself is pulled to, but we left it open last night after somebody had a shower and it's still cold in here.

For a second I pause, surveying the mess. There are jagged shards of broken mirror on the floor and in the sink just beneath the medicine cabinet, little crystalline pieces that glitter faintly. I've no doubt it's sharp, even the pieces that look curved, so I'm trying to think about the best way to clear it up without cutting myself, looking for a towel. But I can't find anything.

The towels that were here are all gone, probably one in each of our rooms, although I was sure there was a spare in here yesterday. Maybe I'm misremembering. There's nothing else I can use, not even a shower curtain that can be detached. I'm going to have to go and grab my towel, or maybe a T-shirt.

'Always left to me,' I mutter.

And then I spot it. On the floor there's a bundle of something tucked under the bath. I get down on my hands and knees, careful to avoid the shards of mirror. It takes a bit of awkward bending, but finally I'm able to pull the bundle out.

It's a T-shirt. Dark blue. It's scrunched up, folded in on itself as if it's been kicked under the bathtub carelessly. It probably belongs to Lucas – actually, no, I'm sure James was wearing one like this yesterday. He probably left it in here last night. But that's fine, because I can use it to get rid of the glass from the mirror.

226

I start to unfold the material and stop.

Something has stained it. Something waxy and fragrant. I peer closer, half my attention still on the shards of mirror by my knees so I don't cut myself. And then my attention isn't anywhere except the T-shirt. Inside it, staining the dark blue a vibrant red in places, is a metal tube. Lipstick. Broken, smudged.

And the same colour as the lipstick on the wall.

I march out into the hallway and head straight for the kitchen holding the T-shirt in my hands like it stinks, as far away from my body as I can handle without dropping it, or the bounty within. Moira and Lucas look up in surprise as I enter, and Lucas gets up when I show them the bundle.

'What is it?' he asks.

'It's not yours, is it?' I demand.

Moira frowns in confusion. 'What? Is that a T-shirt?'

'Yes.'

'It's James's,' Moira says. 'I think. Wasn't he wearing it yesterday? What's the problem?'

'I found it in the bathroom. On the floor.'

'And?' Lucas asks. 'What's the problem? Jesus I thought you'd like . . . I don't know. You said you had proof.'

'I *do*. Look.' I push the bundle at him, still holding the precious tube of broken lipstick in the middle. Lucas peels away a layer of the shirt and then frowns.

'What is it?'

'It's lipstick!' I exclaim. 'Same colour as on the wall. And it's wrapped inside James's T-shirt. Where is he? He's not in his room.'

'He . . .' Moira looks stricken for a moment, her eyes flashing as she considers what I'm showing them. 'He's in the lighthouse.'

227

I spin on my heel, anger burbling, ready to confront him.

'Wait,' Moira calls. 'Hang on. This doesn't exactly prove it was him, does it? Just – one second. Let me think.'

'You can think while I go and find him,' I snap. I'm done playing games now. This has gone far enough and I won't let him treat me as though my feelings don't hurt. I know we have a lot of history, we've both made mistakes, but this kind of behaviour when we're just trying to enjoy a holiday? It's not on. I thought we were friends.

'Wait,' Moira says again. '*Kira.*'

Lucas is remarkably quiet but I know that he's following me as I head out of the cottage, the T-shirt still gripped in my hands. I open the cottage door with my elbow and march across the gravel and grass, my blood boiling. I can almost see red.

The lighthouse is dim. Nobody has bothered to light a fire and there's only one lamp switched on in the lounge to ward off the drab day. I follow the trail of other lights, noticing there's one near the archway into the sunroom, and then more lamps on in there.

The long table stretches onwards towards the wall of glass. The ocean is rough today, buffeted by the wind into peaks that look vicious. The sky looks the same colour as the water, giving the impression that we're underwater.

James sits at the end of the table, his back to me. He's turned around one of the dining chairs and sits on it rigidly, his palms pressed flat against his knees, his back straight as a rod as he gazes out over the ocean.

'James,' I say firmly.

He doesn't react, as though he hasn't heard me.

'James, mate,' Lucas says. He's right behind me, and Moira is there too. I glare daggers at Lucas – for no reason other than I can't control myself, the anger is boiling so hot inside me – but he pays me no attention, just pushes around me and heading for James.

'Are you all right?' Moira asks.

'Fuck that,' I say. 'Is he going to explain this?'

Slowly James turns. It's as if he's waking from a nightmare, each movement stiff and jerky. He's a robot, no sign of life behind his eyes even when he sees us. But then he notices me, sees the T-shirt bundled in my hands.

'What's that?' he asks. Slowly, hollowly. No recognition on his face.

'I'm here to ask you the same question.'

I walk to the end of the table and lay the T-shirt down gently, even though all I want to do is throw it. I peel open the edges of the cotton, spreading it out so that the stain in the middle is stark, so that the damaged tube of lipstick can't be missed.

James looks at the T-shirt. Then he looks at me.

'Where did you find that?' he asks.

'Under the bath. Where you left it last night. After you broke the mirror and wrote on the wall. What, did you think I wouldn't find it?'

'That's not mine.' James's face pales in what might be fear, but I'm too angry to pay much heed.

'Not yours? It's your T-shirt, isn't it?'

'No, I mean – it's mine, but the lipstick isn't mine. Obviously. I didn't do it. Kira, come on, you have to believe me.'

'Why on earth should I believe you?' I snap. 'Tell me the truth. What the hell is going on with you? Why are you being so weird?'

Lucas and Moira are right beside me, flanking me.

It should feel powerful, but instead all I feel is sick. This isn't the James I know. Even the old James, the unhappy James . . . even he wouldn't do this.

'James?' I prompt.

James opens and closes his mouth, his jaw working as he tries to explain. But in the end he just slumps in his chair.

'I don't know what you want me to say,' he murmurs. 'I told you I didn't do it. Why can't we just . . . admit this is ridiculous and then . . .'

'And then?' This is from Lucas. Even he's pissed off, now. This isn't what any of us wanted when we came here.

'Where did you get the lipstick?' I ask when it's clear James doesn't have an answer.

'I didn't get it from anywhere,' he says, 'because it's *not mine*. How many times do I have to tell you?'

His eyes are glassy and I wonder if he might cry. I'm so confused and angry, emotions swirling inside me, that I don't know what to say. I turn to Moira – the sensible one, the one who always has an answer – and she just stares at me.

'You expect me to believe you after everything?' I say. I have to fight the urge to laugh, a bubble of hysteria in my throat. 'Fucking hell, James. Don't you think I'd trust you if you'd proved that I could?'

Moira and Lucas exchange a glance but it's too late. There's too much old emotion in this conversation now, and I can't do this any more.

'Kira,' James says. 'Don't—'

'I covered for you. For *years*. I didn't tell Lucas about what happened. I lied to everybody. And now you're doing this to me?'

'You didn't tell me what?' Lucas asks. He cranes his neck forward, his expression serious.

'When we were at uni. Right at the end of third year. Before graduation, when you went home. I cheated on you. With James.'

Lucas is silent. His expression is as dark as I've ever seen it and I feel as much as see him start to move towards me. I fight the old flinch and stand firm.

'And that's when James got unwell,' I continue. 'After I told him it shouldn't have happened. After I told him that it didn't mean anything. It was a mistake – obviously. Not that it matters now. He lost his temper and the police were called and it was a whole mess. He was sectioned. You all thought he was in Nepal all summer but he didn't go until later—'

'You promised you'd never tell anybody.' James blinks slowly, as if his whole world has crumbled. Although I don't have much to lose where Lucas is concerned, I realise too late that to James, Lucas is still everything. He's never really had a girlfriend, and as far as I know he still spends most of his free time with Lucas.

And I've just wrecked it all.

'Is this true?' Lucas turns to James.

James doesn't move except to swallow.

'I said is it fucking *true*?' Lucas shouts. The words echo inside the glass sunroom, shockingly loud. Moira jumps and crosses her arms defensively across her chest, as though that might protect her.

'Yes,' James says. There are tears on his face. 'It's true. I – I'm not proud of any of it. I had some stuff going on. It was . . . It was a bad time. But I got help and I sorted myself out.'

'What a pathetic excuse,' Lucas grinds out. 'You were unwell so you slept with my girlfriend? Fucking hell, I thought you were my friend.'

'That's not how it was!' James says.

'No,' I agree. 'I played my part. It was what happened afterwards . . . It scared me. That's why I'm bringing it up now, James. I'm worried about you. I'm worried that something is going on, that you're – that you need help again.'

Lucas looks like he wants to say more, but Moira lays a hand on his arm, pulling him back.

'Not now,' she murmurs. 'This isn't the time.'

'James,' I say. I try it softer this time. 'Come on, you have to explain yourself. How can you expect us to believe you didn't do it if you continue like this?'

James rubs his hands over his face and lets out a vibrating breath and then slaps his hands on his knees. Like he's made a decision.

'Jay?' Moira says.

'Fine,' James says. 'Look. I can tell you what happened – what I think happened – but . . . you're not going to believe me.'

'Try us,' Moira says. 'Why won't we believe you, if you're telling the truth?'

James glares at me, all his frustration channelled directly this way, but neither of us budge. I'm too wound up to say anything at all now. And I have to admit, James is scaring me. It looks like he's afraid. Properly scared. He isn't just angry at me for telling his secret. This is something else.

'It's – it's about Friday night. At first I didn't believe it myself. I thought it was a dream. I've . . . I've been having some dreams again, because of my job and stuff. I guess I worried that I was unwell again, that I'd lost touch with what was going on. That I was making stuff up? I don't know.'

'And?' Moira says. 'Now you think otherwise?'

'Yes. Now, I'm almost certain that it wasn't a dream. This is . . . This is it.' He points at the T-shirt.

'This is what?' I say, an icy hand on the back of my neck.

Distantly I hear the front door to the lighthouse open, and then slam closed. Footsteps. Panic worms in my throat, and Moira grips Lucas's arm harder.

'This is proof,' James says. 'She's real. I didn't dream it. She's here.'

# 26

## *Genevieve*

By the time we get back the wind is wild, nipping and snarling at our hair, jackets, legs. Jess and I head straight for the lighthouse, where the lights have winked on one by one during our tumble down the slope from the shack. The day has grown so dark with rain again that we could see them reflecting off – it seemed – the sky, the ocean, the world. Even though I know that's not true, it feels like it.

We hurry for the door, shoving hard to stumble one by one into the lounge. It's stone cold in here, only one lamp in the corner. I glance questioningly at Jess, but neither of us have spoken since we left the shack. Jess knows I'm freaked out – I wasn't able to hide it – but she won't ask why. And I know that just telling her about a candlestick will seem . . . It'll seem ridiculous. But I don't want to tell her.

I'm sure Jess will believe me, and I think somehow that's worse.

There's nobody in the lounge, just the solitary lamp, so I follow the trail of lights, the sounds of life. It sounds like an argument: voices raised and punctuated with silences that seem even louder still. Jess and I glance at each other, but don't slow down. We reach the sunroom and I almost stumble directly into Moira, who holds out a hand to her wife.

'What's going on?' Jess asks.

She's noticed it too, then. Not just me. Everybody looks stricken, like they've had bad news. Even Lucas, who is never bothered by anything, looks like he's been punched right in the stomach, winded and unsure of himself.

'Is it Emma?' Jess gasps. 'Did something bad happen? I tried to call again but I couldn't get through—'

'It's not Emma,' Moira says quickly, almost as if the words rush out in one breath.

'Oh, thank God.' Jess stumbles, slumping against the edge of the table. I'd be worried she might collapse if I hadn't seen her do it more than once this weekend.

'Then what's going on?' I ask, repeating Jess's question. 'You all look like you've . . .' I stop before I can say the rest, but my unspoken words seem to echo into the silence. *You look like you've seen a ghost.*

I look between them, but nobody speaks. Kira's chest rises and falls so rapidly she looks like she's just been running, and James is white as a sheet, his hair wild and unruly as he runs his hands through it again and again in a nervous gesture.

'Guys?' Jess presses.

'Go on,' Kira says slowly. 'James. Tell them. Say what you were going to say. We're all listening.'

It's only when Kira speaks that I see what she's gesturing at. There's a bundle of something that looks like clothes on the table. Dark blue material laid open. And inside it . . .

236

'Is that my lipstick?' I blurt before James can say anything. 'What the fuck?'

'It's yours?' James asks faintly. 'I didn't . . .'

'Oh for fuck's sake James, spit it out,' Kira snaps. 'What did you mean when you said *she's real*? What did you mean *she's here*?'

'Who's *she*?' Jess asks. Her voice wavers. In the beginning I would have found it lightly amusing, maybe commented to Lucas about it. Now I can feel the same fear.

'Can somebody please explain what the hell is going on?' I demand. 'I'm losing my goddamn mind.'

'This is James's T-shirt,' Kira says, pointing to the bundle. 'And I guess your lipstick. I found them in the bathroom. Can you explain what they were doing there?'

'No!' I exclaim. 'For God's sake, are we still on that?'

'No,' James says. He's filled with an eerie calm now, although his face is still pale and his eyes shiny like dark windows. 'It's got nothing to do with you. Or me. It's . . .' He sucks in a breath. 'Look, why don't you all sit down? I'll explain.'

Glances are thrown like punches as we all try to work out whether James is unwell . . . or if we're about to hear something nobody wants to hear. My whole body is tense, the pressure of the lighthouse above seems to bear down so heavily I can't breathe.

'Okay,' Moira says when Jess is beside her, their hands locked on the table. 'Go. This had better be a good explanation.'

'Right. So. It's Friday night, and we're on the beach. We've had a lot to drink, right?'

'Yeah, we were all fucking there, mate,' Lucas snaps. He seems angry – and something tells me it's not just about what James has to say now. I glance at Kira and she looks away quickly.

'All right, well I'm just saying it so you don't think I'm batshit,' James retorts. 'Because I am fully aware that this sounds like I'm imagining things. And – and for most of the weekend I thought so too. That's why I've been so weird.'

'So that's why,' Kira says, her voice dripping with venom.

But James continues bullishly. 'Yes, Kira. I was going to get matches. But for some reason I ended up walking. I don't know. I was pissed as anything and it just – it seemed like a good idea. I think I walked straight past the light-house, just . . . walked up the path. Kept on going right up that little hill.' James is deep in thought. I close my eyes and trace his journey on the map in my head. The grassy knolls, the dirt, the shack.

'And?' Moira says.

'I don't know. I ended up on the beach again. Like . . . I don't know. Listen, this sounds fake but I *swore* earlier in the evening I saw something. I thought I saw something moving down the beach, something . . . I thought it was a ghost.' He rubs his hands over his face. 'Obviously I ignored it. But that wasn't the first. I – God I had this horrible feeling when we arrived and we were looking around. I couldn't place it. Anyway, when I found the beach again it was a different bit and I realised I was totally fucking lost.'

'And this relates to the broken mirror how?' Lucas digs.

I reach out and grab his hand, desperate to force him to shut up. James's voice has grown reedy with fear even though he's trying to stay calm and every interjection by Lucas is driving him this close to giving up and telling us all to fuck off. I can see it on his face. He's teetering on a knife-edge and I won't have Lucas stop him now.

'It's okay,' I say soothingly. 'Go on.'

Lucas rolls his eyes but slumps in his chair, feigning carelessness. But I'm sure everybody can see, as I can, the corded vein in his neck, the way his head isn't quite touching the back of the chair.

'It was pitch black,' James continues. 'Well, not entirely. Just, like, the northern lights? It made everything feel so – like a dream. Anyway I don't know how I got down there but it was like, a slope? I guess. And I walked. And . . .'

He stops. He's looking down at his hands now, rubbing the palms together. I squeeze Lucas's hand tight, forcing him to shut up, and for once nobody else speaks either. The silence stretches, thin and elastic, and then snaps.

'I found a cave.'

'A cave?' Lucas widens his eyes. 'Is that—'

'It wasn't empty, man.' James shakes his head. 'I'm trying to sort through it. Trying to get my brain to work but it just . . . I've had nightmares since and I don't know what happened and what didn't. But there was a woman. I'm sure there was a woman.'

'In the cave.' Lucas glances at me and then Kira.

'Yes, in the cave. And outside the cave.' James looks up and there's fire, suddenly, in his eyes. 'I know it sounds stupid. I know that. Why do you think I haven't said anything? But fucking hell, how else do you explain all the shit this weekend?'

'Wait, you think a random island-dwelling woman broke into the cottage and smashed a mirror?' Kira laughs but the sound is strained. She's trying to make it sound unbelievable, but even she looks shaken.

'You don't get it,' James explains, suddenly animated, as if a huge weight has been lifted from his shoulders. 'She

239

wasn't just a woman. She said she *lived* here. She said that nobody was meant to be here and that . . .' He stops again, choking on the words. 'She said that if I told anybody I'd seen her she'd make sure we never left.'

Jess lets out a squeak, which is the most I've heard from her in minutes. She's fanning her face as though it's thirty degrees in here but it's freezing.

'This isn't fucking funny, Jay,' she says. 'This isn't funny at *all*.'

'I'm not joking, Jess. Honest to God. I wish I was.'

'So this woman,' Kira goes on, a little more gently than before. 'She saw you and threatened you?'

'Yeah.'

'And that's why she's . . . She's angry. She wants us to leave.'

'I told you we should go,' James exclaims. 'I told you. That's why I said we needed to leave. But I couldn't . . . I don't know. It's all fucked up in my head! Don't you get it? I was trying to keep everybody safe. I was trying to make sure we didn't . . . I didn't . . .' He trails off.

Kira turns to Moira. 'What do you make of this?'

But even Moira is silent, now, deep in thought.

'So, what?' Lucas says. 'You just . . . kept your mouth shut and hoped it would go away?'

'I thought it was a dream!' James throws his hands up. 'Jesus Christ. I don't know how to explain myself any more than that. I was pissed out of my brains, Lucas. I got back and you guys were beside yourselves and I just thought . . . Maybe I passed out on the beach and woke up here. Maybe it was all in my head. Maybe I *am* going off the fucking deep end.'

'Verdict's still out on that one,' Lucas says snidely.

'The wine.' This from Moira, who has let go of Jess's other hand and is leaning forward now, suddenly intent. 'The wine that went missing. And this morning James couldn't find his book. The cigarettes that moved.'

'Ghosts?' Jess says. 'Not ghosts?'

'Not ghosts. *Her*.' Moira purses her lips. 'It does sound outlandish, Jay,' she continues. 'I'll give you that. But . . . I don't believe in ghosts.'

'There's nothing to say this woman is alive,' I point out.

Jess blanches again and sucks in a breath.

'No,' Moira concedes. 'But nothing to say she's not, either.'

We look at James. 'I don't know,' he blurts. 'God, don't ask me. It was so dark. I don't know.'

'I don't even think I believe it,' Lucas says. 'It's a bloody good excuse, but absolutely ridiculous.'

'Why would I lie then?' James shakes his head. 'I don't think I could make up this kind of story if I *wanted* to. You all know I'm not that kind of creative.' He turns to Kira, pleading. 'You know I'm straight with stuff. I don't lie. I *never* lie. Even when I'm fucked up.'

Kira shrugs her shoulders.

'So what,' she says mercilessly. 'What does truth count for? We assume you *are* telling the truth, and what does that really explain? I don't understand any of it. There can't be anybody living here. They've had construction crews on site doing all this work for the last year.'

'Crews who swore things went missing,' I explain, giving a brief run-down of the comments I'd found online.

'So? Things go missing all the time. It doesn't mean *anything*. And I don't get why the owners of the lighthouse wouldn't have told us – how they possibly couldn't have known. They own this whole place, don't they? Nobody's lived here for years.'

'I don't think it would take much to grab a boat,' Moira says, weighing her words carefully. 'I mean, assuming she is here, it's not outlandish to assume she's found a way to survive out here. A cave would provide adequate shelter.'

'You're assuming she's alive,' I say again. I can't shake the feeling in my bones. It feels like I'm constantly right on the edge of a shiver. 'You're assuming a lot of things.'

Moira frowns at me but doesn't say anything in response.

'Does it matter?' James says. 'Whoever – or whatever – she is, she wants us gone.'

'Says you,' Lucas points out again. 'We only have your word she even fucking exists.'

'What possible motive could I have for wanting us to leave?' James cries. 'I swear I'm telling the truth.'

'Oh, you mean like you've told me the truth about you and Kira all these years? Christ, Jay. I thought you were my friend. I *thought* we didn't lie to each other. But I was wrong about that.'

I wince. So it's out. Kira's secret – James's secret – suddenly out in the open. It should feel like a relief, I think, but instead it's an open wound. Lucas isn't just upset, he's wild with anger. I can see it in every inch of him. And that hits like a punch to my gut. He and Kira have been over for years, so why does it matter so much to him what happened so long ago?

'That's different,' James says.

'Is it?' Lucas snorts. 'I don't know what to believe any more.'

James opens and closes his mouth wordlessly. The room is plunged into silence, except for a growing pounding coming from above as the heavens open worse than earlier. The rain is coming down so hard it sounds like hail.

Jess looks like she might pass out and Moira is too focused on everything else to notice. I sit, frozen, sadness and confusion and that strange tingling energy-like sensation mingling in my mind so that I hardly know what to say.

'Well, it's simple,' Kira says eventually. 'We need to leave. If that's what everybody wants. I'm done fucking around. I don't care whether this is true or not. I don't care who said what; who did what. If somebody's been in the cottage then we can't stay here: it's not safe, and I don't care about any of it any more. Fuck you all. We can just go.'

'No,' Jess says slowly. 'We can't.'

'Oh?' Kira snaps. 'Why not?'

'There's no boat on Sundays.'

# 27

## *Moira*

'There must be something we can do.' I glance at each of the others in turn, still not sure how to feel. I don't know who to believe; who to *want* to believe. What would be worse: a ghost rooting through our belongings, or a crazed islander wanting us to leave so badly she'd smash a mirror while we slept? Which would put us in the least danger?

'Like what?' Jess says, panic making her reach for my hand again. I want to pull back, to tell her she's hurting me, but I let her hold tight.

'Like we need to see if we can get an emergency boat, since we can't get the ferry,' I say. 'There's got to be provisions for this sort of thing. What if there was a storm?'

'You mean like right now?' Lucas mutters.

'I meant worse, but you're right.' I bite my lip. 'But I guess there's no harm in trying. There's a radio somewhere here, right?' I turn to Kira, who said she'd read the property information several times before we got here. I'd told Jess it was all in hand. Kira knew what she was doing.

'Uh . . .' Kira glances about awkwardly. 'Yeah? I'm not sure where, though. I didn't think we'd need it.'

'Typical,' Lucas interjects.

'Oh fuck *off*!' Kira explodes. 'If you're not going to be helpful then you need to shut the hell up.'

'All right,' I say, in what I hope is a soothing way. Mother Mo, being the calm one again. 'Well, first thing is to look for the radio. Then we'll see if we can get out of here today.'

'Right.'

James is the first to stand, galvanised by the direction. 'I'll look in the lounge,' he says.

'I'll take the kitchen,' Kira mutters. 'God knows I need to be on my own for a bit.'

'Gen, Lucas, why don't you two take the cottage,' I say. 'Jess and I will have a look in the lamp room.'

Jess glances at me like a rabbit caught in full beams but I grip her hand tightly. Everybody gets up and begins to head out. There's a weird tension in the air. It's like a ringing sensation; like somebody's just hit a massive gong and we're all stupefied. But it's good to have something to do.

Kira switches the lights on as she leaves, one by one, until the whole lighthouse ground floor is illuminated. I wonder if anybody will be able to see us from the mainland. If anybody is out on the water today. Though with the rain pounding like that I don't know why they would be.

And I have to admit I'm nervous. If we don't find the radio . . .

'What if we don't find it?' Jess asks. It's almost as if she's read my mind.

I turn to face her, a tight smile on my face. 'We will,' I say.

\* \* \*

246

We search the lighthouse top to bottom. The lamp room feels weirdly empty, after downstairs being so full of us. Jess clings to my hand the whole way up and won't even let go when we get up there. Everything is as still and dark as it has been the entire time, punctuated only by the sweeping, blinding light over the ocean.

'It'll be fine,' I say.

'It's not the radio that scares me,' Jess murmurs.

She's stopped in the middle of the space between the lamp and the window. Outside the rain rages, gusts of wind blowing smatterings of water in loud pops that feel precariously like gunfire. Even though I know it's ridiculous, I flinch.

'Don't,' I say softly.

'If there *is* somebody here . . .'

'Jess, honestly. Let's just focus on getting home, okay?'

'That's just it, Mo.' Jess turns to me and her eyes are wet. She blinks the tears away, almost as if she's embarrassed, but more well as soon as they fall. 'What if we can't? There's somebody here. I had a horrible feeling. I knew I wasn't getting scared over nothing, and everybody made me feel silly—'

'It *was* over nothing,' I say. 'Just Gen's stories. I'm half convinced that James dreamed the whole thing. We have no evidence.'

'The mirror? The lipstick?'

'It could still have been James,' I shrug, trying to remain nonchalant about this whole thing. 'Maybe he did it in his sleep.'

'Are you kidding me? Mo, that's weak even from you.'

'I know.' I sigh, but it's tight and makes my throat wobble nervously. 'I'm freaked out too, but getting upset isn't going to solve anything.'

'I'm not trying to solve anything. I just wanted to talk to you.' Jess lets go of my hand for the first time and wanders right up to the glass. The ocean looks vast and impenetrable from up here, like a wall of blue so dark it's black. The clouds are thick and heavy, and it feels much later than mid afternoon.

'Talk,' I say softly.

'I'm scared.' Jess doesn't turn back towards me but I can feel the way her voice reaches for me, as it always has. 'If something is going on here – if James is right and this woman is here – and she's angry . . . If that's true, then we're both here.'

'We're here together.'

'We're both here. And Emma isn't.' Jess turns now and she's stopped crying, but her expression is deadly serious. 'Did we really consider this? What happens if we get hurt – if both of us get hurt?'

'Jess, this is ridiculous.'

'Stop telling me I'm being ridiculous!' she exclaims. 'Stop it. I know you're trying to calm me down, but it's not working. It never works. It just makes me feel like I can't talk to you about things.'

I flinch, but this time it's not the rain. Not the noise. It's the fact that Jess is right.

'I'm trying to help,' I argue, but it's half-hearted.

'I know. But I'm not a kid who needs to be protected. Not all the time, at least. I need to be able to talk to you.'

'I get it. I get that you're worried, but right now isn't—'

'It's the perfect time to talk about it,' Jess cuts me off. Her hands are on her hips and I know I've lost. She *is* right. 'What happens if we're both here and something bad

248

happens? We haven't got anything in place. Whose parents will look after her?'

'Jess, we can talk about this when we get home.'

'I know we can,' Jess says firmly. 'But we can also talk about it now. There isn't a radio in here—'

A shout from downstairs stops Jess in her tracks, the moment scattering like grains of sand. She lets out a huff of frustration. But her expression has changed. She no longer looks as afraid. As if by taking control she's been able to think clearly.

'Come on,' I say. 'Let's go home.'

As we head back down the stairs Jess doesn't take my hand, but she's not avoiding me. We stumble into the lounge, where Kira is holding the radio triumphantly.

'Next to the fucking matches,' she says, glaring at James. As though if he'd just done as he was told on Friday night we could have avoided all of this.

Maybe she's right.

'Okay,' I say. 'Anybody know how to work one of these?'

It's a bulky set, black and boxy with dials like I've never seen before. If I squint it looks a bit like the radios we have in the auction house, but I've never had to use one so that doesn't exactly help us.

'I can have a swing at it,' Genevieve says. Her hair is wet from the rain and she's quieter than usual, as though she and Lucas have had words while we were all searching. Like us. I guess the tension is getting to everybody. So far she's seemed so entirely unfazed by anything that it still shocks me when she's scared – like right now.

Kira hands her the radio without saying anything and we all watch patiently as she inspects it. There's a small flashing green light in the corner and I focus on that. *Blink*

*blink blink*. Genevieve turns one of the dials on the top and the radio lets out a stream of static. She flicks through what appear to be several channels, but it's just more of the same: a faint *hsssssss* that sounds like the rain on the glass sunroom roof.

'Don't suppose there were any instructions about finding the right channels,' Genevieve says.

Kira shakes her head. 'Nothing with the radio at least.'

'Did they send you anything with your booking info?' I ask. 'Or anything to the magazine?'

Kira shoots me a glare, even though I'm just trying to help.

'Isn't there a way to tell without instructions?' James asks.

'Not without trying all the settings. I can cycle through, but if we're just getting static that probably means the rain is too strong, or it's windy, or something. Sometimes the weather can really interfere.'

If I didn't know better I'd think Genevieve was pleased with herself. She's lost the look of concern she wore before, now that she's had time to settle herself, and is now watching us all as if she's almost amused. She passes the radio back to Kira and sits down on the side of one of the sofas, folding her arms tight.

'Give it here,' Lucas says. 'Let me have another look.'

He snatches the radio again, flicking between several channels and getting an alternating static-silence-static.

'Not like that,' Kira snaps. 'You're doing it wrong. Let me try again.'

She scoops it out of his hands, fiddling for a long minute while we all sit in silence and listen to the progressively quieter static. The last three channels have nothing at all

– or worse than nothing: the knowledge that there should be *something* and instead there's a hollow kind of blankness.

'Pass it to me.' James takes it but doesn't get anywhere. He presses a button on the side which beeps, and we hold a collective breath but nothing happens. We try to talk; to hold the button for longer. We try the same thing on every channel and still there's nothing. Each try is enough to make my heart sink deeper into my stomach. Eventually James hands the radio back to Kira silently.

'We shouldn't waste the battery,' I point out. 'We don't know how to charge it. Maybe we should leave it a while . . .'

'That's it then?' Jess says. 'We just give up?'

'What now?' James adds.

Suddenly they're all looking at me, like I might know the answer. I raise my palms to the ceiling. I'm not a miracle worker, as much as I've wished otherwise.

'Well we can't just sit here,' Kira says. Her camera is on the table next to her and she runs her fingers over it idly: sadly, almost. I wonder if she's wishing we'd never come here. The radio sits dormant in her lap like some kind of symbol of our collective stupidity.

'Why not?' Lucas shrugs. 'If it's a ghost that's been haunting us we'll get proof if she walks through walls. And if she's not a ghost – and that's assuming James is right and she even exists – then we'll be safe enough here, together. We're meant to be going home tomorrow anyway.'

'You're telling me you feel safe enough to just chill?' Kira asks, incredulity obvious on her face. 'Are you kidding?'

'It seems . . . harmless.' Lucas frowns. I'm not sure if he's telling the truth or not, but he has a point. 'I don't believe in ghosts. And I don't believe in bad luck or vibes or any of that rubbish.' He glances at Gen apologetically but doesn't say anything else.

'Nobody's been hurt,' I add quickly. 'This woman – she didn't hurt James when she saw him. She could have. Right? She could have attacked him and she didn't.'

'Which supports my theory, I think,' Genevieve points out, glaring at Lucas. 'Ghosts aren't what people tend to think. They're more like an energy. They don't just go around hurting people. I wonder if she's somebody who died on the island. They often have this feeling, you know; and you get a sense of them but they don't usually hurt you. It would explain – some things.' She rubs at her arms distractedly, as if remembering something, and then says, 'Anyway it would explain why James had such a hazy memory of the other night.'

'Or he was pissed out of his head,' Lucas shuts her down. 'And he couldn't remember because he was beyond blackout.'

'I really don't like the way you said *usually*,' Jess says. 'What do you mean ghosts don't *usually* hurt anyone?'

Genevieve pulls a face I don't quite understand – thoughtful and a little bemused – but there's a bit of fear there too.

'This isn't a horror movie.' Lucas's frown deepens. 'Stop trying to freak her out, Gen.'

'I'm not.' Genevieve shakes her head. 'I'm just being honest. It does happen sometimes. Particularly if they get angry.'

'I'm happy staying here for the night now that everybody knows,' James says. 'We can . . . barricade ourselves in.' He lets out a bark of laughter that doesn't sound pleasant at all. It sounds close to tears.

'I'm not staying in here with any of you lot.' Lucas has been inching further away from the gathering in the centre of the lounge and he's close to the door now. 'I'm sick of this. It's ridiculous. I'd rather take my chances with a ghost.'

'Lucas,' Genevieve tries.

'No, Gen. You can come to the cottage with me if you want, but if we're staying here another night then I'm going to spend it sleeping and playing on my Switch, thank you.'

'For God's sake, Lucas!' Kira exclaims. 'Will you stop being childish?'

'I'm not being childish,' he says calmly. 'I'm being sensible. Moira, you agree with me, right? There's no sense freaking out over nothing.'

'It's not *nothing*. Somebody broke into the cottage last night, Lucas. Somebody broke a mirror. Somebody threatened James.' Kira shakes her head in disbelief. 'I can't believe you'd write that off. What's to stop it from happening again?'

'You were the one who said you didn't care any more.'

'Guys,' I say.

'Maybe I shouldn't have said that,' Kira continues, oblivious, 'but that doesn't change things—'

'Well maybe it should. If we can't leave, then we have to stay. It's as simple as that.'

'Does anybody want something else to eat?' Jess chimes in meekly. She's closed in on herself and I want to go to her and put my arms around her but I can't. 'We should have lunch. Is anybody hungry? There's still so much food.'

'Guys!' I shout, straining my voice so hard that it breaks, creaking in my throat. I really want a cigarette right about now.

Five pairs of eyes turn to face me. I'm standing in the

middle of the room, I realise. But rather than feeling good, feeling like control, this feels like too much pressure. I exhale through my nose.

'Look, we can yell at each other all we want. We can sit here and do nothing. We can eat – I'm actually desperate for some proper lunch. But none of that will get to the bottom of anything.'

'So what do you suggest?' Lucas snipes. 'Since you know everything.'

I glare at him without feeling.

'Well there's only one solution. If we can't leave, but we don't feel safe staying until we have some answers, then we need to get answers. Which means that we need to make sure James wasn't dreaming.'

Jess shakes her head.

'No,' she says. 'Come on, please let's just stay here.'

James shrinks back.

'We need to find that cave.'

# 28

## *Kira*

The mood in the room immediately turns sour. Worse, even, than before. We all stare at Moira like she's got three heads. The wind is howling outside and the rain is coming down mercilessly now, making the lighthouse feel like the last bastion of safety. Except it isn't safe here. It has never been.

I'd pictured revelry for this afternoon. More board games, charades, another family-style meal and trading stories. I'd hoped that this would set us up for another year, draw us together before adult life split us apart again. Now everything is in tatters. Whatever happens this afternoon I can't picture everybody suddenly relaxing enough for a game of Pictionary before bed.

Lucas won't even look at me and James is acting like he's been hit one too many times to bear. Every noise makes him jump. There's a roll of thunder that would be atmospheric if it didn't make me so bloody nervous. In another life, I'd love this. Now all I can think is that the island is punishing us for being here.

'No,' Lucas says, echoing Jess. Except his answer isn't a

plea; it's a demand. 'Why the hell would I risk myself to go out in this weather?'

'You want to sit here and stew?' I mutter. 'Fine. You can stay here, by yourself.'

'Who says I'll be by myself?'

'I want to see it,' Genevieve says, still thoughtful. 'The cave.' I can't tell what she thinks about all of this, but I know that she's angry. Hurt. I can see it and yet it doesn't make me feel anything. I'm so confused that I've lost the ability to figure out whether I hate her or not, and whether I should back her up or just fend for myself.

'Gen,' Lucas warns. 'You can't be serious.'

'What? You've been teasing me all weekend, but I need to know. If what James is saying is true then somebody, somehow, got hold of my lipstick. It was in my bag, in our *room*. So ghost or not, I'd like some answers.'

'Jess?' Lucas says, turning to her. 'Surely you're not stupid enough to go traipsing down to the beach in this weather? We can stay here, get something to eat.'

Jess glances at Moira, her mind already half made up the second Moira suggested it. She can be independent if she wants but there's no way she'd stay up here without Mo. Moira gives her a reassuring nod and Jess crumbles the rest of the way to acceptance.

'I'm not staying here without Mo,' she says quietly, echoing my thoughts. 'If we all go, surely that's the safest thing to do?'

'I'm not even sure I can find it again,' James reminds us. 'It was dark. I was drunk; I wasn't paying attention to where I was walking. I don't know how I got down there.'

'It's an island.' Moira is calm, like always. Practical. At least when she's like this I can relinquish control, and honestly I'm relieved to just follow. I'm tired of making decisions. I'm tired of getting the blame for making the wrong ones. 'It can't be that hard to find it. You mentioned the shack, so we can start there. And we should go soon so we're back well before it gets dark. I know the weather is bad, but this looks like it'll probably only get worse and I want to get this over with.'

'What about food?' Lucas pushes, but it's clear to everybody that he's lost. Moira and Jess are right. We're safer together, no matter what the truth is; whether it's rain or wind or a maniac ghost. 'All I've had is biscuits.'

'We eat first, then.' Moira begins to tie back her hair, plaiting it off her face and looping it off with a practised hand. Her expression is resolute. 'And when we're finished, we go.'

There's no more argument. Once Lucas realises that he will be entirely alone up here if he stays, he decides to come too. After we eat, some of us hungrier than others, we set about gathering coats and scarves and hats. We've got a torch, and Genevieve has managed to find a bigger lantern as well, just in case we manage to locate the cave. The lantern isn't very bright but it's better than nothing.

It's cold out, but the cold isn't the worst of it. As soon as we all pile out of the door to the lighthouse we're hit by the maelstrom. Stinging rain and salted wind whipped wild. The clouds are thick and dark, the sun firmly behind them. It could be any time of day; could even be the middle of the night for the difference those distant beams of sun make. It seems more like nightfall than five in the afternoon.

'I've got the radio,' Genevieve says, shouting over the wind gusting between the cottage and the lighthouse. 'Just

257

in case there's better signal further up. I assume we're going back towards the shack?'

She points up the hill.

Nobody says otherwise so we set off, trudging in single file against the weather. It's hard work, everything fighting against us. My whole body is stiff and tired, muscles aching from all of the tension. And the fear. I can't deny that it's singing inside me now, all joy sucked away until there's nothing but my wounded pride and the heavy *thump-thump* of fear.

I don't know what to believe. I don't know if James is telling the truth, or if we're all just freaking out over – over what? Even I don't believe James would be capable of fabricating a lie this elaborate just to cover up a prank.

But then perhaps it was never meant to be a joke. Perhaps his night terrors are more than just thrashing on a sofa, terrified shouts in a warm, friendly room. It's not too outlandish to believe he could do some damage without realising it. In which case I don't know whether to be relieved that we're heading out in search of a cave which may or may not exist, or whether I wish we'd all just stayed inside. Either way, I make sure I'm walking behind James, not in front of him.

We work our way up the steadily, gently sloping ground that leads away from the lighthouse. The path is thin, bordered by scrubby grass and weeds that bend wildly in the raging wind. Up ahead I think I can make out a sharper rise in the ground, a hulking shape behind it which must be the shack. I can hardly see, my face so wet and cold, but I can't let it stop me. The sea is black and seems very high. I turn back to the lighthouse briefly, taking in the lights that wink as the wind yanks at my hair. I can see the edge of the porch, where the doors lead out of the sunroom onto the thin back veranda; the waves crash against the cliff and the spray climbs so high it seems to claw at the top of the cliff.

'Kira!' James calls. I turn back and he's stopped, waiting for me.

'I'm coming,' I call, hurrying to catch up so we're not too far behind the others.

'Where now?' Moira asks once we reach the rise where the shack comes fully into view, a crooked building that barely looks like it will withstand this storm. There's a path that runs beyond it, but that heads upwards and then, perhaps, inland.

James stops, breathless. He glances about, taking in the shack, then looking back down the slope. From here, it looks like the lighthouse is perched right on the edge of the cliff, poised, waiting to jump in and abandon us.

'I don't know,' James says. 'Maybe we should split up?'

'No,' I say quickly. 'Nobody's splitting up. We should try to get down to the beach from here. What happens if we walk that way?'

I point towards the cliff just beyond the shack to the left. It's not a sheer drop like outside the lighthouse. It seems to roll downwards more softly through tufts of grass and bracken, though it's hard to make out with the weather battering us from all sides, even in the shelter of the shack.

'Worth a shot,' Moira says.

James baulks, but doesn't have a chance to properly argue because Moira starts walking, Jess behind her. Lucas shoves his hands deep into his pockets and bows his head into the wind. Genevieve, I notice, has handed Lucas the lantern and has her phone out, holding it up high as if she's trying to get signal.

'Anything?' I call.

She shakes her head.

'Radio's still static, too.'

As we start walking, it appears I'm right. The island slopes steeply, but not impossibly so. It's slippery, and difficult with the wind and the rain, but there's a sandy path carved into the earth. We head down one by one, grappling with long roots to hold onto, clouds of sand and dirt disintegrating underfoot.

Jess stumbles, letting out a whimper as she skids into Moira and the two of them are knocked off their feet.

They disappear from my vision and I let go of the roots I'm holding onto for one heart-stopping second, almost falling myself, knees buckling as my toes scrabble for purchase in my walking boots.

'Guys!'

Lucas leaps ahead, dropping the lantern and scrambling down after them while the rest of us try to catch up. My hands are sore, my legs aching and trembling from the effort. But then I'm down on the sand and Lucas is there with both of them.

Jess is crying, Moira's arm around her as they sit on the sand.

'I'm fine,' Jess sobs, shaking her hands out. 'I don't even know why I'm crying.'

'Jesus, I thought you'd really hurt yourself,' James says breathlessly, skidding next to me with the lantern in his hands.

'As if you care,' Lucas snaps.

James looks like Lucas has said something abominable. 'What?'

'This is such horse shit and you know it. How can you

drag us down here and then act like you care about any of us?'

'I didn't want to come here!' James exclaims. 'I didn't want to say anything at all. We're not in any more danger now than . . .' He stops as if realising how stupid it would be to continue, his cheeks flushed with more than the cold.

'Exactly. If you'd told us yesterday then this wouldn't have happened, because we wouldn't still be here. This is your fault.' Lucas holds out a hand for Moira to take, and then one for Jess, who limps up and brushes her hands off on her jeans.

'All right,' Moira says. 'Enough. It's okay. We're all wound up and nervous but we're okay. Jess isn't too badly hurt, right?'

Jess shakes her head, wiping her face with her coat sleeve.

'I'm fine,' she says. 'Just the shock.'

'Right. So, what now?' I say.

Finally we look around. We've come to rest at the bottom of the steep hill, a narrow sandy beach stretching to our left and right. Left would eventually lead back to the dock, past the bottom of the lighthouse, but I know that the beach must end somewhere, or else there would be sand at the base of the lighthouse itself and there's only cliff and water that I've seen.

To the right the beach stretches, still thin and pale gold, curving around the island, which is vicious in places, with jagged rocks cropping out precariously, and wild, scrubby grass hiding God-knows-what. The waves on the beach are steady, foaming at the mouth, ready to swallow us up.

'Which way?' Moira demands.

James tilts his head. Left. Right.

'I honestly can't remember,' he says.

Moira looks at me and I know why. There's something in James's face that we all recognise, some way that his expression has seemed to close off. It's how he's been acting all weekend. But now we know. He can't lie any more – not about this.

'Which way, James,' I say. Not a question. The stress and anger must show because James glances skywards before pointing.

He picks the path that heads towards the lighthouse. The path that must end in a dead end. The path that ends in a cave.

'That's settled then,' I say quietly. 'Come on. We need to go before the weather gets any worse. That lantern is fucking useless.'

James holds it up to inspect and notices what I've already seen. It's cracked, the plastic glass broken. And the light has gone out.

'What happens if the tide changes?' Jess asks.

'I don't know,' I say. 'So we'd better be quick.'

Genevieve, who has been silent until now, holds her phone up high again, but I can tell from her face that it's useless. Down here, sheltered from the wind, I can hear the hiss and crackle of the radio, plain as day.

Nothing.

Whatever happens down here, we're not getting off this island today.

# 29

## *Genevieve*

Kira shoves James to get him started, and the rest of us fall into line behind her, keeping in almost single file except for Moira, who helps a limping Jess. I am enveloped in the sound of the radio – a consistent static hum at my hip – and the rustling of damp sand underfoot.

We walk without speaking, the motivation that got us down here evaporating with every step. The others seem terrified but I don't know how I feel. Perhaps we might be getting closer to finding out the source of the strange energy I've been feeling all weekend.

I don't know what we'll find, but I'm almost excited.

I've got my phone in my hand, constantly having to wipe the screen to keep it clear. There's no signal at all down here, but I've still got the pages loaded in my browser from the other day and I run through them, searching for some kind of clue. Did anybody mention a woman who died on the island? Did any of them specifically mention ghosts? But it's hard to see with the rain; the wind making my eyes narrow to slits to keep out the sand; the radio crackling away like a fire at my heels.

The rain picks up again as we reach a wider section of beach where the cliff stands tall at our backs and the clouds are low and angry. James begins to slow down, and that's how I know we're almost there. And it's also how I know that James remembers more than he's been telling us. He knows exactly where the cave is, and he's afraid.

'Oh.' Jess stops walking and I almost crash right into her back. I drop my phone and scramble to pick it up.

Then I see it. There's a section of the island that stretches further into the water: from above, it probably seems like a bundle of grassy earth. But from down here it looks more like a mouth, yawning and dark, over fifteen feet tall at the entrance I bet. What weak daylight there is seems to be being swallowed into the gaping hole, a black maw into which the sand and stones disappear. I'm glad we brought the torch.

'Shit,' Lucas says. He turns to me. I shrug. Lucas doesn't really care what I think about this, so I don't speak, but this does mean something. It means that at least some of James's story is true.

Further ahead I can see the way the island creeps further out, the lighthouse standing on a pinnacle where the point of the land juts into the sea. A warning for all sailors heading this way: *land approaches*. Above, right above our heads, is the path we've been walking this weekend, from the lighthouse to the shack and back again. Traipsing back and forth, blindly. And right underneath our feet this whole time . . .

The cave.

'I don't want to go in there,' Jess says. She's holding onto

Moira's arm tight, hugging it like she might never let go. Even James looks reluctant. 'I don't care what I said before. I – I can't do it. God, just the thought of all of that rock over my head . . .' She looks like she's about to lose it; Moira holds her tight.

'James. Did you go inside on Friday?' Kira asks.

James shakes his head.

'No. No, I was out here. I don't . . .' He stops, clearly realising it's pointless to lie any more. 'I made it to about here. I could see the lights overhead, the lighthouse up there. Everything seemed so dreamlike, I told you. I just stood here for God knows how long, staring and staring at that – hole. And then . . . I blinked and she was there.'

'You're sure she came from the cave?' Moira asks.

'Almost certain, but I guess I could be wrong. But where else? I'd walked this way and the beach ends up there . . . I can't see where else she'd have come from.'

'What did she look like?' I ask. 'What was she wearing?'

'It was dark. I don't know.' This time he isn't lying. 'I'm not entirely sure. Lightish hair, I guess; skinny. Baggy clothes. Her voice was rough, but it wasn't deep. That's all I know. It was too dark and she was all in my face, yelling, too close for me to take it in, and then too far away, and I was drunk, so drunk. And then she was gone and I didn't . . . I didn't stick around long enough to see where she went. I just . . . I just went back. And I tried to pretend I hadn't seen anything at all. It felt like she was there. All the way back. But she wasn't. She can't have been. I don't know.'

'I'm not going in there,' Jess says again, calmer now. 'We don't know what might happen. We can't even call for help if somebody gets hurt. What if there's a pool in there? What if somebody drowns?'

Moira pulls herself free from her wife's grasp and squeezes her shoulders tight.

'You don't have to go in,' she says. 'You and Lucas stay out here. Keep an eye out, make sure that we're okay. And if anything happens – you'll have the radio.'

She gestures that I should hand it over. And honestly, I'm glad to be rid of the thing, hissing and spitting like that. I miss the peace and tranquillity of before, back when it was just energy – at least for us, if not James. Even the excitement I felt as we came onto the beach was better than the nervous bubbling I'm feeling in my belly now. It's starting to feel like fear, even though I know there's nothing to be afraid of. Ghosts don't hurt people. James was probably just dreaming.

But, of course – what if she isn't a ghost?

'So the rest of us are going in then,' Kira murmurs. She wipes a hand over her forehead to clear the rain that's dripping under her hood.

'We're going to have to.'

'Oh for goodness' sake,' I say. I'm not waiting around for the rest of them to make their minds up. 'I'm going in. Give me the torch.'

I march across the sand, aware that the others are watching me, and then I hear James hurry to my side. The others – Moira and Kira, anyway – follow. I'm half convinced that we'll get in here and there will be nothing except stagnant water and seagull droppings, but we won't find out by standing around.

As we reach the mouth of the cave I realise that I was wrong before. The opening might be fifteen feet high, but it rapidly gets narrower. Ten feet, then seven. Lucas would be lucky to even fit. The walls are slick and wet from the rain at the entrance, but they seem to dry out as we go further in, the torchlight bouncing off them in shallow pools.

'Watch your heads,' I murmur. My voice echoes.

It's not as cold in here as I thought it would be. Not as cold as the beach. The entrance to the cave isn't just narrowing in height but in width, too, and it isn't long before I could touch both sides without even stretching my arms all the way out if I wanted to. I've never been claustrophobic but I can feel it now, the sensation of all that earth and rock pressing in over my head, waiting to bury me.

I let out a breath, which turns into a small laugh. And I hear it echo in Kira, who releases a whoosh of air.

'I don't want to be here,' James says quietly. 'We shouldn't be here. She told me to leave. She told me if anybody found out about her—'

'Shh,' I hiss. He shuts up.

The path is narrow but fairly straight. The sand is waterlogged underfoot but soon progresses to stone, polished pebbles and larger, more jagged rocks that don't look inviting. I'm careful to avoid them and whisper to the others to watch their step.

And then the path starts to widen again. It's not far enough in that I can no longer hear the roar of the sea and the whipping of the wind, but the light is gone, only my torch beam and the light from James's phone behind me.

And then it opens up into a bigger space, an antechamber of sorts. A proper cavern, maybe fifteen feet high again, a strange oval shape. The energy in here is wild. I can feel it like a flame in my chest. It feels like life, like darkness. Like sadness. I've never felt anything like it.

My torch beam picks out sparkling flecks in the dark and grainy rock, and then I flick it down.

Kira is beside me. I can smell her body cream, feel her warmth more than I can see her. She makes another gasping sound, but this time it's not laughter.

'Do you see that?' she says.

'What?' Moira asks.

'It's—'

I train my torch back down again, following the line of the wall until I find the ground, which is uneven in places but packed with dry sand. And then – blankets. Pillows. An old cast iron pan, and the candlestick from the shack.

My heart leaps but it's not excitement now. It's a bone-deep feeling, regret and fear mingling to make my blood freeze sluggish in my veins.

Not a ghost.

'Somebody has been living here.'

# 30

## *Moira*

'You have got to be fucking kidding me,' Kira mutters. 'This is . . . What the fuck is this?'

I think of my wife, keeping vigil outside, and I'm so impossibly glad she didn't follow us in.

James swings the faint light of his phone torch back and forth, picking up detail after detail. The blankets are thin and moth-eaten but there's a bunch of them, layered thick. I force my eyes to peer into the dimness, to search every roll and divot in the cloth to make sure there isn't a sleeping soul nestled somewhere deep inside them. The thought makes me feel a bit sick, that we're even in here, that we're intruding. That I don't feel any less scared than I did before.

There's a faint smell of burning in here and my eyes find the skinny pillar of a candle poking out of a small metal candlestick. I cross to it, my boots kicking up dry sand, and up close I can see that I'm right. It hasn't been extinguished long, the wax still cooling and the scent of smoke still rife in the air.

'Whoever was here hasn't been gone long,' I say.

'What the fuck,' Kira repeats. 'Who . . .?'

'Somebody's been living here.' James shuffles from one foot to the other. '*She* has been living here. This whole time. I bet she's been here for ages. The builders, those stories they had about stuff going missing. I bet it was her.'

'Who is she, though?' Kira demands. 'Why the fuck don't the owners know about her? You can't just – you can't invite people to an uninhabited island if it's not fucking uninhabited!' She's shouting now, her voice echoing, and I rush over to her.

'Kira,' I soothe. 'Just calm down a second.'

'I'm so fucking calm I can see the future,' she spits.

'I know. And it's – it's unbelievable. But shouting won't help.'

I don't say it, but we don't know for sure yet that we're on our own. Genevieve continues to scan the shape of the room with her torch but until I know that there's no other way out of here, a crack or crevice we haven't noticed, I don't want us to make too much noise.

'Just calm down,' I say. 'Breathe. Let's look at this logically. We don't know that this woman – whoever she is – is dangerous.'

'Not dangerous?' Kira scoffs. 'She broke into the cottage. She smashed the mirror.'

'And she didn't hurt anybody.' I clench my fists, trying to fight the nerves that are desperate to make my hands shake. 'She told James to leave, she threatened him, but she never touched him. Did she, Jay?'

James shakes his head, a trembling silhouette in the darkness behind his torch beam.

'No.'

'Exactly.'

Genevieve wanders towards one of the walls and I watch her with half my attention, the other half fixed firmly on Kira, who looks like she's about to break down into a puddle of tears.

'Look,' I say. 'This is weird. We know this is weird. But . . . it's human. Right? It's not ghosts. We're not being haunted by some . . . some . . . sailor's widow or lighthouse keeper's mother. This is just – human.'

Kira blinks slowly, her dark eyes very shiny in the dim light that criss-crosses back and forth as Genevieve kicks up blankets. She picks up something thin and white and holds it between two fingers, inspecting it.

'That's what I'm afraid of,' Kira says quietly. 'Ghosts I can deal with. Ghosts aren't *real*.'

'And we'll deal with this.'

'Guys,' Genevieve says. She lifts the object up to her torch beam. It's a cigarette. I feel a tremble in my gut. It's the kind of cigarette I would smoke if I was still smoking. The kind I bought and then couldn't find.

'And this.' James picks up a book. Red, clothbound. Hardback. The book James has been leaving lying around the lounge all weekend.

'Fuck that,' Kira mutters. 'Maybe we don't know that she's dangerous, but does this seem like the actions of somebody who isn't unstable?' She turns back to me again. 'Does it? Stealing stuff? Breaking in and scaring the shit out of us? James said she was acting wild, threatened. *Threatening.*'

I can't argue.

'Let's just keep looking,' Genevieve says. 'Maybe we'll find something useful.'

James grunts and we fan out, kicking up more blankets.

I discover a whole set of cutlery, old but still in good condition. There's a cast iron skillet and a big, heavy black pot that's filled with water, a metal cup and a Thermos-style bottle next to it that looks new.

'Wonder if she took that when they were having the renovations done,' I say. 'Some of this stuff looks new, but the rest of it . . . I dunno, it looks really old.'

Kira doesn't answer but she holds up a pair of rusted scissors in one hand. I feel a shudder of something like revulsion run through me. I can't explain it but the idea of Kira and the others touching all this stuff when it doesn't belong to them – when we don't even know who it does belong to – feels incredibly wrong.

'I'm not sure we should be in here,' I say. 'Like, I want to have a good look around like you guys do but it's clear she isn't here. It feels wrong. Intruding—'

'Bullshit,' Kira says. 'She's been intruding on us all weekend. This is just payback.'

Genevieve shakes her head. 'It's not about paying anybody back,' she points out, her voice low. 'I just want some answers. Don't you?'

'We don't even have proof it was her,' I say. 'This feels – it's just wrong. Okay? I'm just saying how I feel.'

'If it's not her, then who could it be?' James gestures at the detritus of human life around us. 'It's not like there are a hundred people on the island. There's us, and there's her.'

'That we know of.'

My words feel heavy, and having spoken them I realise that it's what I'm really afraid of. It's scary that this woman has been here all weekend, perhaps taunting us, trying to make us leave. But what proof do we have that she's the only one?

'Mo, what are you saying?' Kira asks.

'I'm saying that we don't know for sure that she's the only person here.' I mirror James's gesture, picking out piles of blankets, pillows, genderless clothes: shirts, trousers and sack-like dresses that look old-fashioned, as though they once belonged to somebody a long while dead. 'Look, none of this stuff says it's just one person living here. Jesus. I'm just pointing out that we don't know for sure. It wasn't long ago that we were thinking maybe the guy who brings the boat might have had something to do with it. Now we're just ready to write everything off as being her? She could be in as much danger as us if there's somebody else hanging around.'

James looks like he might be sick. He's dropped the corner of the blanket he was lifting, exposing a sheet of blue tarp, and he folds his arms.

'That's not funny, Mo,' he says.

'I'm not trying to be funny. I don't want to stay here. Please, let's just go back to the lighthouse and try to get hold of somebody with a boat. Surely we must be able to get the emergency coastguard somehow? Do we have flares or anything? I don't like this at all.'

'I don't think we need to rush off,' Genevieve says quietly. 'But you might be right. We don't have any proof. And that shack – it looks like more people used to live there, doesn't it?'

'Exactly,' I say. 'Surely that alone is reason to leave?'

'We don't know why she left the shack though,' Genevieve says. She doesn't look as afraid as the rest of us: more thoughtful, although the glimmer of fear is there under it all. She is still inspecting the cave, her torch beam picking out a rug that's been placed carefully over a thin, flat rock,

273

a pile of leaves stacked there beside a wooden board with a knife laid carefully on top.

'We don't know that she ever lived in the shack,' I reply. 'And what does it matter?'

'I think she did.' Genevieve points at the candlestick. 'I saw that there. The other night. I don't know why I remember it but I do. And when I was there earlier I realised it was gone. Look at this stuff. It looks like stuff you'd have in a cottage like that. Some of it's fairly rudimentary but the rest has been well-used.'

'Well there's nothing to say she didn't steal it,' I point out.

'Is it even stealing if nobody owns it any more?' James says. 'Probably she just saw it and took it.'

'But then why not stay there?' Genevieve is pacing back and forth, nudging things with her toes and bending down occasionally for a closer look while the rest of us stand clustered by the tunnel back to the beach. I can feel a cool breeze snaking down my spine, my clothes drying slowly and crisping up with the salt from the air.

'You mean, if she was going to steal things anyway, why not just stay in the shack and use it?' I ask.

'Exactly. If she had the motivation to steal, she'd also have the motivation to find somewhere warm and dry to sleep. This is fine, but it's not exactly cosy. And it'll only be worse in the winter. Now, if you took all this stuff up there and set it up in the cottage, I think that could be quite a nice life. There are probably rabbits and birds on the island you could eat. Plenty of fish. You could make a comfortable life here.'

'And yet she's living in a cave.' James is shivering now, but whether with fear or the cold I can't easily tell. I'm sure we're all tormented by the same combination and it's impossible to tell which is winning. 'So there must be a reason for her being here and not up there.'

'That's exactly it,' Genevieve repeats. 'So why hide like that? And why does she want us to leave so badly?'

'And you think we'll find answers in here?' Kira says. Her voice is cold but it's tinged with curiosity.

'I don't care,' I say. 'Don't you realise how dangerous this is? We need to go back to the lighthouse and try to get home.'

'You were all for coming in here before.' Genevieve is frowning in confusion. 'I don't get it. Why the one-eighty?'

'That's before we found *this*.' I point indiscriminately. I can feel the panic worming up inside me right now and it feels like seaweed, slimy and thick. 'Lucas and Jess are out there waiting for us. Can we at least go out and tell them that we're okay?'

'I just want to finish looking,' Genevieve says.

'No. Okay, you know what, you can do that. But I'm done. I've seen everything I need to see. I stand by what I said, Kira. There's no evidence that whoever James saw on Friday is dangerous, but that doesn't mean I'm going to dig around here in somebody's life to try and figure out what on earth has driven them to live in a *cave*.'

'Oh.'

James has abandoned Kira and me by the exit and walked over to where a small part of the cave wall juts out in an overhang, the rock worn smooth by the years. I can make out more blankets beneath it, burrowed up tight like this is where somebody sleeps, safely cocooned against the wall. My panic surges again and I don't want to see it, don't want to take any more fear in.

But then he lifts up what he has seen and I don't know how to feel.

It's a drawing, beautifully etched in charcoal shades of pencil on a crinkled piece of lined paper that looks like it was just torn out of a jumbo notepad. The perfect lines of the lighthouse stretch across the middle, top to bottom. To the side there is the cottage, and beyond that the hill that leads to the shack. The ocean looks peaceful, perfectly calm against a pale sky. There's real love there, a real sense of longing.

And for a second I'm in awe. Until I realise what this might mean. It feels dangerous, like standing on the edge of a cliff and looking down into the roiling water. It feels like hidden depths. If somebody could love the lighthouse this much, and didn't want anybody else to experience it . . .

What would it make them do to protect it?

# 31

## *Kira*

By the time Genevieve has had her fill of the cave I'm itching to leave too. Moira is right. It does feel wrong to be in here. This is somebody's home, no matter what we might think about that. But there is anger, and there is fear, and they both war inside me right now. Guilt barely factors in.

Genevieve bites her lip as she moves past me and leads the way out, the torch beam bouncing so much it makes me nauseous as she practically jogs towards the entrance. The ground feels much more uneven now, slippery, and I start to worry. What if the tide is coming in? What if the others have had to leave us? Or worse, what if *she's* on the beach?

But they're only the same puddles that we trod through on the way in, and it's only the same horrid weather, gusty and wet and wild. There is nothing to take away the sour panic that bites my tongue. The pressure builds inside my body, a storm in my rib cage, and I almost wish she was there, that the danger was tangible and proven, so that at least I might stop feeling like I'm losing my grip on reality.

Moira is close behind me, eager to get out, and when

she spots Jess on the beach she lets out a gasp of relief and runs to her. The freezing air burns my lungs.

Lucas looks at Genevieve, who pulls her phone out immediately with her free hand and taps the screen, although it doesn't look like she's having any more luck than before. When Gen doesn't look at him, Lucas turns to me, a question mark in his gaze.

'There's a whole fucking house inside there,' I blurt.

'What?' Jess's eyes are like dinner plates, wide and round with fear. 'What do you mean?'

'Somebody has definitely been living there,' Moira murmurs, so quiet the wind whips her words away. She raises her voice as she goes on: 'Blankets, clothes, knives and forks, some of my cigarettes. A whole life.'

Jess doesn't say anything, just grabs hold of Moira and holds her tight, her head tucked under her wife's chin. Moira doesn't move, just clings to her and stands silent.

'How long?' Lucas asks.

'What do you mean?'

'How long have they been living there?' His eyebrow is raised in that cocky way I used to find so irresistible, but I think he's more afraid than he'll let on.

'I don't know,' I say. 'It's hard to tell. Could be weeks, months – years, even. Some of the clothes look really old.'

'She looked . . . I don't know.' James shrugs. 'She looked normal? I didn't think . . .'

'What do you mean normal?' Genevieve mutters. 'You mean she didn't look *homeless*?'

'Well, yeah.' James's face colours, and it's almost a relief to hear the same old tone to their voices, even if it's a calling out. Even if it's embarrassment and anger. It's better than fear.

'You didn't have a torch on Friday night,' Moira says. 'How could you even tell what she looked like?'

'Oh I don't know.' James groans. 'I'm sorry. I didn't mean anything by it, just . . . I'm just trying to say . . . She scared me, right, but I thought she was – Jesus, I thought she was a *ghost*. Like, I actually got that into my head. She was just an apparition. She was so close but I couldn't really *see* her, like she was – greyed out. I guess the northern lights, the moon . . . I even thought I saw her other times through the weekend, but then she was always gone before I could confirm it was her. And on Friday she didn't attack me. She could have, if she was as scared as me, but she didn't get close enough. It wasn't like she was . . .'

'Feral?' Jess suggests, peeling back from Moira's chest. 'You mean she didn't seem dangerous. Even though she scared you half to death, even though you're afraid enough that we're here right now.'

'Yes? No. I don't know!' James flings his arms up. 'There was this . . . feeling? Right down in the pit of my stomach, that something wasn't right. I wasn't scared at first, just curious, so I tried to get closer to see if I was seeing things. But then I just got this horrible feeling. I went all cold and panicky. It was like my brain was telling me to get away. That she wasn't entirely – human. Like a wild animal, you know?'

'I don't think you can tell how long she's been here,' I say to Lucas again. 'But I do think she's probably been living in there a while. There's all sorts of stuff inside. Pots and pans, a candle, stuff for everyday life.'

'Did you have any luck with the radio?' Moira asks urgently. 'Any signal or anything while we were inside?'

Lucas shakes his head.

'Nothing,' Jess says. 'No phone signal, no radio signal. Just static and wind and rain and I'm actually freezing.' She looks it, too: her cheeks are chapped pink and the rest of her face is alarmingly blue-tinged.

'So, what do we do now?' Lucas asks. 'I don't know what we're meant to do. It's not like she's hurt us, but I don't like it. This place is supposed to be deserted, right?'

'Right,' I say. 'And the thing is, we don't know if it's one person living there, or more. That's what's freaking me out the most. There's no way to tell.'

'There were men's clothes in there, but women's stuff too. Shirts and jackets and dresses. It all looked old.' Moira stares at the entrance to the cave. I can feel it behind me, burning into my back. 'I don't want to get worked up about it, because we need to stay calm. But it's really getting to me.'

'It's possibly just the clothing that was available,' I suggest. 'If she's taken stuff from the shack, from whoever left it there, and brought it down here, it makes sense that she'd just take whatever fits.'

'Why doesn't she just live there?' Jess asks. 'In the shack. If she's taking stuff from there and using it? I don't get it.'

It's the same question, and we still don't have an answer. Because that feels like the crux of it. If I had somewhere warm to live, even if it was old and rickety, or a cave? I know what I'd pick.

'We don't know,' I say. 'Unless—'

'Unless she's trying to stay hidden.' Lucas shields his eyes from the rain, peering up the cliff face as though he might be able to see the shack above us. I imagine it, leaning into the wind, and shudder. 'When the people came to the island to renovate – I wonder if she left then. If she was scared.'

'That doesn't really answer the main question, though.' Genevieve puts her phone away and turns back to the rest of us, a frown on her face. 'My main question isn't why did she leave the shack, or why she's living in a cave, or even how long she's been hiding. That's all important, but honestly what I want to know is how did she get here in the first place?'

We keep trying the radio as we begin to head towards the slope that will take us back to the lighthouse. The static is so persistent that it's doing my head in and I'm this close to smashing the thing on the rocks when we reach the sandy path up the hill where Jess fell. She's still limping, worse now than before, as if standing in the cold has made her leg seize up. I'm not filled with hope that any of us will make it back up the path, never mind her.

'Do you think you can make it?' Moira asks her when we get very close.

From down here it looks much steeper, and the rain that's pelting has made the sand even wetter than before. Water runs in rivulets between the tufts of yellow grass and roots from the trees that grow up near the wooden shack.

Jess's lips narrow.

'I'll have to,' she says.

'There's got to be another way around.' Lucas backs up, as if that will help him to see better, but I'm sure all he gets is more of a glimpse of grass and sand and dark, angry sky.

'James?' Moira asks.

'Don't ask me. I do not remember getting back to the lighthouse.'

'You said that last time,' I mutter. 'Forgive us if we don't believe you.'

There's still something about this I don't like, and the further away we get from the cave the less I like the dark turn of my thoughts. James says there is a woman. And there's certainly evidence that *somebody* has been living there. But . . . if she exists, if he's telling the truth, then why haven't any of the rest of us seen her? If she wants us to leave, then why hasn't she just asked us? Why trust James, drunk and stupid with tiredness, to heed her warning?

It's not that I think James is lying. I just . . . don't trust him enough any more to believe it. I can't push aside the feeling that's been growing inside of me the last couple of days, of something growing in this place. Something dark and rotten. A stain spreading across the island. It's not something I can explain, but I can *feel* it. And all I know is that James hasn't been himself lately.

'I can do it,' Jess says firmly. 'I'll just go up last and maybe you can help me . . .'

But Moira isn't listening. I follow her gaze, round the edge of the island where the beach follows the curve. She looks like she's thinking furiously.

'Maybe there's another way,' she says. 'Maybe . . .'

Standing like this, the rain pounding, the wind howling, it's hard to think. We're huddled together in something of a circle, all six of us. Genevieve is quiet, but at least she's finally given up and put her bloody phone away. Lucas is staring at Jess, and I wonder if he's sizing her up, trying to figure out if he could carry her. But it's ridiculous. He maybe could have ten years ago, but years of office living and Netflix, even alongside a monthly gym direct debit, mean

I'm not sure he could now. At least not for long. And it would definitely be dangerous.

'We need to make a decision,' Moira says. 'Either the rest of you go up and Jess and I try to figure out another way, or . . .'

'Or we all stay down here together and find another way up.' Lucas is solemn.

'Fucking hell,' I mutter. But they're right. And would any of us feel safe splitting up right now? We've all seen enough horror movies to know that's a bad plan.

It feels like it's decided and I feel a swell of panic overtake me. We were so close to getting back to the lighthouse, and now . . . it's like it's been snatched away.

'I could go up to the cottage,' Genevieve says, hesitant but growing more convinced all the time. 'I could take the radio.'

'Why on earth would you do that?' Lucas turns on her. 'Really?'

'I know how badly you all want to leave,' she says calmly. 'I don't exactly think it's the best plan but maybe it would be better, if – if there's no way up. If we're all together and we get stuck down here and the weather gets worse, that's not exactly safe. I'm sure I could climb up there. I can go and try to find a rope, even.'

I can't help the laughter that bursts from me. It's not funny. Nothing about this is funny, but I can't control myself.

'It's not safe!' I exclaim.

'Well, okay.' Genevieve shrugs. 'I'm just thinking about this logically. We didn't try the radio from the top of the lighthouse. Maybe we should. Maybe there'll be a radio signal from that high up even if the phones are no good up there. And the sooner we can get through to anybody the better.'

I can see the indecision on Lucas's face and know it's mirrored in my own.

'It's not safe,' I say again, this time quieter.

Lucas opens his mouth to say something and then clamps it shut. And then James nods his head.

'Maybe she's right,' he says. 'The quicker we can get somebody to come and help us, the quicker we can get away from here. And like, I could go too so she's not on her own?'

'I don't like it,' I blurt. I want, immediately, to take it back, but I carry on. 'I don't want us to split up.'

'I'll go instead,' Lucas says.

'No.' James shakes his head. 'I'm not being funny, but I'm smaller than you. If somebody needs to carry Jess then it's gotta be you. I've got no hope.'

There's silence among us as we weigh up the options. Much as I hate to admit it, I think Genevieve is right. I don't like the idea of anybody being on their own – and I don't like the idea of anybody being on their own with James, either – but what else are we going to do? And James is right, too. He's bean-pole skinny with arms like twigs; he'd never be able to carry Jess, even if he had to.

'Maybe I should go with you,' I say.

Genevieve shakes her head. 'No sense all of us going. No offence, but I'm worried that we'll struggle enough getting up there and we're both stronger than you are. It'll be fine.'

I want to argue. I really do. And yet I'm relieved. If Genevieve goes with James, then we can focus on getting back up to the lighthouse our way without having to try to climb up the slope and risk hurting ourselves doing it.

'Do you think you can make it?' I ask. The slope is slick, mud running in rivulets so that the path we came down is barely visible.

'I have three older brothers,' Genevieve says as though that answers it. I think of the yoga, that quiet strength she has in her body that I've been a bit jealous of, and it does make sense. I am tired, worn out from this weekend, but Genevieve still looks fit and strong.

'And you?' I turn to James.

He shrugs. 'I think so. It's worth a shot, right?'

The others say nothing. Not even Moira, who looks sick with guilt but holds onto Jess's arm tightly. It seems a decision has been reached. I want to ask Genevieve if she's sure. I want to ask her if she knows what she's doing, going up there alone with James.

I've always loved James. Not like I loved Lucas, but James is soft and gentle and kind, and for years he was my best friend. But this weekend has reminded me of the darkness of those months after it happened, the violence and the instability and the fear that coiled within me waiting for him to tell Lucas everything. Waiting for that other James to show himself again: wild and angry and unrestrained. He might be telling the truth now. He *probably* is telling the truth. And yet I can't bring myself to believe him completely.

'As long as you're sure,' I say.

Genevieve nods once, firmly, and then reaches out to take the radio from Lucas, clipping it onto her belt. He looks like he's about to say something to her, his whole body rigid, but instead he just crushes her tight to his chest and kisses the top of her head. She lets out a huff of surprise but hugs him back.

James stands awkwardly, waiting until they're done. And then they head for the slope. Genevieve wipes her hands on her leggings and grimaces when they come away wet. She pushes the sleeves of her coat up and breathes deeply, hooking her hands around the first tufts of grass. And then she begins to climb.

The rest of us watch from the beach as she and James make their way up the hill. I can see the strain on James's face, red with exertion as he scrabbles for handholds amongst the grass and roots. Sandy pebbles skid, clumps of dirt tumble under their feet.

We watch until there's little for us to do except panic if they fall, and then we wait another few minutes, hearts pounding and rain clawing at our backs before we start out.

Jess and Moira are slow, but Lucas and I slow down further to give them a moment to check in with each other. Jess looks like she might cry; like she's disappointed that she's held us back and, if I know her at all, angry at herself for not being able to put on a brave face. But I'm not angry at her. In fact, I'm grateful she didn't insist on trying to climb back up with her ankle the way it is. It's not my job to protect everybody now; Genevieve has taken the mantle. Frankly, I'm glad that Gen and James are up there and the rest of us are down here. And I think Moira probably feels the same.

We trudge along the beach, which is empty and seems to go on forever. The wind picks up as we hit a big stretch punctuated only by jagged rocks and seaweed. The sand along here is damp and I suspect the tide comes all the way in here, which does nothing to still the panic inside me. If we are stranded; if Genevieve and James don't come back to help us . . .

Jess and Mo murmur to each other, their words hidden by the roar of the wind. Lucas walks next to me in sullen silence, refusing to even look at me. If not for the tension in the air, the dull ache of my limbs, I might be able to pretend that we're not all terrified right now. I can feel Lucas's anger radiating towards me, as if now he's finally thinking about what we said earlier.

'Are you going to ignore me forever?' I ask.

He says nothing.

'Lucas,' I snap. 'Come on. Don't be a child. It happened so long ago.'

Now he's looking at me. I wish he wasn't.

'Does that matter?' he asks. 'Does it matter whether it was ten years ago or last week? You betrayed me, Kira. With *James* of all people.'

'It wasn't meant to happen.' I'm embarrassed by the thickness of my voice. How can I tell him that he will never make me feel worse about what happened than I already felt? It ruined everything. It was the death knell I heard before he did, and which brought it all skidding down. 'It was a mistake.'

'Right.' Lucas shakes his head. 'Whatever. Now isn't the time to talk about it.'

'Maybe it is, though,' I push, glutton for punishment. I want the wind and the salty air to cleanse me. 'I never meant for it, but it happened and I'm sorry. If it's any consolation I'm pretty sure that's why things didn't work. Between you and me.'

Lucas blinks. 'You think this makes me feel better? You think I ever wanted that?'

'It seemed like it.' I shrug, fighting the tears that well up. 'You wanted to be able to blame me, and now you can.

Anyway, that's all done with. And you've got Genevieve and you guys are perfect.'

Lucas snorts. 'I thought so. But this weekend . . .'

'This weekend is a royal fuck-up,' I say. 'Which is why we need to talk about it. Because I'm scared, Lucas. I – I'm actually scared. It's all my fault, *again*, and I just want to go home.'

Lucas doesn't say anything for a minute, giving me the benefit of pulling myself together before he finally sighs, the wind tearing the sound from his lips.

'I was going to ask her to marry me this weekend,' he says. 'Can you believe it?'

'Why can't you now?'

Lucas rubs his hand over his face, wiping the rain from his cheeks.

'I guess I can.' He scans the beach ahead, and I see what he sees. Long stretches of cliff, dark seaweed, no way up. No way out. And Genevieve and James alone up there, together. 'But we need to get through this first, and I'm scared too.'

# 32

## *Genevieve*

I already regret my bravado. It seemed like a good idea that I go up to the lighthouse, but I realise as I climb, James close behind me, that I wish they'd let me go alone.

The climb is hard. The sandy soil is treacherous, twisting underfoot so many times that I've lost count how often I've burnt my hands grappling for chunks of grass, rocks biting into my palm, roots tangling my fingers.

But we manage it. By the time we reach the top of the hill I'm out of breath, my face dripping with a mixture of sweat and rain that makes me shiver. My legs scream and my arms feel like they're vibrating with the focus it took to claw my way up that hill.

I turn back, giving James my arm. He grabs it, tight. For one stomach-clenching second I feel my feet skid on the wet grass, wonder what it would be like to fall from this height, how badly it would hurt. Then James's fingers sink deep into my skin, bruising hard, and he hauls himself over the final lip, tumbling to his knees and letting out a grunt.

'Fuck,' he pants. 'I thoroughly regret my decision.'

But his attempt at making light of everything just makes it all seem worse. I wipe my hands on my leggings for what seems like the hundredth time today, feeling the damp material cling to my legs. I'm freezing from the waist down and wishing I'd worn thicker trousers.

I head for the shack, and the path that will lead us back to the lighthouse. It takes a lot of effort; my legs are tired from the climb and the ground here is so uneven. But when I reach the path I don't follow it directly down the slope. Instead, I pause.

'Wait, what are you doing?' James asks. 'I thought we were going straight to the lighthouse.'

'We are,' I say. 'But I just need to have another look.'

James runs to catch up to me. I can already feel the wind buffeting us again, clawing and yanking, its fingers nudging at the gap between my coat and my neck, insistent.

'Why?' James demands. 'Why do you need to go back in there? I thought . . .'

I ignore him and start walking again.

I tell myself that I don't have to explain myself to him. But the truth is that I don't know why I need to see inside the shack again, that little wooden cottage that houses so many ghostly memories of people long past. I just know I won't rest until I have.

'Gen,' James tries. 'Come on. We said we were just going to go to the lighthouse.'

'Let me think,' I say.

'Gen—'

I'm already at the door, the sagging porch creaking as I step onto it. Suddenly the wind and the rain drop away and I feel like I can breathe; like I can finally see. The salted air fills my lungs and I inhale deeply, catching whiffs of rot alongside the icy sea air. I'm shivering now, the cold worming deep inside my bones.

Indoors it's dim – so dim I can hardly see – but it's familiar now. The brick and mortar hearth, the dining table. I hadn't checked properly before, but there is a small kitchen at the back, hidden by another door. And a bathroom. Modern enough plumbing; a toilet and a bath. Some of the decor is maybe seventies or eighties, floral motifs that have faded and begun to peel at the corners in the damp. We've called it a shack, but that's not fair. This was a home once, warm and welcoming. Only now it's as if the island is clawing it back: seeding rot into the walls as if it's planning to drag the whole thing back down into the earth.

'There's a ladder here,' I say, surprise barely surviving the fear. 'In the bathroom.'

I pull back, gesturing for James to have a look.

He reaches out gingerly and extricates it. It's a heavy, sturdy-looking thing, and he wobbles with it at an angle, precarious to say the least. I stand with my arms out, waiting for him to drop it, but he doesn't.

He drags it into the middle of the room and then attempts to prop it against the mezzanine above our heads. There's a groove there, just to the right, and the ladder fits perfectly. I see the shack with different eyes. I gaze past the darkness, the cold. Past the mouldering walls, the damp that has seeped in, greedy fingers grappling for mulch, and realise that once this would have been a nice place to live.

The windows are thin and dirty but they block out the worst of the wind, and I close my eyes, picturing what it might have looked like filled with cosy blankets, cushions, the armchair in the corner not threadbare but plush and freshly upholstered. I picture a fire in the grate, food on the table, chicken and spices under my nose.

'This was a home,' I say, my voice low.

James looks at me.

'I wonder if it was *her* home.'

'Why would she leave?' James asks. 'Was she scared of *me*? Why?'

'I don't know,' I murmur. 'But I don't think it's just you she's afraid of.'

I wander to the ladder, tugging on one of the thick, wooden steps. It seems sturdy enough.

'Hold the bottom,' I say.

James does as I ask and I climb up to the top, feeling it sway only slightly under my weight. The upstairs is a revelation. There's a double bed against the far wall above the kitchen, and a single bed against the wall on the right, tucked under a small window that lets through a bruised kind of blue light.

The beds are both bare, and so is the floor, but I can see the outline of the rug that once sat there, the wood underneath darker than the rest. There is a box up here filled with thin white candles, and a stack of magazines, all dating from the nineties. There's another box full of clothes, old dresses similar to those we found in the cave, so worn and thin they're little better than paper. The wall above the smaller bed is decorated with pencil drawings, right onto the white paint: sketches of trees, chickens, and then a small lighthouse.

I climb onto the bed, feeling bad about it, but not bad enough to stop myself. The springs in the mattress creak and the bed itself lets out an unearthly groan.

'You all right?' James asks.

'Don't come up. Not sure how sturdy the floor is.'

That's not something I'd thought about before I say it, and it's probably true, but more than that I just don't want James up here. This feels like my discovery. I bend my knees slightly, getting close to the window. And, standing with my knees bent and peering through the dirty, rain-streaked glass, I can just about see the lighthouse, small and thin from here.

I clamber down off the bed. The cold has bitten me right the way through now and I'm shivering again, knuckles aching as I lower myself back down the ladder. James is still standing at the bottom, holding the sides so tightly his hands are white with it.

'Bedroom,' I say tersely. 'I think she must have lived here with her family. I don't know how long ago, or whether she had any children.' I shrug. 'There's a single bed up there, though, and drawings of the lighthouse on the wall.'

James doesn't say anything but his lips grow thin. He glances around the room, properly taking it in.

'I wish I'd looked around before,' I say.

'We need to go,' he says firmly. 'You've had a look around now, and it's not done anything to help us.' As if to illustrate his point the radio static seems to grow louder again, and I notice the little green power light flash amber. Instinctively I snap the volume right the way down.

'I'm trying to figure things out,' I say.

'Are you?' James stares at me. 'Or are you just trying to prove a point?'

'What?'

'You've been going on about those ghost stories all weekend. I thought it didn't matter, but now I'm starting to think you're enjoying this.'

'Enjoying it?' I raise my eyebrows to hide my hurt. 'James, I'm just trying to figure out what the hell is going on, same as everybody else.'

'Why?' he demands. 'What does it matter if we understand who she is? Why she's here? Surely all that matters is she broke into the cottage. She scared the shit out of us. And that means she's unstable and we could be in danger.'

'You seem pretty eager to judge her as dangerous now, considering your refusal to talk about it all weekend.' I put my hands onto my hips and it feels like I'm back at work, reprimanding Adam for his stupid Twitter post two weeks ago. This isn't how I wanted things to be with them this weekend. '*You* put us in danger, James,' I add.

'I didn't mean to! I was confused.'

'And now you're not?'

'Well, no. I've seen the cave. You saw it, too. You must know that she's—'

'All that proves is that somebody lives here. What proof do we have that it wasn't you who broke the mirror? It's your T-shirt that Kira found.'

'And your lipstick.' He glares at me. 'If this was a joke don't you think I'd have backed down by now?'

'I don't know, James!' I exclaim. 'I'm not sure I know you well enough to make that call. And while we're arguing here we're not accomplishing anything.'

'That's what I'm trying to say!' James is getting wound up. I can see it now, and I realise that I *have* seen this behaviour before. There have been times, at home, when he's come round looking like he does now, glassy-eyed and his cheeks flushed, panic glazing every movement. I always assumed he was maybe high, or a little drunk.

'James,' I warn. 'Look, just calm down.'

'I wish people would stop fucking telling me to calm down,' he growls. 'This isn't just about me. For God's sake. You're all so eager to make it about me!'

'James, I'm not—'

'Why is it always my fault? Why can't I ever do anything right?'

He presses his hands to the sides of his face and lets out a rumbling sound that hits me right in my chest. Suddenly I'm aware of our isolation. It's just us here, and the others don't know that we haven't gone straight to the lighthouse. If they go there now, and we're not there, will they think to check here? How long will it take them?

'James,' I try again. 'Look, it's okay. I'm sorry. I'm sorry I upset you and I'm sorry that today has been so awful. We should have asked more questions.'

'No,' James spits. 'No. Questions are half the problem. When Kira said about what happened between us, you didn't seem surprised. I knew she couldn't keep it to herself. She's probably been whispering behind my back for years. She exaggerates, you know? She *lies*. But nobody ever believes that because she's so brutally honest that people assume she must *always* be telling the truth. But she twists things. That's why you're assuming that I broke the mirror.' He rubs his palms hard over his face. 'Did she tell you about us? Before she told everyone?'

'Did she—'

'She swore she'd never tell anybody and I swore it too. I thought we'd been keeping that a secret for *ten years* and then suddenly you come on holiday with us and Kira can't keep quiet about it any more. When it suits her to tell people I'm unstable. She was as into it as I was, you know. She told me so.'

'James, I don't care about you and her. I don't care about any of it. Why would I?'

'Don't you care that Lucas cares?' James looks at me with such clarity now that I take an involuntary step back. I know this doesn't matter. I know that this is a conversation we should have later, somewhere warmer and more populated, but James is right. I do care.

'I don't want to get dragged into this with you,' I say. I'm trying to be calm but my voice betrays me, shaking like a child's. 'Look, we need to go.'

'Sure.' James chews on his lip. 'Sure. But listen to me when I say I'm telling you the truth now. I don't care what Kira said about me. She was the one who instigated *everything* back then. She told me how she felt about me, and she made it happen. She enjoyed it. And it happened more than once. I thought . . . I thought it meant something. That's why . . . It's why I was so upset.'

'James . . .' I say softly.

'No. I get that it's easy to blame me because I'm such a screw-up. But that's why I beat myself up about Friday night. It's why I didn't say anything. I was afraid that nobody would believe me. That Kira would say I made it up to ruin her perfect weekend. And now you know. You've seen it. I just want you to believe me when I say I'm telling the truth about the other night, and I'm telling the truth when I say that I don't *know* if that woman is dangerous but I'm scared she could be. But it doesn't matter what I think.'

He turns away, jaw clenched hard, and I'm relieved that he's no longer looking at me. That I can no longer see the pain and the anger in his face. The feeling slowly returns to my fingers and I clench my fists a few times to get the blood pumping. I realise that we've been standing here for so long that it's getting dark outside now and a chill sweeps through me. How long until the others can no longer see where they're going to find their way back?

I turn the dial on the radio again so that the room is filled with the fizz and pop of abandonment. James nods, once, but the tension is still so thick I can hardly breathe. I don't know who to believe. What proof do I have that James is telling the truth? Kira said he lashed out, that it came out of the blue, and I can see that in him now – that coiled anger and the unpredictable swings from hot to cold. What's to stop him from accidentally hurting me too? I don't know.

Which means the only person I can trust is myself.

'Let's go,' I say, my voice croaking. I can't be in here any more. I need the feel of the wind, honest and brutal, and the rain in my face to wash away the growing confusion and fear inside me. All the energy I could sense on the island when we arrived is mixed up now, as if the mist off the water has descended into my mind, as if everything has been devoured by terror.

We stumble out into the darkness of the storm. It feels colder now than it did before, but I don't know how much of that is exhaustion. I've hardly slept all weekend and I feel so out of control that it takes me a second of blinking into the rain to realise that I'm not moving.

I push myself into a trot, hurrying down the hillside as carefully as I can as the rain runs in untamed torrents along the path. The lighthouse grows, towering above as we get closer. I recall the first time I saw it, breathless and in awe. Now it fills me with dread.

I can see the lights from here, winking at us almost

mockingly. We left them on and it looks like somebody is home, and the fear that hums through me at the thought is tight and hot. But as we reach the doorstep it's reassuring to see that everything is as it should be: the door is closed, the lights warm and dim.

'We need to go right to the top, I think,' I say to James as I turn the handle and start to step into the lounge.

Suddenly, though, something makes me stop. I hover on the threshold, the door handle still under my palm, my ears straining against the distant sound of the wind and the rain. Fear bundles inside me like pinpricks.

'Go on,' James demands, pushing at my back, his fingers insistent. I don't like the way they needle at me, how close he is. I want to shove him back but I can't. I won't.

'James,' I say. 'Wait—'

'Gen.'

Maybe he just wants to get dry. He's in a hurry to get to the top.

Or maybe he wants me inside for another reason. Inside, where nobody would hear me if I put up a fight . . .

And something is different. The energy of the lighthouse isn't the way it was when we left it, warm and full of life. The lounge seems brighter, as if somebody has turned on all of the lights. Everything is too blinding; too wrong. Panic engulfs me as James pushes me again, his eyes shining.

'No,' I say urgently. 'James, please. Wait.'

# 33

## *Moira*

It's getting darker all the time, the sun inching towards the horizon as the rain lashes down, leaving us wandering along with the lights on our phones for direction. My battery is dipping into the red and Jess has already switched hers to flight mode.

Kira and Lucas walk silently just behind us. It's almost as if they're guarding Jess. The thought would normally amuse me, but now it just makes me feel uncomfortable. I can feel them there, like shadows pressing at my back. I have to force myself to keep facing forward; not to turn and check over my shoulder.

I told Jess everything would be fine. I told her not to worry. I didn't mean for it to be a lie.

'What if we can't find another way up?' Kira shouts as we pass another tide pool, deep and rippling under the wind. There have been two or three places where the cliffs seem to dip, but not low enough for us to climb. At this rate we'll have to walk around the entire island before we can find a way to get back to the lighthouse. And that's assuming the beach keeps going.

I don't want to think about what will happen if we can't make it. We've already been out here for long enough that it's starting to get dark. How long could it be before Genevieve and James can get help? I refuse to even think that anything might stop them – but every sound makes my heart jump, my palms clammy. We are totally at the mercy of the island.

'It can't go on like this forever,' Lucas says. 'That's not how islands work.'

'Since when did you become a geographical expert?' Kira snaps, the words loud as the wind drops suddenly.

But I'm no longer listening. Up ahead the beach broadens, the golden sand, pitted by the rain, opening to what looks like a small slope to our right. I squeeze Jess's arm excitedly and point.

'Look! That looks promising.'

The cliffs here are soft and dip into grassy mounds, sand dunes rolling ahead. I don't know how far we've walked from the lighthouse, from the dock, but it seems like miles. I'm exhausted. And still I feel a little trill of hope in my chest. We will be okay. We will climb this hill, cross through the trees I can see cresting from here, and find our way back to the lighthouse. Genevieve and James will have managed to call for help. And we will sit and wait in the warm, with a cup of tea, until somebody comes to the island to bring us home.

But then I stop.

'What's that?'

The others come to a halt by my side. They've seen it too, now, amongst the grass and the sand and the rocks, hidden like treasure. Or like a ghost, hunched and white against the gathering dark.

'It looks like a . . .'

'A boat,' Jess says excitedly. 'It's a boat?'

'A boat.'

We hurry towards it, Jess dragging her bad leg eagerly. It isn't unlike the one we came here on, only it looks older, worn by the wild weather and the ocean. It's come to land just beside the dunes, empty and broken, a long gash along its hull. I glance at the others.

'How did it get there?'

'It looks like it crashed,' Kira says faintly. 'I wonder – I wonder when that happened.'

'Ages ago,' Lucas says firmly. 'Look, it's old.'

'Yeah, but . . .' I wander towards it. Lucas is right: the interior of the boat is shabby. But the gash on the hull looks newer. The sand here is mostly dry, dampened only by the rain, not by the tide. So how did the boat end up so far in? 'How do we know for sure? I don't like it.'

'It's probably from one of Gen's stupid stories,' Jess says, trying to make her voice sound light, but I can tell from the way she's standing that she's in more pain than she'll let on with her leg. 'I bet it's been here years. It doesn't mean anything about . . . about anything.'

Suddenly I'm angry – at what, I don't know. At the world, I guess. At Kira for bringing us here; at James for not telling us. At Genevieve for scaring Jess. At myself for the feelings I have, deep down. Belief that maybe Gen is right. There is something very wrong about this place.

'Yeah, maybe.' I peer into the body of the boat and find nothing but the seats and the panels and I don't understand how any of it works. 'I don't like it, though. I really just want to get out of here.'

'Maybe we should see if it works,' Lucas says. He gives

301

me a grin that normally I'd find charming, but right now it fills me with dread. 'I bet I can test it real quick—'

'No, don't touch it.'

'It's *fine*, Mo,' he says. 'Look.' He swings a leg over the side and clambers in. It's small, built probably only for two people with a bit of space in the back. I wonder if it belonged to somebody who lived here once; the owners Kira has never met, maybe. Or James's woman in the cave . . .

'Lucas, get out!' Kira shrieks. 'You'll probably get tetanus.'

The boat creaks under his weight, sinking deeper into the sand. Jess lets out a small cry and I panic, gripping her hands tight. Lucas rolls his eyes but doesn't waste any time jumping back out, his nostrils flaring with barely disguised emotion. I know we're all trying to keep it together, but I'm on the verge of yelling, so I take a deep breath and turn back towards the dunes. For the first time, I think, standing here with the dunes ahead and the roiling ocean at my back, it truly hits me how isolated we are. How we know nothing about this place. If something happened to us right now it might be hours – days – before anybody knew.

It's like a punch right to my gut, leaving me breathless.

If there's somebody else here with us . . . I don't know what to think any more. What would be worse – if there was truth to Genevieve's stories, or if there wasn't?

'It could mean something else,' Jess says slowly.

'What could?'

'The boat. Being here now.'

I shake my head, barely wanting to ask, but Kira has heard and now she's interested.

'What do you mean?' she asks.

302

Jess swallows hard and wets her lips, glancing back at the boat and then at the dunes. Her fear echoes off the rest of us and I think to myself that I might lose control if we carry on like this. I feel like I might explode.

'Come on,' I say, desperate to move on. 'It doesn't matter. It doesn't affect us. It's just a boat.'

'Yes,' says Jess, 'but what if . . . What if it means there's more than just this woman on the island?' She winces as she says it. 'I don't know. Maybe it even belonged to her. But how do we know she's the only one who's here with us? Gen's stories—'

'We can't think about it,' I say firmly. 'We're just going to wind ourselves up and wind ourselves up until . . . We just can't. Okay? We need to focus on getting back, getting home.'

'Jess is right though,' Lucas says. 'What's to say we're on our own here?'

'It doesn't matter,' I say again, teeth grinding. 'Guys, we can speculate for hours and never get anywhere. Please, let's just go. Look, we can get up there. It doesn't look too steep. Jess, we can carry you if you can't walk it. Right, Lucas?'

Lucas doesn't say anything but he does reluctantly tear himself away from the boat, and Kira follows, still glancing back over her shoulder, as if she's afraid it might move when she's not looking.

'It'll be fine,' I say to Jess. 'Let's just get back to Genevieve and James. Then we can think about it. And only then.'

But I can't deny that our pace has picked up since we found the boat. Even Jess, who is obviously struggling to put any weight on her ankle now, is determined. She walks with a grimace, her head bent into the wind. I offer my arm for support and she clings to it, the two of us dragging ourselves on.

Lucas takes the lead now, guiding us through the rain with what's left of his phone battery, the light pale and white, casting a hollow circle that draws us through the dunes, up a sandy slope that is steep but not impossible, and we climb until we reach the top and then stop to give Jess a break. She lets out several sharp breaths and then nods once, firm. We can keep going.

'This will be a fun story to tell Emma one day,' Jess says. Her voice is tentative, but we've reached the copse of wind-stripped trees we could see from the beach below and I can hear her much better now that the howling storm is held at bay.

A few days ago I'm certain I'd have been annoyed at Jess's mention of our daughter in this moment. I wouldn't want to bring her here, even if it's just in memory. But now I find myself warming at the thought of Emma, her baby-powder scent, the soft, rich curl of her hair, and the way she grabs at my hands, wrists, clothes with such ferocity it feels like a bargain.

'She'll think we're lying,' I say. 'There's no way she'll believe a word of any of it.'

'We'll get Kira to tell it.' Jess ducks under a low-hanging branch and I have to step aside. 'She'll believe her. Or Lucas, if Emma ever stops being afraid of him.'

I grin.

It feels good to smile, even if it doesn't last long. The path through the trees is uneven but Lucas does a good job of navigating us, twigs cracking underfoot and the sound of the rain outside feeling a million miles away. But then we come to a small crest, where the land starts to slope upwards, and I can see the shack up ahead, tucked in its little bump of land.

And then the lighthouse. Its beam slashes through the growing darkness. I should feel relieved. I know I should be grateful that we've nearly made it, that soon we will be warm and dry even if we don't feel entirely safe. But there's something about the harshness of that white light and the fake warmth of the golden pinholes from the kitchen windows that just feels treacherous, now. It feels like a lie.

'God, it seems like it's miles away,' Jess says, breathless.

The anxiety is building again between us. I can feel it, almost like a hum. I think, if I was alone, I would want to hide from the fear that's burrowing deep inside me, but for Jess I have to be strong. Even if that's not what she says she wants, it's the deal I made when I married her.

'Lucas,' Jess adds, and I realise she's been looking at me, watching me stare at the lighthouse ahead. 'Can you . . . Do you think you can carry me? So we can get there faster?'

Normally Lucas would be offended. The Lucas we've spent years making fun of would be eager to show his strength, upset that anybody would question it. But this Lucas, the one from this long, long weekend, just weighs it up quietly and then nods.

'I think so,' he says. 'If not all the way, then I can certainly get us closer. Come here.'

Jess limps towards him and he thinks for a moment before bending forwards and gesturing that she should try to hop onto his back. It's a fumble, but they manage it, and then we're moving, driven by the gold lights and some impending sense of danger.

All of us are aware that the walk has taken longer than

we'd hoped. That it's dark. That the cave was empty. That Genevieve and James are alone. That James has not been himself.

I run with my heart in my throat, the bitter taste of iron on my tongue. I'm not fit any more. Too many late nights; too many afternoons where all I've eaten is two cookies and Emma's leftovers. Too many takeaways when even Jess couldn't be bothered to cook.

But my body is still strong. It hasn't let me down so far, and it doesn't now. We slip and slide our way down the slight slope and back up towards the lighthouse, where it stands proud against the black sky. The chance of us getting a boat tonight seems so slim, growing slimmer by the moment, but I refuse to think about that.

Lucas has to let Jess drop to the grass just before we reach the cottage, panting madly. She lands awkwardly but I'm there to catch her, and it feels like the most graceful thing we've managed in a long time. She shoots me a small, grateful smile.

'Do you think they're upstairs?' Kira asks, pushing the door open.

We all follow her inside, just about ready to start shucking off coats and scarves. I'm already thinking of lighting a fire, getting the kettle on or opening one of the last boxes of wine we brought. I'm hungry again, too, and wishing for something more substantial than a sandwich. Jess had a bolognese planned for tonight but I can't see that happening now. Maybe there's something easier that we can cobble together from the stuff in the fridge.

And that's when we stop. It's cold in here.

Too cold.

Kira looks at me out of the corner of her eyes, breath

coming in foggy puffs. The lights are all on and it's too bright. Jess shivers.

I creep forward, my jacket half-unzipped, my hair plastered to my forehead. And then I notice Genevieve and James. Together.

They're standing completely frozen in the entrance to the sunroom. James glances back in panic.

I inch closer. Closer. My boots too loud on the floor, even as I try to be silent.

And as I get to the doorway I feel the temperature in the room plummet, as though we're surrounded by spirits, their fingers clawing at my skin drawing goosebumps. I'm reminded of my nightmare again, of feeling a cold just like this, a draught so icy it felt like hands pawing at me, and I shiver.

Then I see what has the others frozen in place.

The long dining table stretches down the sunroom, the slowly greying windows reflecting the many electric lights and the candles dotted on every surface. It seems like a party. Like a question.

And at the head of the table, sitting in one of the beautiful new chairs, with the veranda doors open at her back, wind crackling at the tablecloth and rain splashing onto the terracotta tiles—

It has to be her.

The woman from the cave.

She's here.

# 34

## *Kira*

Shit.

I don't know what to do. I shove Moira gently, trying to push my way into the room until we're all gathered at the sunroom entrance. I can feel the panic in my nose, my throat, threatening to close it all off so I'll never breathe again. But instead I force myself to look.

She's small, skinny and birdlike. Blonde. She has a thin, angular face and big, dark eyes. A smattering of freckles that bridge her nose. She's sitting at the table but it's awkward, as though it's been a long time since she's sat at one, her hands poised nervously on the surface where just last night it was spread with plates and bowls, wine glasses, cutlery.

She reminds me of a ghost, in every way. Her clothing is tattered, stitched carefully in places but obviously old. She's wearing a baggy black sweater that looks like something out of the late nineties, a skirt, and long stockings that stop at her knees. Nothing looks like it belongs to her – or it didn't to start with, anyway. Everything is too big, as if it was all bought for a person larger than her petite frame.

I inch forward. Moira shoots out an arm to hold me back, but Genevieve doesn't stop me – why would she, after everything I've said and done – so I move to the side and step around them both, until I'm in front of all of us. The woman, who so far doesn't seem to have said anything, cocks her head slightly.

'Erm,' I say, 'hello.'

It's stupid, but it's all I can think to say. The woman twitches her nose thoughtfully and then leans forward.

'Hello,' she mimics. Her voice is surprisingly high, soft and rasping, as though she doesn't use it very often.

'I'm Kira,' I say hesitantly. I pause, waiting for her to respond, but she doesn't. 'Can . . . Can we help you?'

She sits very still, watching all of us. Her gaze flicks from one to the next of us, slowly. Curiously. James was right. She doesn't seem outwardly violent, but there's something about her that's got an edge to it. A brittleness to her movements that belies a speed most of us would not be able to compete with.

'Did you need something?' I try again. 'We don't live here. We're just visiting. But you're welcome to help yourself to – well, anything that you need.'

She watches us still. It's starting to creep me out, the lack of movement, the way she sits as though she's made of stone, except for her eyes which go back and forth and back and forth . . .

'What's your name?' I try. 'Is there a name we can use?'

The woman watches us.

'Ask her what she's doing here,' Lucas mutters. His voice

carries and the woman snaps her attention to him like a cat tracking a bird in a tree. Lucas steps back.

'You might remember my friend here . . .' I say. I gesture at James. 'You met him the other night.'

'Hi,' James croaks.

'I just want to – apologise, I guess. We're sorry if we disturbed you. We didn't know you lived here. If we'd known, we'd have been much more careful. Hopefully it didn't cause you too much distress.'

There is a long stretch of silence. I can feel the coldness in the air, snaking down my spine, making my fingers numb. I pick idly at a loose thread on my coat sleeve. I don't know what else to say. What else to do.

And then her soft voice breaks the silence.

'Why are you here?' she asks, mimicking Lucas's question.

I glance at the others. My camera is on the table, so I point to it.

'I'm a writer,' I say. 'I take photographs too. The people who own this lighthouse were – are – planning to turn this into a holiday cottage. For people to come and stay on the island. We came to test it out. Take pictures. To advertise.'

But the second the woman sees the camera, the moment she comprehends what it is, I know I should have lied.

She lets out a low, rumbling groan, panic stretching her mouth taut. I freeze, but Genevieve reacts quickly and snatches my camera off the table, cradling it like a child.

'There aren't any photographs of you on here,' she says quickly. 'Just of the lighthouse. Of the sea. The cottage out back. I promise.'

The woman's fingers are like claws digging into the arms of the chair as she strains against it.

'Yes,' I blurt. 'I can show you them. There's nothing bad on there, I promise.'

'Is there a reason you don't want us to have a photograph of you?' Genevieve asks, words tumbling out fast. 'Are you hiding?'

'*Genevieve*,' James hisses. But she goes on.

'How long have you been here on the island? Don't you want people to know you're here?'

The woman is moaning now, her head in her heads.

'No, no,' she murmurs. 'No, no, no.'

I look at Moira, at Jess, then Lucas and James in turn, but they all look as confused as me.

'Tell us your name,' Genevieve says. 'Will you tell us who you are?'

The woman is crying, I think, but it's hard to tell. The noises she makes remind me of a child: grunts and keening moans that quickly die to silence as she calms down. She breathes deep and slow. And then when she lifts her face, I see that the tears are drying already. And in their place is something hollow and cold.

Genevieve hands me the camera, slowly, as though we're being watched by a predator. And then she begins to creep closer.

'What are you doing?' Lucas whispers. 'Gen—'

She ignores him. She's halfway down the length of the long table now, and the woman is watching her like a bird – no – like a raptor – her head bobbing slightly with every step Genevieve takes, as she traces every ounce of movement.

'Can we talk?' Genevieve tries, calm and quiet. 'It's – Samantha, right?' she adds. 'Samantha Buchanan?'

\* \* \*

312

The rest of us watch in silence as Genevieve reaches the edge of the table, drawing up so she's about six feet away, her back to the big, open stretch of black glass. Outside the ocean roars and the rain continues to fall, but all I can hear is the pounding of my blood in my ears.

The woman shakes her head.

'You're not Samantha Buchanan?' Genevieve asks.

The name tickles the back of my brain. I've heard it before.

'No.' The woman tilts her head again, birdlike, thoughtful, her lips a pout. 'And I don't know you. Why are you here?'

Genevieve lowers herself slowly into the chair closest to her, the one to the woman's left. I feel my heart squeeze. I want to join her, to be closer so I can help her if she needs it, but I also can't move. The others stand frozen next to me and I wonder, distantly, if they feel the same.

'We told you,' Genevieve says, slowly. Carefully. 'We're on holiday. We're meant to be going home tomorrow.'

The woman looks at James, suddenly, and I jump, my heart hammering in time with the rain that lashes against the glass.

'You said you would leave,' she says. 'You told me you would *go*.'

'I . . .'

'We didn't realise,' Genevieve soothes, 'that you needed us to leave so soon. We didn't understand what you wanted – but we know now. We got your message.'

'Message?' mutters the woman. 'What message?'

'In the bathroom. In the cottage.'

The woman shakes her head again.

'In the cottage there is a bathroom with a medicine cabinet,' Genevieve explains with more patience than I could

313

muster. Frustration is making me dig my nails into my palms. I try to suck in a breath to calm myself. 'And there's a mirror on the cabinet. Last night somebody broke the mirror and wrote on the wall in lipstick.'

'I don't know anything about a mirror,' the woman says. 'But I told you to leave and you're still here. Why are you here?'

'We're leaving tomorrow.'

'Yes,' says the woman. She looks at Genevieve now with such clarity that it seems wild that we've been talking to her like a child, like she's unwell. There's intelligence in her eyes, and quiet resistance too. 'I understand that. What I don't understand is why you are *still here*.'

Genevieve doesn't baulk, but even I can tell that it takes everything in her not to. She places her palms on the surface of the table as if she's trying to ground herself and I flinch, wishing she wouldn't get so close to the other woman.

'You didn't tell us to leave,' Genevieve says. 'You told James. And James didn't understand. He just thought you wanted him to leave you alone. Why didn't you come to ask us? What is your right to the island?'

'It is my home,' the woman says proudly. 'I have always lived here.'

Genevieve thinks for a moment. It's like watching somebody play chess, and for the first time I truly realise why Lucas fell for her. And why she's so good at her job. It's the same reason I've always disliked her. She knows how to communicate with people, to get right to the heart of them.

'So, if you've always lived here, why haven't we seen you before?' Genevieve asks. 'Were you hiding from us?'

314

'No.' The woman shrugs. 'I don't see people. People don't see me. It's the way it's always been. The way it has to be.'

'Why?'

The woman presses her palms to her cheeks as a particularly cold wind howls through the open doors. It's freezing in here and I don't know whether it's the wind, my soaking clothes, or the fear that's making my whole body hum. I can see Moira gripping Jess's hand and Lucas hovering on the balls of his feet as if he doesn't know whether to run or fight.

'My parents used to go to the mainland,' the woman says, her voice wistful. 'They'd come back with boatloads of things. Sweets and chocolates and once we even had *beef*. Have you ever had beef? It's so dark and flaky.' She smiles wistfully. 'But they are dead now, so I don't go anywhere except here. I don't see people. I don't like people. I like nature. Chickens – I used to like chickens. But I had to kill them when I left my home. They couldn't live in the cave. Now I like rabbits and fish. It's very loud here, if you know how to listen to the world. My parents taught me that.'

'Your parents,' Genevieve says. 'Isabelle? And David?'

The woman frowns. 'No. No, those weren't their names. My mum was . . . Pat,' she says thoughtfully. As though the memory is buried deep. 'My dad was Andy. They lived here and their parents lived here and their parents before them. We've always lived on Ora. It's our home.'

'Okay.' Genevieve glances at me, and then at Moira and Jess, a silent question on her lips. But I don't know what she means. 'And what about the wooden cottage? Up the hill? Is that where you used to live with them?'

The woman shies away at the mention of it, shrinking into herself.

315

'I can't talk about it,' she says quietly.

'Why not?'

'I'm not allowed to tell. They said I should never tell because it's dangerous. I'm not allowed to go anywhere else. I'm not supposed to be in here . . .' She glances around the room, taking in the lights and the darkness beyond them. The room looks like a hall of black mirrors. 'But I thought . . . I needed to see it. I stayed away before. I did what I was supposed to do. I stayed away, *always*. But then I saw you and you were here . . .'

'And you wanted to come and see the lighthouse?' Genevieve asks tentatively.

I think of the short distance between here and the shack. How could you spend your whole life there and not be drawn to this place?

'Yes,' the woman says. 'My whole life I wanted to see inside. I wanted so badly. But I didn't because I couldn't. And then . . . people came. And I thought – well. I'm old now. I can do what I want. I've always lived here. And so has the lighthouse. And I think it should be mine too, like the rest of Ora. Don't you?'

She smiles a small, sardonic smile.

'If you've always lived here,' Genevieve says, pushing the conversation back again, 'then I think I'm right about you. I think we need to talk about it. I've done some research, you know, and I think you must be Samantha Buchanan.'

The woman tilts back in her chair, scraping it across the tiles like she's been shot.

'No,' she says. 'Why do you keep calling me that? That's not my name.'

'You've lived here your whole life,' Genevieve says again. 'You're the right sort of age. You look like her – and your

316

mole. The one on your cheek, just under your freckles. I've seen a photograph of a girl with the same mark.'

'I'm not somebody *Buchanan*. My name is Sammy,' she insists. 'S – A – M – M – Y. Sammy McDougall. My parents were Pat and Andy. The McDougalls have run this island for generations. We tend the island. We watch over this place.'

'Samantha. Buchanan,' Genevieve says again, slowly. Like she's trying to provoke her.

But my fear is swallowed by realisation.

'Samantha Buchanan,' I repeat breathlessly, suddenly hit full force by where I've heard the name before. 'The owners. Their *daughter*? But she died.'

'I'm not dead,' the woman – Sammy – says. 'I'm alive as anything. As you. Or them.'

She peers at the rest of us and I feel myself go cold. Her eyes have lost the warmth, the curiosity of before. And then she grabs Genevieve's arm, yanking it so hard that Genevieve cries out, pulled to her feet. In that split second everything shifts, and the woman has both of Genevieve's arms and spins her with surprising strength, drawing her close so that her back is pressed to Sammy's chest.

Lucas shouts.

'Just look,' Sammy murmurs. 'I promise I'm very alive.'

317

# 35

## Genevieve

'Samantha,' I say, quietly, as calmly as I can with a stranger pressed to my back. My heart hammers and I feel dizzy. 'Sammy,' I correct myself. 'Can you let me go? This is uncomfortable.'

Her breath is hot on my neck and I feel my limbs go liquid with fear, but I try to stand, to be centred. There is still no evidence that she's dangerous. Right? If I don't provoke her, maybe nothing bad will happen. She's just confused and scared. Probably as scared of us as we are of her. I inhale and catch a whiff of salt, of something green, and of very human sweat.

'Let her go.' I realise I've got my eyes closed, but this is Lucas's voice. He sounds like he's about to lose it, so I interject as quickly as I can.

'Sammy,' I say again. 'Do you want me to show you round the rest of the lighthouse? There's a whole lot more of it and I'm not sure if you've seen it, but it really is very cool. We can talk – or we don't have to. It's up to you. And I promise to get your name right.'

Sammy considers for a second. I can feel the tightness of her grip on my arms, fingers biting into the flesh of both of my biceps. She's surprisingly strong, and incredibly quick on her feet, but it feels like the kind of energy that might burn white and hot and, hopefully, *fast*.

'It can be all of us, if you want. Or just me. I don't mind.'

'Gen,' Kira warns. I want to shake my head but I daren't even move.

'And then we can come and sit back down here and have a nice cup of tea. We've got milk – I don't know if you like that. And cake. We've been trying to get the radio to work so we can leave early, but the weather—'

'Please stop talking so much,' Sammy says, her voice soft again. 'You're hurting my head will all those words.'

She releases me and I stumble forward with a whoosh of breath into my lungs. I make sure that I turn my back to the window again so that we're face to face. It means I can't see the others, but I'm not sure that matters. Jess has her phone in her hand – I can see the bright screen – but it won't do any good. I haven't managed to get signal in here since last night.

'Can we go right to the top?' Sammy asks.

She looks, in this moment, like a child. Her eyes are alight and she gazes upwards, towards the glass ceiling. If I craned my neck I know what I'd see: the lighthouse, impossibly tall, like a giant with light pouring from his mouth. I keep my eyes firmly trained on her.

'Yes,' I say. 'Right the way up.'

'Okay.' She looks at me again. 'And then you leave. And you don't tell *anybody* about me.' Her eyes are steel.

'Yes,' I agree quickly. 'That's a deal.'

320

'Gen,' Lucas mimics Kira's warning, but this time I do shake my head.

'Stay here,' I say. 'Try to get that goddamn radio working before the battery dies.'

'I don't want you—'

'We will be fine,' I say, even if I don't believe it.

Sammy has her fists clenched by her sides and she looks at each of the others in turn, sizing them up. I try to keep Sammy distracted from Jess and her phone. I don't know how long she's actually been here, and it's possible she's never seen a mobile phone before – it's probably why she didn't recognise Kira's camera – but I don't want to take any chances.

'This way, then.' I point to the door, and the others scoot awkwardly out of the way.

It feels like I'm back at work, giving a post-interview tour to a new intern. I try to pretend that this is true, that it's exactly what I'm doing, and it helps to steady my hands as we reach the staircase and Sammy is right behind me and my hands tremble and tremble.

'Did you say you've never been inside the lighthouse before?' I ask. I want to keep her talking, if only so I know exactly where she is.

'Only this weekend. Only downstairs. Only when it's dark. Only . . .' she trails off.

We've come to the first landing. The bedroom. Secretly I'm glad she's spotted it and I come to a stop. She eyes the door with what almost seems like curiosity, her head tilted like before. As if she's never encountered it before.

'Do you want to go inside?' I ask gently.

Sammy's gaze snaps to me and then back to the door.

'Yes. I want to see it all.'

I lean over and unlatch the door. It swings slowly inwards, a faint creak the only sound as the woman steps towards it. She is wearing a pair of boots that are so well-worn they look like they might fall apart at any moment, but they're silent on the concrete stairs and on the wooden floorboards too.

She stands in the centre of the room and stares.

'What.' Not a question. Not even a sentence. Just one word that feels like a thousand thoughts all bundled into one.

'Your bedroom.'

Sammy's nostrils flare.

'You've been in here before. Haven't you?' I ask.

She ignores me and walks towards the bed with its pink gingham sheets, running her fingers along the dusty white frame, the soft linen that the sun has bleached pale over the years. She trails to the back wall, to the stencilled animals and then around to the windowsill, where the line of trinkets sits.

She picks up the tortoise with his racing stripes gingerly, as though she might break him.

'The door was locked when we got here,' I go on, tentatively. I step into the room. 'We couldn't get in. We didn't know what was in here. But then it was suddenly open. Did you open the door? Do you remember it?'

'Too many words,' Sammy mutters. 'You speak too many words. Too many questions. You remind me of a very annoying little bee living right inside my ear.'

She glares at me and I clamp my lips shut.

'Sama— Sammy,' I forge on. I can't stop myself. 'Do you remember this room? Have you been here before?'

Sammy puts the figurine down and wanders to the

322

bookcase. She runs her index finger down the spines of each of the books in turn, mouthing the words to herself.

'I haven't read a new book in a long, long time,' she says. 'My dad used to bring me books, sometimes. Magazines mostly. We read them together. And then sometimes in the winter we burned them. No sense keeping them around, he'd say. Take up space. But look at these.'

'Yes. I think they have been here for a very long time. Do you remember any of these?'

Sammy's eyes look like they're filling with tears but when she spins towards me I realise it's anger brimming there.

'Stop trying to make me say I remember things that aren't true,' she snaps. 'I am only here because I want to see. Because I want to *look*. You're making me feel stupid. You are a *liar*.'

'I'm not trying to lie,' I say. 'I just – have you seen the photograph? Up there on that shelf?'

But Sammy won't look at it. She marches back to the window and stares out over the ocean, watching the rain lash against the glass. It's not as heavy now, but distantly I think I hear a rolling boom of thunder. I'm trying not to think of what might happen next. What if Sammy won't leave the lighthouse? Worse, what if she won't let *us* leave?

'Can you tell me more about your parents, Sammy?' I ask.

'Why? You didn't know them. They're dead.'

'No, but I like to hear people talk about their families.'

Sammy picks up the hare next and turns it over and over in her hands, her fingernails finding the pits and grooves. She doesn't answer right away, but stares at the little statue, thoughtful.

'My parents were kind. They protected me. They taught

323

me how to raise chickens. That was when I was very small. We grew carrots and potatoes sometimes. And tomatoes. We had a little garden at the back of the house. I have not been very good at growing my garden, but there is enough.' She shrugs. 'Sometimes my dad would go to the mainland. But he would say I had to stay here. So I stayed here.'

'Why?' I ask gently. 'Why did he ask you to stay here?'

'It's safe,' she says. 'Ora is safe. Ora is the sort of place everybody wants to be. And we couldn't tell people about it because . . .' she begins to scowl, 'because people like *you* would come and try to take it. Make it yours.'

'No,' I say. 'We didn't make anything ours. We're just – borrowing it.'

'And those men who came,' Sammy goes on. 'They took things. They found my carrots and took them. The last ones I had. They walked all through my house. They made me *leave.*'

'They didn't know you were here,' I say.

'Well they should have.' Sammy's chest is rising and falling rapidly now. 'They should have known. I am a McDougall. McDougalls have lived on this island since the beginning of time! They should have known I was here and they should have left me alone.'

She's panting now. I realise that she has noticed the photograph again and this time she's looking at it. Her eyes flicker over the family portrait: Isabelle and David Buchanan tucked in tight, their daughter between them. The blonde hair and bright blue eyes, so like her own. The freckles, and the mole just beneath them. All hers.

'There used to be other people who lived here,' I say softly. 'The people in that photograph. They are the people who sent the builders to fix up the lighthouse. They didn't know you were here. But – they would be pleased to hear it, I'm sure. Can you tell me about how your parents came to have you?'

'I won't tell you any more about my parents!' Sammy hisses. 'You are a liar. You're trying to make me believe things that aren't true.'

'No, I'm just—'

'You don't know anything about the island! You don't know anything about me!'

'I'm asking you so that you can tell me,' I beg. 'Please, can we just talk about it? I don't think you're Pat and Andy's daughter. I don't think you can be. I think they must have raised you, but you are *their* daughter.'

I point at the photograph.

Sammy lets out a shriek and buries her face in her hands.

'*No,*' she whispers. 'You are a liar. You're lying to me. Why are you here? You shouldn't be here. Nobody should be here but me. This is my home and you are ruining it.'

She begins to rock backwards and forwards again, her arms wrapping around her waist. Her blonde hair hangs in sandy curls, her face a mask of torment. I don't want to do this. I don't want to hurt her. But I'm almost certain I'm right and I need to know – we all need to know – how this happened. How this woman came to be here, by herself, believing she was somebody else entirely.

'What happened?' I push. 'When you were little?'

'I don't know,' she says. 'I don't know what you're talking about. We lived here. We always lived here. It wasn't safe to go out for a while and I could only see the lighthouse from my window but then we had the whole island and I could go anywhere except the lighthouse because the lighthouse is dangerous. You could fall right from the cliff. You could fall from the roof. You could break your neck. You could die.'

She looks around the bedroom, absorbing the pink gingham, the love and effort that went into designing this bedroom with its Laura Ashley bedding and the beautiful rug right in the centre, so thick and plush it could swallow your toes. The toy box in the corner, the books, the paintings and stencils on the walls . . .

'Why is this room here?' she asks. 'Why is it here? Who lives here?'

'You did.'

'No, I didn't. Who lives here now?'

'Nobody lives here now,' I say. 'The room was locked when we got here on Friday. You opened it. You saw it. And you panicked.'

'No, I didn't come here. I've never been here before. Why would I come here? This isn't my home. I'm not allowed in here.'

'You are allowed in here,' I say forcefully. 'I think you are very much allowed in here. Look at that photograph, Samantha. Those are your parents. Isabelle and David Buchanan. They own the lighthouse. And look at the little girl they're holding. Look at her face. Doesn't that look like you? It *is* you.'

'I don't believe you!' Sammy lets out an ungodly shriek. I realise, seconds too late, that I've pushed her too far.

Sammy runs towards me with surprising speed, the little figurine still in her hands. She hurls it at my head and it connects with my nose with a sickening crack and a pain like a lightning bolt that is black and white simultaneously. I shout in surprise as much as pain, cupping my face as I feel blood trickle from the wound.

'Sammy!' I yell. 'Please, just let me explain!'

She rushes for the bookcase, grabbing the photograph from its perch and slinging it hard against the wall. The picture frame explodes in shards of glass and metal and wood, splinters flying across the room and glittering on the ground. I can hardly see and my ears are ringing from the blow to my nose, but I try to reach for her, to calm her.

But she's already running down the stairs, and now she's wild. Wild like the island, like the ocean. I glance around and realise that one of the bigger bits of glass from the picture frame is missing. Panic engulfs me.

Sammy must have it.

# 36

## *Moira*

'Shit,' Jess says. 'What was that?'

She glances upwards from her phone screen at the same time as the rest of us hear it, the webpage still open on her browser and her fingers hovering over it, where I can see she's returned to the Google search we managed to get to load: *Buchanan McDougall Ora*. There's a thud, like something hitting the boards on the next floor, dulled by the distance and the glass roof above our heads that echoes only the stars.

'Sounds like—'

Lucas barely gets his words out before there's a shout, and then another one about an octave higher. There's a smash and then a thunder of footsteps. Lucas pelts from his position hovering in the doorway and is out into the lounge in seconds.

It's not long before the blonde stranger flies down the stairs. Her hair flies behind her, long and tangled, and she grabs at the bannister attached to the wall and swings to the ground so hard I hear the wood crack. I'm only seconds behind Lucas and I see her come skidding to a stop.

She's aiming for the door, but Lucas is in her way now. He doesn't move. The two of us stare at her, and she stares back, and then Genevieve comes into view on the stairs. There's blood running hard from a cut on the bridge of her nose, smeared down her chin.

'What happened?' Lucas demands. For the second time today I'm glad for his size, his sheer width as he stands in the doorway. I half think we should just let her go, but then—

I notice the broken glass in her hand, half-raised, ready to strike.

'Lucas,' I say, my voice low with warning.

He ignores me. 'What did you do to her?' he barks.

'She didn't mean to – I pushed too hard.' Gen swipes at her face quickly.

Sammy is like a wild animal. James said she wasn't feral, but he was wrong. Her eyes are wide, flicking back and forth. Her attention catches on the kitchen door and she looks like she might bolt that way, but then James makes a break for it, shoving past me and blocking it before she can react.

She lets out a frustrated wail.

'Why won't you let me leave!' she shouts.

'Maybe we should,' Jess starts. But Lucas shakes his head.

'Not until we get some answers. How do we know she won't try to come back in later? How can we trust her now? We need to get to the bottom of this.'

'She hasn't done anything,' Jess whispers.

'She's done enough,' Kira says.

I step forward, my palms raised in surrender. 'Look, let's just everybody calm down a minute, okay? There's no need for this to get out of hand. Sammy, I'm sorry Gen scared you. I'm sure she didn't mean to.'

'She didn't scare me,' Sammy hisses. 'She's telling lies. I hate lies. I hate liars. My dad said nobody would ever come here. He told me nobody knew this place existed. He *said* we were the only ones who ever lived here.'

'The bedroom upset you,' I say, understanding blossoming.

'Yes.' Her voice is throaty now, full of feeling. I can see the warring emotions flitting across her face. She's angry but she *is* scared. And she's confused.

'Why don't we talk?' I say. 'We can try to explain everything. Would that help? If we tell you what we know?'

Sammy is on the balls of her feet, eager to run, eager to slash with the glass. I don't know what she hopes to achieve, but something deep in my belly says that if we're not careful she'll think nothing of shutting all of us up. There are no consequences that would seem real enough to her. Not here, not now. We *need* to be careful.

'Why don't we go back into the sunroom?' I say calmly. 'It's big, it's open. You can leave through the veranda door at any time. But it will give us a moment to talk and explain what we know. Would you like that?'

I don't know if it's my tone, or if she's simply tired, but Sammy begins to sag and I think I'm getting somewhere.

'We can make tea,' I suggest, 'or just sit quietly. You can ask the questions and we won't talk unless you ask. Sound fair?'

'Mm-hmm.' Sammy's lips are clamped shut but she nods slightly.

'And then, when we're done, we might have questions for you. But we will only ask them if you're willing to answer. Okay?'

331

'Mo,' Jess whispers. I open my palm behind my back, the sign we always use at home if we want somebody to hold off for a second. And Jess wilts reluctantly.

'Does that sound okay, Sammy?' I ask.

'Yes. Okay. Yes. But – no lies.' She glares at Genevieve.

'No lies,' I confirm.

We wait for a second, all of us on tenterhooks. Lucas squares himself against the door, ready to tackle her if she gets close. But the glass in her hand . . . It looks sharp. There's already blood on it, I guess from her hand. She looks down at it, as if following my gaze, and seems almost surprised to find it there.

And then she walks through to the sunroom, calmly as anything.

I let out the breath that's been building in my chest, feeling my body start to shake as the adrenaline surges. This is madness. Genevieve slowly descends the rest of the stairs and Lucas opens his arms to her. She doesn't go to him immediately, but when she does I see her rest against him, as though the last twenty minutes has taken it out of her.

In the sunroom I find Sammy already sitting at the head of the table again, just as she was earlier, except this time the chair is pushed further back from the table for an easy escape, and there's a glinting piece of glass sitting where her plate would be if, in an alternate reality, she'd joined us for dinner.

'Okay,' I say as we all take seats around the table. It feels formal, forced, and a hysterical part of me wants to laugh, but I hold it together. My clothes and feet are still soaked and I'm so cold that my teeth clamp together and I have to force them apart. 'So, what do you want to know?'

Sammy looks at Genevieve, who is the last to take a seat, and then at me.

'You,' she says, pointing at me. 'Explain why she keeps calling me Buchanan.'

I purse my lips and try to find a way to tell her without it sounding harsh, but all I can think is that I need to tell her the truth, especially now I've seen the webpage that Jess and I found; the article with an interview that was given only a couple of years ago. She could bolt at any moment anyway, so there's no use dressing it up.

'There were people who used to live on this island, who still own the lighthouse, called Isabelle and David Buchanan. They lived here in the late 1970s until 1980. They were the official lighthouse keepers on the island, but I believe they hadn't always been.'

'My parents were the lighthouse keepers,' Sammy asserts. Her suspicion is like a blindfold. 'Not these other people.'

'I suspect they cared for the land and the lighthouse together,' I say. 'Sort of like a team. I don't think the Buchanans were traditional lighthouse keepers, but they bought land on the island and probably hired the McDougalls to continue looking after it.'

'We didn't find information that says when they moved here, but it looks like the McDougalls were here before the Buchanans,' Jess says, turning her phone in her hands, the screen dark but ready. At the time, we had discussed using the brief moment of Internet access to make a call. It wouldn't have worked though. The hotspot had barely given us enough juice to load and screenshot two webpages. Besides, Sammy was here right now. Any help wouldn't arrive for at least twenty minutes – twenty minutes we still might not have if Sammy doesn't like what we have to say.

'I think the McDougalls already lived here in the sh— the cottage,' Jess continues, 'and the Buchanans hired them to stay on when they bought the place. It's possible they even sold the lighthouse to the Buchanans themselves, but I don't know for sure.'

'Sold it?' Sammy raises her eyebrows and then dips them into a deep frown. 'No, that's not right. They would never sell it.'

'It says, in the article we found, that both families were living here on Ora,' I agree. 'We can show you . . . if you want. And I think that makes sense. Don't you? And it makes sense that you wouldn't remember. You were very young at the time.'

'I don't remember them.'

'You wouldn't.'

Sammy thinks about this. There's something about her that seems to have fractured, an openness in her that wasn't there before, but it feels like broken china, jagged and hungry for blood.

'So, these people. Why did they leave? Why did my parents never tell me they owned the lighthouse and not us? Why is all of this happening?'

I glance at the others. Kira looks like she's about to launch into an explanation but she manages to hold back. James is sitting on Sammy's right side as I sit at her left, leaning back in his chair as if he wants to be as far away from her as possible while still protecting Kira.

'They left,' I say, watching Sammy and that piece of glass closely, 'because something terrible happened to them. They had a daughter, you see. A little girl. Samantha.'

'Samantha.' Sammy stares at Genevieve, but to her credit she just looks back calmly. Her nose has stopped bleeding

334

now but her face is a sight, already bruising. It's lucky she didn't lose an eye.

'Yes. She was two years old, and they lost her.'

'Lost her.' Sammy mimics my words again and it's eerie, like an echo bouncing off the black glass like the reflections from the lamps. 'She died? That's what you said before. She died.'

'They thought she did. She was playing outside, and the rocks were slippery, and they – I suppose they must have taken their eyes off her. She vanished. They found her cardigan later on, in the ocean, caught on some rocks. They assumed she must have drowned and been swept away by the tide.'

Sammy doesn't say anything. She angles the piece of broken glass upwards, catching a beam of light and chasing it across the table ahead of herself.

'There was a reason they thought she'd drowned,' Jess says. Her voice is softer than mine, gentler, and I'm glad. She goes on slowly when Sammy doesn't react. 'Because a few years earlier something terrible had happened to the McDougalls, too.'

Sammy's head snaps up at this and she focused on Jess. 'What something terrible?'

'They also had a daughter. We found an interview online – on the Internet. In a newspaper,' Jess fumbles, trying to explain how she knows that it's true in a way that this woman might understand. The differences between her life and ours stretch between us. 'They said that their daughter – a little girl called Elsie – had also fallen into the ocean. Drowned. The island . . . it's a force of nature. The girl was swept into the ocean from the cliff just outside here, where the porch is now. She was never found.'

'No,' Sammy says. 'They didn't have anybody called Elsie. My parents never said anything about anybody called Elsie. I would know. They would have told me. I would have . . .'

'She was their daughter,' Jess says.

And it all comes together in my mind, exactly the way it must have happened. I feel a swell of excitement as the nub of it appears, and then guilty dread as the truth settles in a hollow in the pit of my stomach.

'I think Gen was right earlier,' I tell Sammy, my voice smooth but my whole body alert, 'when she called you Samantha Buchanan. I think that – I think that your parents, the people who raised you, were so desperate after their daughter died, and so sad, that they could only think of one way to carry on.

'I think they saw you. A little girl who didn't belong to them. But maybe you reminded them of their daughter. Maybe they wanted you to grow up on the island like she would have. And maybe it all made sense to them – they were so unhappy. Perhaps the Buchanans were going to move away; perhaps they couldn't bear to lose another little girl. So they made sure you stayed with them. On Ora.'

'No.' Sammy shakes her head; shakes it so hard it must make her sick. 'You can't – they wouldn't. They wouldn't have done that. Why would they? I can't be. Why wouldn't these people have known? How couldn't *I* know?'

'You said they kept you inside when you were little,' I say urgently. 'You said that it wasn't safe to go out and that they made you stay indoors a lot. Do you know why it wasn't safe?'

'Because . . . Because it's easy to—'

'To drown?' Jess says softly.

336

Sammy inhales, a gentle gasping sound.

'And because they didn't want anybody to see you,' I add. 'They needed to keep you hidden from the world, in case the Buchanans suspected anything. In case they figured out what had happened. But they didn't stay on the island after they lost their daughter anyway. They were overwhelmed, they said, with grief. And so they left the McDougalls in charge to look after things while they were gone. The lighthouse. The island. Only I guess they didn't think this meant they would be looking after their daughter.'

'That's not true,' Sammy whispers. 'It can't be.'

'It has to be.' James's voice feels like a rumble, sudden and unwelcome. 'It's the only thing that makes sense. Why would your parents keep you here without teaching you to look after the lighthouse if they wanted you to stay after they died? They should have taught you how. But they couldn't, because they were scared you might remember something if you came inside.'

'No.'

'And they knew you were smart, that you would put the pieces together. And you did, didn't you? You came here and you saw your old bedroom.'

'I didn't go in there!' Sammy exclaims, her face darkening. 'This is not my house. I don't remember anything!'

'James—'

'And *that's* why you needed us to leave. Why it got urgent. Why suddenly you're so mad. That's why you broke the mirror – to scare us, to make us leave sooner so you could go back to pretending you don't remember the truth.'

'That's not true!'

'When those men came – the contractors – you hid because you were scared of what would happen if they

337

found you. If you had to face the truth that you've suspected for years. Haven't you? What happened? Was it after they died? Did living in this big open world suddenly make you realise that you were never meant to be here alone?'

'Stop!' Sammy screams.

'*James!*' But my voice goes unacknowledged.

And Sammy lifts the broken shard of glass.

# 37

## Kira

It takes less than a second. It's like flash paper. One moment things are relatively calm – it's a conversation; a *dialogue*. The next moment it's like the world has exploded and everything goes a hundred miles a second.

Sammy lashes out. She swipes at James with her bit of broken glass and he yelps, diving to the side just in time. But I don't think she even intended to hit him, because seconds later the glass is arcing through the air, coming to rest on the middle of the table.

'Sammy!' Moira exclaims. Genevieve shouts, too.

Sammy hurls herself at the table. She flings ceramic place settings, wooden candlesticks – their candles still alight – to the ground, dashing them so hard that one of the mats shatters. Lucas and Jess dive for the candles, snuffing them out, while I try to grab hold of Sammy.

But she's slippery and determined. She begins to lift one of the dining chairs and I let out a scream as I throw myself at her, desperate to stop her before the heavy seat collides with the glass windows. Everything in here is so fragile.

And she is out of control. It's like, suddenly, she's a thousand times stronger, driven by denial and fear and confusion. She doesn't even seem human. There is only me – it's always me – between her and the rest. My body collides with hers and we tumble hard to the tiled floor but she's out from underneath me in seconds as I try to drag myself upright, stunned by the impact.

Still she doesn't stop. I can see her glancing around, looking for something else to grab, something to destroy. Her eyes land on one of the place mats that has skidded to land at her feet. It's heavy enough to do some serious damage.

'Sammy, please!' I shout. 'Just calm down. It's okay. Everything is going to be okay!'

She's not listening. I'm not even sure she could stop now if she wanted to, a one-woman wrecking machine, driven by fear and anger and hurt. Something inside me screams with recognition. That urge to break, to smash – so familiar. Tears stream down her face.

'It's not true,' she cries. 'None of it is true.'

Jess has dropped one of the candles and it rolls under the table. She curses, cradling her hand. Moira rushes to her side.

'Just a burn,' she murmurs. 'Watch—'

And then the heavy place mat flies through the air, driving them apart. The corner catches Mo in the upper arm. She shouts, a hoarse pained noise that reverberates deep in my chest.

'Enough!' Lucas bellows. He dives at Sammy but she's quicker than him: years of racing with wind and rain; years of outdoor living making her strong and fast.

She slips out of Lucas's reach and goes for the broken glass again, this time her anger flaring hot.

340

'You need to leave,' she growls. 'You all need to go. It's clear now. It's so clear. You have to forget this place.'

She scrambles over two overturned chairs and reaches for the glass. This time it's James who manages to grab her, and he doesn't do it by half. Unlike the rest of us he doesn't seem to care if he hurts her. He hurls himself at her and catches her square in the chest. The two of them tumble backwards, towards the door to the veranda.

'James!' I shout.

Jess screams.

And it seems like only seconds as we watch. They roll together, a ball of limbs, Sammy lashing out with that piece of glass clutched in her fingers. There's an arc of blood and a loud *oof* as Sammy's foot connects with James's stomach.

I kneel, motionless, unable to make my body obey. All my strength is suddenly gone as Sammy kicks James again, and then his fist lands under her jaw. Her head swings back and the two of them half scramble, half skid through the door.

They crash into the railing of the veranda outside with such force that I hear the wood splinter with a loud crack that sounds like thunder. The rain is still coming down in sheets and the sun has dipped low behind the horizon now.

Lucas is faster than me. He manages to get to the door, but he can't intervene, fists and feet lashing out, the piece of glass lost somewhere on the wooden decking. I finally get my knees to respond and drag myself to my feet using the side of the table. I follow the others, skidding out into the rain and the frigid salty air, almost catapulting Lucas right into the ocean.

It's dark on the veranda, despite the lights from within the sunroom, and I can hardly see James and Sammy through

341

the rain. I can just hear their grunts, as James tries to hold down her arms, her legs, anything at all, and she fights with every fibre of her being.

'James!' I shout. 'Just let her go!'

It isn't worth it. I know it isn't. But James is like a creature possessed now: something inside him is fighting against her, determined to win. A brief spark of that dark strength inside him I remember, vying to be free. And I'm grateful for it now. I grab hold of Lucas's arm as Moira, Jess and Genevieve run to join us. The wind snarls down the length of the cliff and I feel it in my bones: a strong tug that almost lifts me off my feet.

There is another gut-wrenching crack of wood.

A scream. A shout.

And then – a jagged bolt of lightning surges and I see James. Only James. Alone on the veranda with his eyes wide, his mouth agape.

'Where is she?' Genevieve yelps.

James is frozen for a solid second, his face a pale oval. And then he rushes to the balcony, looking like he's going to throw himself over the edge.

Lucas is quick, Moira not far behind, and together they grab James's arms and haul him back. His feet scrabble against the slick decking and he lets out a groan that is more a sob, kicking out once, twice. They hold fast.

'Let me go! Let me— I've got to— She went over,' he cries. 'I didn't mean – I was trying to stop her from hurting herself. From hurting *us*.'

I hurry to stand beside them and I peer over the balcony. Down, far down into the murky darkness. The waves are unhinged, clawing at the cliff and the rocks beneath. Rain sluices from the sunroom roof, torrents soaking the decking.

There's no sign of her.

'I have to go in,' James pants, fighting against Mo and Lucas again, but they are stronger together. Lucas pulls him into a bear hug, locking his knees. 'I have to help her!' James screams.

'No,' Moira asserts, her voice strained as she tries to pull them both back, out of the wind and the rain that still howl like wild beasts caught in the night. 'It's too dangerous!'

'You could die.' Jess's words are quiet but we all hear them as though they are crystal clear.

He could die.

Like Sammy.

*Samantha.*

'It would be no use now anyway,' I say quietly, pulling myself back from the balcony. 'She's gone.'

'We don't know that,' James sobs. 'She might have landed – she might reach the beach. I didn't mean for this. It was like something pulled her out of my hands. We have to do something!'

Lucas twists James, pulling him back until all of us are crowded inside again. Jess, Genevieve and I block the doors, as if James might bolt. Instead, he sags against Lucas, tears and rain streaking his haunted face. Jess hugs her arms to her chest.

'It's too dark,' Mo says firmly. 'By the time you get down there it will be pointless. And if she's in the water . . . what could we do?'

Genevieve shakes her head, looking like she's about to argue. 'Mo's right,' I cut in before she can speak. 'There's nothing we can do.'

'We need to tell somebody then,' James begs. 'We have to get signal, try to phone somebody. The police or the coastguards. We can try the radio again. We've got to tell somebody – anybody.'

'And even if we can get through, what exactly would we say?' I hold in the squirming, sick feeling in my belly. All of us against her? How would that look to anybody else? They'd never believe us. And James . . . 'They'll think we hurt her on purpose.'

'Why would they think that?' Jess's eyes are wide. 'She attacked us. James was just protecting us.'

I stare at James. He meets my gaze and I can see the hollowness inside him. He knows what I'm going to say.

'Because of me,' he answers before I can. 'Because of my past. What happened between me and Kira. The police were called. I have a – record.'

Mo and Jess exchange a glance and Genevieve lets out a breath that is full of sadness. Before she had been ready to run, too; to rush down to the beach and find a survivor. Now she seems to realise how futile it all is.

'But Lucas said that happened years ago,' Jess says. 'Surely we could explain. We can tell them about the cave, about the broken mirror . . .' She trails off, her voice growing weak. Moira shakes her head.

James won't look at me now. He won't look at anybody; he just stares at the floor like he wants it to swallow him.

Lucas lets go of James as though the thought of holding on sickens him now – as if he has the urge to wipe his hands on his jeans to clean them. I avert my gaze, focusing instead on Jess, who stands beside me trembling.

'It won't look good,' I say softly. 'The six of us against her. One small woman who there's no record of. They won't understand that she was wild; that we were afraid. They'll

344

ask why we couldn't stop her without hurting her. And if they know James has a history of violence . . .'

The silence is deafening.

'It was an accident,' Genevieve says then, soft but determined. She bites at her lip. 'We can tell them it was an accident.'

I don't say what I am thinking: that we have, each of us, got something to lose. There is *always* something to lose. Lucas has his new job, and Genevieve has her position at AdZec to think about. Mo and Jess have Emma. And James . . . It's the worst for him. He could lose everything. They might send him to prison.

I don't want something that happened ten years ago to ruin his life now.

'We can search for her in the morning,' I suggest, fighting the guilt and the sickness inside me. This is wrong – everything has gone so horribly. How can we ever fix this? 'When there's daylight it'll be easier to see. Maybe she'll turn up on the beach like James said, and if we find her we can apologise; make sure she's okay. We can play with the radio until then, try to come up with a plan. If we find her we can figure out what to do next.'

Lucas nods and I can tell he understands me. He knows how much we have to lose. Moira is frowning but she knows it too.

'And if we don't find her?' James asks. 'What do we do then?'

Nobody answers.

# MONDAY

# 38

## *Genevieve*

We don't speak. I don't think anybody has said anything at all since the early hours, when we all decided to try to get some sleep. The radio was a waste of time again – just static, or worse, *silence*. Like a black hole that eats everything up. We took turns to scroll through the options, and tried to get enough phone signal to do more than load a Google search. There wasn't enough to make a phone call: the line just crackles and dies. And what would we say anyway? Kira is right about that at least.

I don't think any of us managed sleep. Lucas lay stiff as a board for three hours, before getting up to have a shower. And when I repeated what I'd said to everybody earlier on, that I thought we shouldn't use it just in case we decided to speak to the police, he just sighed and sank back down onto the bed and sat, still and silent, for another hour.

Long before the sun has fully risen I get dressed and find Jess and James in the kitchen. Jess holds a mug between both hands but the tea has been cold for a while, a scummy ring forming on top. James clearly hasn't slept either. Both wear dark clothes, jumpers and jeans, as if they dressed for the atmosphere here today. Bleak.

'Does it hurt?' Jess asks when I step into the kitchen. For a second I'm confused, because everything hurts. I ache all over, as if I've run two marathons back to back. Then I notice she's looking at the cut on my face, my swollen nose, and I shrug.

'Yes, but I'll live.'

The choice of words is poor but I'm beyond worrying now if I might upset anybody. Jess's lips form a straight line and she finally pushes the cold tea away.

'We need to tell somebody,' she says, glancing between James and me. 'We can't just pretend that nothing happened.'

'I don't want to pretend anything,' James agrees. 'I'll take the fall. I deserve it. It's my fault she fell and it's my fault w—'

'This isn't just about you any more.'

All three of us whip round as Kira's voice startles the stillness in the room. She's already dressed in jeans and trainers, her hoodie pulled up high around her ears, which look pink in the pale light spilling through the window. She stares at James and he flinches.

'You can't just act like this didn't happen,' I say. 'She is still human.'

'I'm not saying we pretend it didn't happen,' Kira snaps. 'I'm saying we don't tell anybody about it.' She reaches out and takes the mug away from Jess, dumping the contents in the sink before wiping her hands on her jeans. 'But it's not that simple.'

'How will you sleep at night?' I push. 'If we just leave today and never say anything? How will you sleep knowing we just abandoned her?'

350

'I won't,' Kira says simply. She turns towards me with her hackles raised but I can tell now it's not me she has a problem with. She's doing what she thinks is right. We are backed into a corner and there's no way out. 'It doesn't matter if we sleep, though. It matters if our lives fall apart. This wasn't our fault – no, James. It wasn't. We didn't do anything wrong. Do you want this to ruin everything? For all of us? We've got to do what's right. I don't think Sammy would want police crawling all over the island either.'

We're all silent again, only the gentle *tick-tick* of the clock near the kettle betraying that time is moving at all. My limbs feel locked with sadness. In the end it's Moira who breaks the silence, appearing with Lucas at her side. They're both dressed now, too, in coats and boots.

'It's light enough, I think,' Moira says. Her voice creaks with disuse. She gestures outside at the pale rose sky. 'We'll see her if she's washed ashore. We've still got a few hours before the boat should be back to pick us up.'

Lucas hands me my jacket as Jess and James grab theirs and we walk towards the door of the cottage. The others follow us quietly. We trek down to the beach dressed in hats and still-damp coats, scarves wrapped tight around our throats, but nothing is enough to dull the chill in my bones. I don't care what Kira says: this is selfish. This isn't about Sammy, about doing what's right. This isn't about protecting the island.

This is about us. About lying to protect ourselves.

We search the beach as a group, silent between rumbling arguments. There is no sign of life on the sand. If Sammy had come out of the water anywhere along this stretch there would be something: some evidence. There is nothing except the thrash of waves and the threat of more rain.

351

James demands, again, that we try to call the police, clutching the radio as we walk, even as it continues its static hiss. Jess echoes him, begging Kira to reconsider. Moira disagrees with her wife with a vehemence I was not expecting, her whole body taut as she kicks at the remains of the fire we built on Friday night. The thing that started it all. We've circled this beach twice and still seen nothing. No sign of Sammy at all.

'You've got to be kidding me, Jess,' Moira cries angrily. 'Can't you see what will happen if they think we did it on purpose? If they don't think we did enough to help her? They will punish all of us.'

Jess stands her ground. 'What sort of example do we set for Emma if we don't say anything?' she retorts.

We're firmly in two camps now: James, Jess and me in one; Kira, Lucas and Mo in the other. And I don't know which way this will go. I feel sick with it.

'The kind of example that we're actually fucking around to set!' Mo throws her hands up, her face contorted. 'You said yourself: what happens if she loses us? Both of us? That's what you're suggesting. Emma growing up without us, or watching us suffer through it. They won't just let it drop.'

'Don't you dare turn this on me.' Jess trembles with barely subdued rage. 'This isn't about us.'

'Of course it fucking is,' Moira snaps. 'This whole thing is about all of us.' She gestures at James, at Kira. 'What, you honestly think we'll all walk away from this clean?'

'I can tell them it's my fault,' James argues. 'Nobody else will get in any trouble.'

'Can you promise that?' Lucas demands. He stares at James and then at me, and as much as I love him I can feel the weight in his gaze, the fire when I don't immediately agree. 'How do you know?'

'And anyway, we can't let you take the fall for all of this,' Kira says. 'It *isn't* your fault.'

'It doesn't matter whose fault it is,' I say. 'It's not *right*. Sammy doesn't deserve this.'

'Fuck what's right!' Lucas rubs the stubble on his jaw. 'None of this is right. But I'm not letting this stupid accident – which she engineered, by the way – take away everything we've ever worked for.'

'We don't even know if she's alive,' Moira adds softly. She glances from Jess to me, and then to Lucas who wavers indecisively between us. 'If she isn't, then what harm does it do? It was an accident. Like so many accidents on the cliffs. We can just go home. Nobody knew she was here.'

'We knew,' I say.

'Apart from us.' Moira's eyes are dark and unclouded. She's been thinking about this all night and even I can tell that her mind's made up. Kira nods. She agrees. 'And if she somehow managed to survive the fall . . . the waves . . . then isn't leaving today exactly what she wanted us to do?'

Jess wavers. It's in her expression, the way she leans towards her wife. I know she's about to cave. My heart thuds and I feel sick but I don't argue. What's wrong with me? I glance at each of their faces: James's eyes are bloodshot, haunted; Jess looks like she'll never sleep again; Kira's angry fire hides her bone-shaking fear for James, for all of us; Moira is stoic, the fight sucked out of her. And Lucas . . . Lucas won't look at me. He's ashamed.

'Maybe it's for the best,' I whisper. 'We're running out of time and we still have to clean up before we leave.'

The wind whips my words away but they all hear me. There's a collective sigh – not of relief, but of agreement. A pact.

We know without saying it that we will have to accept this. We will have to carry our silence, whether this is right or not. We can never tell anybody what happened here this weekend. If Sammy is still alive then she'll get half her wish at least: we will leave. But we will never, ever be able to forget this place.

It *isn't* right, but it's the only option we've got.

We board the boat with Sammy's ghost between us. Ben arrived exactly on time and said nothing about the state of my face, of the solemnness between us. Moira explains quietly about the broken mirror and the fractured railing outside the sunroom, conveniently ignoring the smaller damages, and perhaps he thinks we're embarrassed. It's better that he doesn't talk to us. I'm not sure I would be able to hold it in.

My nose throbs from the cut above it and I wince, waiting for the painkillers I took to kick in. I turn away from Lucas, who won't let me out of his sight, and pull my phone from my pocket, holding onto it tightly as the boat tugs and bobs against the waves.

The motor is a steady thrum that reminds me of the sound of the rain on the glass roof of the sunroom. The weather is clearer now, just a smattering of grey clouds obscuring the sun. No mist. No rain. The wind has dropped right down, too, and the air smells fresh and green.

I inhale deeply, taking in the salt and the grass and the dark grey rocks that still smell like rain, the wood of the dock as it grows smaller and smaller, the faint pine tinge of the trees. There's smoke somewhere on the breeze, from somewhere far away. The lighthouse stands, as always, proud and silent; but now I wonder if it *is* pride. Or whether it's guilt that makes it stand so tall, so defiant.

We will never know, I suppose, what really happened between the McDougalls and the Buchanans. We will never know for sure if Sammy – the Sammy who was wild and tough and grown from Ora – was the same Samantha who was born on the mainland to David and Isabelle. Who came here as a babe in arms to start a fresh life. All we have is our silence, our memory of last night, and her abject refusal to believe it could be true.

Kira paces somewhere behind me. I feel the steady thud of her trainers across the surface of the boat, hear the urgent undercurrent of her voice as she speaks low and fast on her phone. It's somebody from the magazine: she's giving an explanation about the damage before she can get in trouble. It's not important that she do it right away, but she's doing it now anyway.

I know what she's doing because I've considered doing the same: picking my phone up and ringing Sarah about the stupid paperwork she didn't file, giving myself something to focus on. If Kira's thinking about that, she's not thinking about *this*. About what we're doing right now by fleeing in silence. This distraction is welcome, even as the signal drifts in and out and she swears heartily.

James stands to my right, his arms hooked over the edge of the boat. He's not watching the lighthouse like me, not got his eyes half-closed against the sun like Lucas. Instead his gaze roams the water below the sunroom, combing the rocks and waves as though he might find treasure. Find *her*.

*She's gone*, I want to tell him. Surely there is no way she could have survived.

I think of his face after she fell: the horror. The way he almost threw himself in after her. And I think, as well, of what Kira told me. About the way he lost his temper with her, and how badly he regretted it. I know I can't say anything to make it right, so I bite my tongue.

I wait until the lighthouse is out of sight. I wait a long time. Jess and Moira sit together on the bench, their heads pressed together. Moira is holding Jess's burnt palm as though she might be able to heal it with intent alone.

I wonder how we will ever move on from this.

Finally there is only the ocean, sapphire blue and stretching as far as I can see. Then I click open my phone and pull up Google again, watching the page load inch by inch as I loop back to the site I found on hauntings reported on Ora over the years. I only made it back a few years last time, but there are more posts. More stories from people who know people who say . . .

I know I should leave it. There are some questions best left alone. But I can't let it lie.

I think of the cold patches of air around the cottage, how it had felt to me so much like a *presence*. Like a clawing pair of hands. I think of little Elsie's fall from the cliff – an accident that led to her parents' grief and perhaps even Sammy's kidnap – and can't help picturing a pair of hands locked around a tiny ankle. I think, too, of the way Sammy disappeared over that railing, the ocean dragging her down. Just like Elsie.

Sammy said she didn't break the mirror in the bathroom. She swore blind she didn't go into her old bedroom, didn't leave that door unlocked for us to find it. James said he hadn't meant for her to fall, that it had been like something pulled her away from him.

And, despite everything that has happened this weekend – or perhaps because of it – some part deep inside of me believes both of them.

# ACKNOWLEDGEMENTS

This is the most fun I've ever had writing a book and I owe a debt of gratitude to the following people for its pleasure: Diana Beaumont, champion agent and the absolute best person to have my back. Katie Loughnane and the entire Avon team for truly bringing this spooky book to life. My deepest thanks to all of my friends, especially those who agreed to forget about me for a month while I drafted my little heart out. Book people are, genuinely, the best people. All the usual suspects have supported me through the writing process, including Doomsbury, Crime Kissers, Sauv Life, and the Waterstones Dream Team. Special thanks goes to Michelle Robins for listening to me cry about grammar – all errors are absolutely, positively, one hundred per cent my own. Endless thanks as always to my best friends and to my family (and my furry family – especially you). I would not have been able to write this book without you. I promise to only stare off into space half of the time we spend together on my next deadline!